Daffodil Season

Daffodil Season

a novel

✳✳✳

by Melanie Lageschulte

Daffodil Season: a novel
© 2021
by Melanie Lageschulte
Fremont Creek Press

Kindle: 978-1-952066-14-6
Paperback: 978-1-952066-15-3
Hardcover: 978-1-952066-16-0
Large print paperback: 978-1-952066-17-7

Cover photo: yanikap/iStock.com
Cover design: Melanie Lageschulte
Author photo: © Bob Nandell

* 1 *

A plume of dust rose from the storage room's floorboards as Melinda shoved the next cardboard box to the side.

"Did you find them yet?" Diane wanted to know. "There are some crates over here, but none of them seem to be what we're looking for."

Melinda answered her mom's question with a sneeze. Grace, who had been sniffing the closest box with a flicker of curiosity in her feline eyes, looked up in surprise.

"Nope," Melinda finally said. "This one's marked 'tax forms.' I doubt they're in here." She picked up the dusty box and started for the entrance. "I wonder how these got left behind? If Kevin and Ada don't need them, I'll get them shredded."

"It's amazing what one family can collect over a hundred years." Diane wiped her hands on her faded jeans and went back to her search. "Actually, it was even longer than that. I can't imagine how overwhelming it was to sort through everything in this room, much less the entire farm."

The sun was bright outside the dormer's east-facing windows, but the late-February air held little more than a promise of warmth. This was the one room of Melinda's farmhouse she didn't bother to heat, and she wished she'd grabbed pairs of gloves before asking her mom and aunt to join her on this scavenger hunt.

Aunt Miriam didn't seem fazed by the room's chill, but had donned a kerchief to protect her gray curls from the dust. She found her way through the sea of boxes to the dormer, and started to remove the tired, beige curtains from their warped metal rods with careful hands.

"Goodness, they're stuffed with dust! I bet these things could stand up by themselves. And I can't believe how many boxes and crates there are to sort through. I thought the Schermanns made a clean sweep last spring, before the auction."

"Well, yes and no." Melinda sat back on her heels and rubbed Grace's ears. "They did what they could in a few days, but had to focus on the furniture and other items for the sale. Between that, and dividing family heirlooms, all this random stuff was left behind."

The storage room was a mess, and it would stay that way for some time. Because while Melinda Foster had lived at this farm for almost two years, her to-do list never seemed to get any shorter.

Horace Schermann's side of the bargain had been clear: He'd needed someone to care for his animals after he moved to a nursing home, and the rent had been laughably cheap as a result. As for Melinda, she'd had no idea what she wanted, or even needed. But what she got was far more than anything she could have expected.

When she left Minneapolis behind, she found a whole new life here in northern Iowa: A job at her family's hardware store, an expanded circle of friends, more time to live in the moment. It hadn't come easily, or quickly, but as the months rolled by, her new life had slowly revealed itself.

Today's task, by contrast, seemed incredibly simple: Locate the meeting minutes from the now-defunct Fulton Township women's club. Ada Arndt, Horace's youngest sister, was fairly certain the files were still tucked away in this storage room.

But more than an hour of diligent searching had already passed, and the documents had yet to be found.

"Are you sure Ada doesn't have the club's records?" Diane pushed a few stray gray hairs out of her face and weighed where she might look next.

"No, she checked again last night. Went through everything in the cedar chest, the other boxes she took home. Nothing."

"And they're not at Mabel's?" Diane gestured north toward the farm of Mabel and Ed Bauer, Melinda's closest neighbors. Mabel's mother, like Horace's, had been a member of the Fulton Friendship Circle for decades and served as president several times.

"Mabel doesn't have them." Melinda sighed. "She's looked high and low. I still think they must be in here, somewhere. Let's dig for another half hour. Those cranberry-orange muffins cooling on the counter should be ready by then."

"Do you think they are safe from Hobo's prying paws?" Diane's eyes sparkled when she mentioned her grand-dog. Hobo had been Horace's best friend, but over time had turned his affections toward Melinda. Most of them, at least. Whenever Horace visited the farm, they were inseparable.

"He's outside," Melinda said with an edge of resignation in his voice. "The temptations of puddles, dirty snow and mud are too much for him to ignore. You know Horace always let him run, and I gave up trying to curtail his whims long ago."

"That's what old towels are for." Miriam stuffed the last of the faded curtains in the sack. "I personally could go for a muffin or two. Let's push on, and see if we get lucky."

Diane started for a stack of wooden crates along the north wall, a move that earned a growl of disapproval from Grace. The long-haired calico never allowed her humble beginnings as an abandoned kitten to dampen her considerable pride.

"Excuse me, Princess Grace." Diane made a mock bow as she passed. "I shall endeavor to stay out of your way. Oh, it's so much brighter in here with those curtains gone. Just look at that sunshine! Another few days of this weather, and the rest of the snow should melt. Sure, we'll get a little more, but maybe we've turned winter's last corner."

Miriam's face broke into a wide smile. "Spring's not here yet, but it's on its way. Can you feel it?"

Melinda glanced at the dingy plaster that sloped sharply over the room's corners, and tossed up a quick prayer. "As long as I don't feel anything dripping on my head, I'll be grateful."

A Schermann relative patched the shingles before Melinda purchased the farm, but the house's roof needed to be replaced. That was on her list for this year, along with painting the house. And that wasn't the half of it. Right now, today, there was laundry to do, and she wanted to get some seeds started, and the bathrooms needed to be cleaned ...

She crossed her arms and looked around at the clutter. "Maybe this is a wild goose chase. Besides, I have so much else to do, as do the two of you. It's possible something happened to the records, that they were thrown away."

Miriam chuckled. "Oh, I can't imagine Horace and Wilbur tossing anything out." The bachelor brothers had remained at the farm for more than two decades after their parents passed away, and had been as reluctant to part with any of their possessions as they were their money. "But then, I can't say much. Our family's owned Prosper Hardware for a hundred-and-twenty-years, and I can't think of the last time anyone did a good purge. The file cabinets at the store are overflowing, and there's even more stuff in the attic at home."

Diane lowered herself to one of the wooden crates and opened the one to her right. Hazel, Grace's sister, saw her chance and vaulted into Diane's lap. Hazel's long, brown-tabby fur was a bit ruffled from her expeditions, but her white paws were immaculate despite the dust.

"I always say, the journey is just as important as the destination, if not more so." Diane gave Hazel a quick pet and turned to the task at hand. "Let's not give up yet. As for everything else, Melinda, you'll get it done, one way or another. You always do."

"Look at it this way." Miriam held up her sack in triumph. "You don't have to wash these old curtains, at least. They're ready for the burn barrel. By the looks of them, they're at least fifty years old. Who did you say last slept in this room?"

"Ada and her sisters, before they left home. She remembers picking those out of a catalog, as a teenager." Melinda gazed out at the bare branches of the front yard's largest maple, and wondered if the towering tree had been there fifty or sixty years ago. It surely had been, albeit shorter and with a smaller canopy.

The lawn was still drab and brown, and the gently rolling fields on the other side of the gravel road were barren except for patches of snow. Late-winter scenes outside these windows hadn't changed much over the decades, and that filled Melinda with a feeling of comfort and stability. And she knew that even now, on a chilly day like today, all of her farm's trees were preparing to push out new leaves as soon as the weather turned for good.

Miriam made her way to the room's only chair and tested its scuffed wooden legs before she took a seat. "Oh, my knees. This might be a daunting task, but it's nothing like what Frank and I will face when we move."

The Langes had decided to downsize after living in their grand Victorian for over thirty years. Tiny Prosper didn't offer many real-estate options, so Frank and Miriam were thrilled to find a ranch home that would suit their needs as they aged.

"We'll help," Diane promised. "You know we will."

"I wanted to make a dent in things over the winter, but never got it done." Miriam looked at her sister and niece, and the start of a smile tugged at one corner of her lined face. "And now, we'll have even less time to box stuff up."

"What do you mean?" Melinda frowned. "I thought you weren't planning to close on the new house until at least early May?"

"We aren't, since our friends aren't moving out until April." Miriam leaned forward, as if sharing a secret. "I wanted the two of you to be the first to know: Frank and I are going on vacation!"

"What?" Diane was floored. "But you never ..."

"And that's exactly why we're going. Neither of us is getting any younger."

Melinda was surprised at first. But then, why not? Frank and Miriam had operated the store since Grandma and Grandpa Shrader retired, and rarely took time off. They had no children; Prosper Hardware was their life's work, as well as their legacy.

"A long weekend might be just what you need," she told Miriam. "Chicago is always fun. Minneapolis is, too, but you've been there several times. Maybe Kansas City?"

"Oh, we're going much farther than that." Miriam's eyes sparkled with excitement. "Girls, we're off to Hawaii! For two whole weeks!"

Diane blinked, unable to speak. Melinda finally found the words.

"Two weeks?" She swallowed. "You're going to be gone for two weeks?"

"Oh, it'll be more like three. I mean, as far as being away from the store. We'll need some days to pack, and we might tack on more days at the end, since we're already taking the leap. We're still trying to narrow down our options, but the plan is to ship out at the tail end of March."

Miriam squeezed Melinda's arm. "And honey, we have you to thank for this opportunity. Bill's responsible, and your parents can help out, but having you back here makes this possible. We know we can trust you to run the store while we're away."

Melinda widened her eyes at her mom. "Sure. Of course."

"I think it's a wonderful plan." Diane plastered on a wide smile. "You're right, Roger and I will chip in. We're retired, we certainly have the time. Don't worry about a thing! You two are overdue for a break."

Miriam hurried over to hug her sister. "Oh, thank you! This is going to be the trip of a lifetime." She studied the storage room with renewed energy, and zeroed in on an old dresser slumped against the far wall. "Those records have to be here somewhere. Let's get back at it."

"What are we going to do?" Melinda whispered to her mom after Miriam moved away. "What about the accounts, ordering supplies? Bill's worked there longer than I have, but I doubt he knows how to do any of that."

Diane took a deep breath. "We'll figure it out. At least we have a month's notice. I can't believe I'm saying this, but I'm no longer in a hurry for spring to arrive."

Melinda suddenly felt the same. Would a few weeks be enough time for a crash course in running Prosper Hardware? So far, her role had been limited to manning the register and stocking shelves. Sure, Frank and Miriam added her to the business' board of directors in the fall, but she never could have guessed her role in the day-to-day operations would expand this quickly.

Miriam rummaged through the old dresser's drawers, but her occasional sighs and grunts made it clear she wasn't having any luck. Diane started on a stack of boxes in another corner, with an alleged assist from Hazel. There was one place they hadn't looked yet, and Melinda climbed over and around the room's contents to reach the closet next to the boarded-up window in the north wall.

That was something else that needed to be fixed. The storm window over that ancient frame was cracked, and the stains seeping out from under the plywood told her there were leaks to be addressed. She'd check the closet walls for more while she rooted around for the club's records.

"I don't even remember what's in here," she muttered as she tugged at the door's iron latch. Grace and Hazel were suddenly at her feet, ready to investigate. "I guess we're all going to find out, huh?"

Finally, something clicked. The thick varnish squeaked as the door flung itself inward, and Melinda stumbled after it. A cardboard box caught the toe of her sneaker, and she banged her elbow on the paneled door.

"I thought there was more stuff in here." Melinda pulled her now-smarting toes back from the box and eyed its lone neighbor. "But I guess not."

Although it qualified as a walk-in closet, it was small, and half of the space was compromised by the steep slope of the roof. Melinda reached for the dingy string that dangled from the ceiling's bare bulb. The light sputtered before it glowed steady, then threw shadows across the iron clothing hooks embedded in the wall's strips of stained wood.

These walls were rough, their condition far worse than the slight imperfections found in the rest of the room. While Horace's grandfather had insisted on solid craftsmanship when the house was built, no one would have bothered to smooth the plaster in such a hidden space. But years ago, someone had cloaked it in a surprisingly cheerful shade of yellow. And there, in one corner, were the water stains Melinda expected to find.

"Oh, great. What a mess." She stepped around Grace to get a closer look.

Squeak.

She froze mid-step, and cringed. But there was so little left in this closet, where could a mouse even hide? "Girls, come on; you have to have heard that." Grace and Hazel ignored her, and continued their baseboard sniffs as if nothing was amiss.

Melinda gathered her courage and stepped forward.

Squeak, squeak.

Diane popped in. "Oh, I'm sure it's just a loose floorboard. Look at those thick wooden planks; they're not like the narrow oak strips in the main parts of the house. Any change in humidity, and these would really let you know."

Melinda shifted one shoe, and tried to find the instability in the floor. This might be something she could fix on her own. Given the advanced age of all the buildings on her two-acre farm, she'd learned fast how to make minor repairs to just about everything.

Grace and Hazel crowded around, and Melinda crouched down to investigate. That's when she spotted the hole. Or really, it was more like a notch, right where two lengths of board came together.

"Well, we can't have this. That's the door to a mouse house, for sure. Maybe some wood filler would be enough, I wouldn't have to ..."

The board shifted easily under her hand. Too easily. And just there, only a foot away, was another short seam. The other lengths of flooring were several feet long.

"What is it?" Diane joined Melinda in the gloomy half-light. "Miriam, get over here. I think we're on to something."

"The club's records?" Miriam's sneakers beat a staccato across the floor. "Are they in there?"

"I can't imagine they would be, unless those two boxes are mislabeled." Melinda edged her way back into the room. She kept a small toolbox in the little office across the hall, and needed something to lift the loose board. "There's a notch in the floor, though."

"Ooh, I can't wait to see this!" Diane's enthusiasm was contagious. "This might be even better!"

Melinda returned with a large, flat-head screwdriver. "Kitties, stay back! I don't know what's under here, or where the hole leads to." Diane handed a protesting Hazel to Miriam, then tried to corral a squirming Grace in her own arms.

Melinda took a deep breath and angled the wedge into the hole. The short board rose easily, and she closed her eyes for a second before she lifted it away. What if some creature slipped out of the darkness and scampered over her hand?

Thankfully, that didn't happen. The cavity wasn't as deep as she expected, and went down only a few inches to the rough-hewn subfloor. But there was a small wooden box waiting inside, and she pulled it out with trembling hands.

"What is in here?" She carefully lifted the lid, mindful of its delicate, rusted hinges. "Oh wow, look at this!"

A worn, leather-bound ledger, not much bigger than a checkbook. Inside, several columns of numbers scrawled in faded ink. "Is that ... 21? Like, 1921? And does that say 'gal' ... like gallons? What could this be? Some sort of accounting book for the farm?"

Miriam crowded into the closet, Hazel still in her arms. "Wait a minute. When were Horace's parents married?"

"Spring of 1922." Melinda's answer carried the air of certainty only found in family members. But her ties to the Schermanns were so strong, she might as well be a blood relative. "And Henry and Anna didn't take over the farming operations for a few years after that. I'd bet Jacob, Horace's grandpa, kept these accounts in order. Whatever they are."

She carefully flipped through the ledger, and tried not to snag her fingers on its fragile pages. There were countless more references to what had to be gallons. All had dates, but none were attached to names. Only initials.

"How odd." Miriam frowned. "We have the store's records going way back, in our attic at home. I've never seen an accounting book that small, or so ... abbreviated."

These records had obviously been kept with great care, but why the secrecy? And then, Melinda's mouth fell open. "Do you remember the old still, the one we found in the machine shed?"

Diane gasped as she tried to gather her thoughts. "Yes! There was something ... Ada said there were rumors about a bootlegging operation, and then Horace confirmed it."

"And the haymow floor." Miriam jumped in. "There's that secret space where they kept the bottles!"

"This has to be the ledger." Melinda's heart pounded in her ears. What a find! "Jacob would have hidden this away, somewhere no one could find it. This was during Prohibition, so he was breaking the law, and ... oh, I have to call Kevin!"

"What about Horace?" Diane wanted to know. "Do you think he knew it was here?"

"Well, I'm going to find out. I'll call Ada, too. But Kevin was so fascinated by the still. Remember how he and his cousin flipped a coin to see who got to take it home?" Dave had won the toss, but Kevin hadn't minded. He'd spent several years coming down from Mason City on the weekends to help Wilbur and Horace, and Horace had let his favorite nephew pick out several family mementos before the auction.

Another one, however, was also tucked away in this wooden box. Melinda pulled out a smaller, square container covered in faded velvet. "There's something else in here. It's a pocket watch!"

She rubbed her hands on her sweatshirt, trying to get them clean, before she lifted the timepiece from its case. It was made of silver, or maybe platinum, and the face was still in excellent condition. There was even part of a chain nestled in the cream satin lining the box. Vines and leaves were etched on the back. And there, in the middle of the design, what appeared to be a name.

"Wes?" Melinda frowned, then looked closer. "Oh, there are periods. W.E.S., and the last one probably stands for Schermann. Maybe William ... William Edward? Who would that be? I can't remember."

"I bet Horace will know." Miriam reached out, and Melinda gently passed the watch to her aunt. "Well, doesn't that beat all?" Miriam shook her head. "Here we were, rummaging high and low for those club records, and so discouraged when they didn't fall right into our hands. Turns out, those are nothing compared to what we actually found."

Diane let Grace finally have her freedom. "Sometimes, life has surprises for us that are bigger, and better, than we could ever imagine."

Once it was clear nothing else was hidden in the small space, Melinda slipped the protective floorboard back in place. Hazel scooted over to help Grace continue her search of the closet's cobwebbed corners, which made Melinda laugh.

"Sorry, girls, you can look all you like. We already found the buried treasure."

✻ 2 ✻

Melinda deposited the rest of the muffins on the sideboard, then rolled open the wide drawer below the metal counter. Out came the paper plates and napkins, and a handful of plastic forks from Auggie's coffee-club stash.

"I wonder where he is this morning." She glanced out Prosper Hardware's plate-glass windows to study Main Street, which was nearly vacant at this early hour. "The co-op isn't that busy this time of year, and he prides himself on beating me through the door."

A blanket of heavy clouds had moved in yesterday evening, a sudden change from the afternoon's cheerful sunshine. But that was typical weather for this time of year in northern Iowa, when spring's arrival drew closer but winter still firmly held the upper hand. The skies had darkened further while Melinda hurried through morning chores and now, as she checked for any sign of Auggie's truck, the first flakes of wet snow appeared on the sidewalk.

Melinda's outlook was certainly more cheerful, given what was stashed in the canvas tote that waited on the back shelf of the antique oak counter. A call to Kevin had reinforced her suspicions about the ledger and confirmed her hunch about the pocket watch's initials. While she'd been hesitant to bring the watch, given its sentimental and monetary value, she had packed the ledger for a bit of show and tell. That, and muffins and coffee, would surely raise the men's spirits on this gloomy morning.

And while it was dreary outside, Prosper Hardware was warm and bright. Heat pushed through the iron floor vents in the gleaming oak floors, and the ceiling lights' beams made the pressed tin above them glow. The oak showcase had been polished by Esther Denner, the store's only part-time employee, before she closed last night. Even the large mat inside the oak front door was marginally clean.

But it wouldn't stay that way for long. Melinda had barely tossed the coffee grounds into the percolator when veterinarian John "Doc" Ogden pulled up out front. The wet snow was coming down heavier now, and Doc's lean frame braced against the driving flakes as he hurried for the shelter of the store's dark-green awning.

"The door's still locked!" Melinda snapped the coffee pot's lid and hurried to the entrance. Auggie normally came in the front, using the same key as when he'd worked at Prosper Hardware in high school. But Melinda, who always let herself in through Bill Larsen's wood shop in the back, had missed a step as she'd tried to fill Auggie's shoes. Where could he be?

"Sorry." She held the door as Doc stumbled in, his navy work parka nearly soaked with melted snow. "Auggie's not here, and I ... goodness, look at you!"

Smears of dirt mixed with tiny chunks of ice covered Doc's snow pants, and his work boots were worse. Thanks to the store's comforting warmth, rivulets of water and mud soon rolled down to the mat and out onto the floor.

"Miriam will have a fit." Doc looked around for a moment, then gave a grateful smile as Melinda hurried back with one of the metal folding chairs. "Thanks." He dropped into it with a sigh and started to undo the knots in his frozen boot laces.

"Had a call already this morning. It started out in the barn, at least. A sick cow, but everything was going fine until she slipped the halter and bolted for the pasture door." He raised an eyebrow. "Which, apparently, hadn't been tightly latched the last time."

"Oh, no! Did she ..."

"Yep. Thought she'd run halfway to Eagle River before we could catch her, she was so angry. But the mud slowed her down, and we got her cornered before she made it around the side of the barn. Of course, I had to go for the tackle. I quit football thirty years ago, after high school, but it's amazing how often I use those skills in my line of work."

"Good thing we have these economy-size trash bags handy." She pulled one from the box on the counter's shelf. "Here, put your stuff in this. Actually, take two. I'll get the mop."

"Might want to wait." Doc peered out the water-streaked glass toward the curb. "Here comes Auggie. If his boots are half as dirty as his truck, there's more mess coming in the door."

Auggie Kleinsbach blew in with an angry gust of wind and wet snow. "Good Lord!" he barked before he even pushed back his parka's hood. "What a mess! I don't know about you two, but I'm beyond tired of this crap. When's spring going to get here?"

"Well, you're the weatherman. What's the long-term forecast?" Doc handed over one of his plastic bags and pointed at Auggie's boots, then motioned for Melinda to bring reinforcements. She did, then decided to put the box of trash bags beside the door. Jerry, Frank and George had yet to arrive, and Bill would also show up before the hour was out.

"I checked the models this morning." Auggie took his usual chair in the makeshift circle. "This stuff won't last long, but we're supposed to get another rough round in a few days."

In addition to running Prosper Feed Co., Auggie served as an amateur observer for the National Weather Service. It was a role the co-op had held for over seventy years and, as far as Auggie was concerned, his predictions were as professional as any of those made by the television meteorologists.

"And Melinda, I apologize for being late." Auggie's tone carried the weight of someone dedicated to public service, perhaps a little too much. "It's imperative that I keep up with my reports. I got a bit behind on my weekly dispatch, had to file it before I came over. The really big spreadsheet, at least, isn't due until the end of the month."

"Just one more week until March," George Freitag said wistfully as he slowly unwound his woolen scarf. "But we won't be home free for quite a while yet."

"I started the coffee." Melinda went back to check the percolator. It was an ancient thing, and sometimes the cord needed a jiggle. "Auggie, how many scoops do you usually put in? I did two."

"Oh, no, that's never enough. Three." He gestured for her to keep going while she remedied the situation. "Toss in some more, while you're at it."

With his filled trash bags now stuffed by his chair, Doc stretched out his long, lean legs. Even the hems of his worn jeans were soaked. "No wonder I feel like I can conquer the world when I walk out of here in the mornings. Your coffee has a kick that's worse than any mule."

"I hope it's almost ready." Mayor Jerry Simmons wiped his wet tennis shoes on the mat. "I have a mean stack of paperwork waiting for me across the street." A former principal, he'd taken an early retirement buyout from the school district only to find himself elected mayor within the year. "George, you're living the quiet life these days; how about you come over and give me a hand? I know you enjoyed the bookkeeping part of managing your farm."

"I'll pass, thanks." At eighty-four, George was the oldest member of the coffee group. "Once we moved to town, I've kept my business dealings down to keeping our taxes in order and Mary's grocery lists up to date."

"Anything you need today?" Melinda looked up from organizing the displays on the counter. Doc was right; it would be useless to mop the floor until just before the store opened at eight. "I can get you a pile started."

"Oh, just some bran flakes and a dozen eggs." George gently insisted on pouring his own coffee, although Doc offered to get him a cup. "Our hens' production is down, of course, even with that fancy new coop I built. Just too cold. But another month or so, and they'll be back in the swing of things." With barely two-hundred human residents, and nearly all of them with ties to farm life, chickens had always been legal within Prosper's city limits.

"I can't wait, either," Melinda admitted. "My girls have been giving me enough eggs for myself, but I've got a list of buyers who can't wait for things to pick up again."

"That includes me." Uncle Frank rubbed his hands after he pulled off his gloves. "Mercy, it's a bear out there. Melinda, I told our supplier to keep our usual order coming for now, since we can hardly keep eggs in stock as it is. But we'll cut back a bit once your chickens get going again."

"Sounds good." Melinda smiled even as her stomach dropped. What exactly was the store's 'usual order' for eggs? What about the milk? Or the rest of the groceries? And that was just a fraction of what Prosper Hardware offered. So far, her efforts to keep the store stocked hadn't extended beyond ensuring the shelves were full. How would she handle everything when Frank and Miriam were gone?

Miriam had insisted the Langes' vacation stay secret until the itinerary was finalized. Word that Frank and Miriam planned to fly the coop for three weeks would cause quite a stir in town, and Miriam had said there was still a chance Frank would change his mind about such a long trip. Although Melinda wanted to see her aunt and uncle get a much-deserved break, she almost wished they wouldn't go.

Once the men were settled with their coffee and muffins, Melinda set aside her dust cloth and pulled up another chair for herself.

She waited for a lull in the discussion about basketball scores and crop prices, then reached into her tote. "Everyone, I have something exciting to share!"

Before she could even pull out the ledger, Auggie was sure he had the answer. "Let me guess, you're getting married!" That brought curious expressions and a few chuckles from the rest of the guys.

"No." Melinda shot him a look. "Come on, you know it's not that."

"Why not? Josh is a real catch, from what I hear." Auggie's smirk indicated he heard everything in a thirty-mile radius; or at least, he thought he did. "Better lock it down before someone else reels him in."

"Really, Auggie." Jerry rolled his eyes. "They haven't been dating that long."

"That's right. It hasn't been much more than a month." Melinda pretended to study the calendar on the wall by the refrigerated case as she weighed the best way to steer the conversation in a less-personal direction.

"Come on. It's been two months." Auggie looked to Frank for confirmation, but Frank was suddenly busy adding sugar to his mug. "Christmas Eve morning, am I right? That's when you went over to his clinic and ..."

"Who told you that?" But Melinda was sure she knew. Josh Vogel was a small-animal veterinarian in nearby Swanton. Norma, his vet tech, was Auggie's wife's cousin, or something like that. Norma was kind and understanding, but even she hadn't been able to keep such news to herself.

And it was good news. Melinda and Josh now spent as much time together as possible, and she was very happy. But it wasn't something she wanted to discuss with the guys.

"Never mind," she finally said. "I have something to show you that's far more interesting than my love life. Look what I found!"

"What is it?" George adjusted his glasses and leaned forward.

Auggie set his mug on the floor and took the little book out of her hands. "A ledger of some kind." He wiped his palms on his jeans and carefully turned the yellowed pages. "Accounts, looks like. Money in, money out."

"Where was this?" Jerry circled behind Auggie's chair for a closer look. "At the farm?"

"Yeah, in the closet in the front bedroom, which is now just storage. Miriam and Mom and I were going through the boxes Horace and Ada left behind, trying to find the minutes of the old Fulton Township women's club, but no luck. And then, I found this!"

"Why would the club need something so detailed?" The ledger had passed into Doc's hands, and he frowned as he studied its faded notations. "I can't imagine they were collecting dues more than once a year."

Frank, who already knew the story, contributed only a smug smile to the discussion. George had to barely glance at the book to know something was afoot. "Look at this, money was changing hands several times a week! And this was back in the twenties, looks like. No way was this just for club dues; the ladies must have been selling something."

Melinda burst out laughing. "George, you're partially right. But it wasn't the good women of the township peddling eggs and vegetables. It was the Schermanns, I'm pretty sure; and they were pushing something far more valuable."

"And illegal!" Frank added. "Hooch, as a matter of fact."

The men's chatter ground to a halt. It was so quiet that Melinda could hear the wet snowflakes, driven by a relentless north wind, hitting the store's front windows. She explained where she'd found the ledger, then told them about the family rumors and the worn-out still and the hidden compartments under her haymow's floor.

"They hid it in the barn?" Doc burst out laughing, a glint of admiration in his eyes. "A secret stash, with easy access for when a customer came around. Remind me about this the next time you need a vet. I have to see it for myself." Doc shook his head. "Oh, Horace, you sly dog."

"He wasn't involved, it goes back farther than that. And he was a little boy when Prohibition was repealed. But I heard Wilbur took it up again for a while, when he got home from World War II."

"Booze was legal again, by then." Auggie rubbed his chin. "Wonder why he bothered?"

Melinda only shrugged. Horace once told her Wilbur was heartbroken when he discovered his love had married someone else, and had tried to numb his pain with alcohol. But she felt such affection for Wilbur, who now suffered from dementia, that she kept that bit of gossip to herself.

George had his own rumor to share. "I was too young to partake, but there was still a market for bootleg hooch around here in the late forties. There were several roadhouses, if you want to call them that, scattered around the countryside. Seems like there was one west of town, somewhere."

"And one over by Eagle River, I think." Auggie thought for a moment, clearly disappointed that he didn't know all the details. "Well, Melinda, that's quite a find, either way. I bet Horace can't wait to see it."

"I haven't told him yet, I just called Kevin last night. And that's not all! I found something else in that wooden box that's far more valuable than this ledger."

"Money!" Jerry slapped his knee. "I bet that's it! Horace and Wilbur were always careful with theirs. Growing up during the Great Depression, it wouldn't surprise me if they were still a bit distrustful of the bank."

"My parents were," George said. "We had our accounts, of course, but there was always an emergency stash at the farm. In a big pickle jar, buried in the dirt floor of the root cellar."

"Grandma Kleinsbach kept hers right under everyone's feet." Auggie chuckled at the memory. "Rows of bills, lined up under the rug in the parlor. Why, once my parents went in on a side of beef with Grandma and Grandpa, and she rolled up that rug and handed over their contribution, as smooth as you please."

Melinda described the pocket watch, down to its filigree carvings and initials. After consulting with Kevin, she'd decided to take it to the jewelry store in Swanton and get the watch cleaned before giving it to Horace.

"Sounds like you'll have to make a trip to Scenic Vista, then." George made it sound like a major trek, even though the nursing home in Elm Springs was only a fifteen-minute drive from Melinda's farm. "I can't imagine Horace wanting to leave their cozy apartment in this kind of weather."

Auggie had picked up his coffee mug again. "Just because you didn't find the women's club's records doesn't mean all is lost. Why don't you start the group back up?"

"That's a great idea," George said. "Why, Mary was in one of those for years, back on the farm. My mother was, too. Seems like it was always a highlight of the month."

"People are busier than they used to be," Doc reminded George. "And that goes for the ladies as well as the men, even in the rural areas. Working off the farm, kids' activities, you name it. Life moves at a faster speed these days."

"All the more reason to spend time with your neighbors when you can." George gently shook a finger at Melinda. "And you're just the person to get it up and running."

Melinda had considered that very idea, but didn't want to admit it to the guys. It wouldn't take long for word to spread, and then, how would she be able to say no? It took dozens of volunteers to keep activities afloat in a rural area like this one, and Melinda had been badgered to pitch in as soon as she'd unpacked her boxes at the farm. Between the town's annual festivals and its nearly completed community center, as well as countless fund drives and other projects, she always seemed to be on the go-to list. And while she found all these efforts rewarding, they were almost too much to juggle.

"Oh, I don't know." She rose from her chair and went back to the counter. Doc and Frank were still studying the ledger, trying to guess names that might be tied to the initials. "Last spring, when I was preparing to buy the farm, it seems one of you had the name of a great handyman. I want to get the house shingled and repainted this summer, and I need to start asking around."

Auggie let out a low whistle. "That'll cost a pretty penny. Where are you going to get the cash?"

"I've been saving up for it." That was true, but it was also true that Miriam planned to give Melinda and Bill generous bonuses for taking charge of the store during the Langes' vacation. It would be just enough to finally put Melinda's projects within reach.

Jerry sighed and took a sip of his coffee. "You're not the only one looking for a good painter."

"Fixing up the house?" Doc frowned. "I thought you had vinyl siding."

"Sure do. I wish this was for our place, it would be much easier. Nope, the water tower's starting to look shabby. We need to do something about that."

"I hadn't noticed." Auggie chuckled. "I mean, it's been shabby for years."

"Well, it's getting worse, and it just happens to fall on my watch." Jerry generally enjoyed being mayor, despite his occasional grumbles, but any project that might incite unrest among Prosper's residents added lines to his already-wrinkled brow.

"But I have a bigger problem. Or at least, one that has to be dealt with first. There's a property owner here in town who's so far behind on their taxes that we'll be forced to take legal action."

Eyebrows went up around the circle. "You don't say?" Auggie was all ears. "Who is it?"

"Now, Auggie," Frank warned him. "This is official business. Jerry might not be able to reveal it." Frank was a member of the city council.

"That means you already know." Auggie sounded like a little boy whose favorite toy had been taken away. "You know everything, and the rest of us are in the dark."

Doc had served a few terms himself, years ago. "Well, Auggie, the suspense won't kill you. You'll just have to wait until it comes up at a meeting."

"I can still find out, if I try hard enough. I'll just get on the assessor's website and start poking around."

Melinda shook her head. "Yeah, and even in a town this small, it would take you hours to find the right property."

"Or, in this case, the one that's in the wrong," George pointed out.

"OK, I'll tell you all this much." Jerry leaned in. "It's on Main Street. The storefront's empty, has been for years."

"Wow, I think that really narrows it down," Doc said sarcastically.

"Anyway, I don't know if the owner's going to put up much of a fight. They're from out of town, and I think they'd sell in a heartbeat if they could find a buyer. Which isn't likely, or they would have done something before now."

"Just like the building next door." While Melinda wasn't as curious as Auggie, the idea was still intriguing. "Those people weren't behind on their taxes, but they wanted to sell. And Prosper got a new business out of the deal. Vicki and Arthur bought it, and now we have Meadow Lane. It all worked out."

"Are you thinking about foreclosure?" George frowned. "Oh, I hope it doesn't come to that."

"Something will need to be done." Jerry drained his mug. "This town needs every tax dollar it can get. But it's not just that. The county's cracking down on delinquent properties. I don't think we have a choice."

✳ ✳ ✳

The heavy, wet snow continued to fall the rest of the morning, but it didn't slow the stream of shoppers coming through Prosper Hardware's front door. Or the piles of muck and slush that gathered on the sidewalk, under the awning, and across the floor.

"I give up." Esther set the mop aside with an exasperated sigh. "It's almost noon. I've been at this off and on for two hours. I'll never get the groceries restocked, at this rate."

"Just let it go." Melinda pushed the stray hairs out of her face. Her brown waves tended to slip from her ponytail when the store was this busy. She'd been on the run since the door opened. "I appreciate you trying. The 'wet floor' sign is up, at least. We can tackle it later."

"Oh, I can't wait for winter to be over." Esther wiped her hands on her dark-green apron and peered outside. "What do you think? Should Bill put out more ice melt? I can ask him before I take over the register for your break."

Even under the bustle of the store, Melinda could hear the hum of Bill's table saw in the back room. "Sounds like a plan. We might as well use up more of what we have, rather than store it until next winter."

A gust of damp wind slapped Melinda's face when she stepped onto the sidewalk, and she tightened the drawstring on her parka's hood in preparation for her trip across Main Street. It was long past the part of winter where a gentle padding of fresh snow frosted the four-block avenue and highlighted the old buildings' quirks and charm. Even city hall, a towering, golden-brick structure with limestone accents, looked tired and dull today.

The next-door library was a single-story building with a welcoming picture window, but much less style. It shared a wall with city hall, and seemed to lean on its neighbor for support as the last days of winter dragged on. But the lights were on inside, and the library promised a visit with a good friend as well as the new book Melinda wanted to curl up with by the fireplace that night.

"You're just in time!" Nancy Delaney looked up from the circulation desk, which was an ornate, walnut cabinet that had been planted by the picture window decades ago. She pointed at a nearby cart. "I just got all the new holds processed. Yours is on the top row, to the left."

"I love the online notifications. I know that when I open one, it's always good news." The novel was the latest from one of her favorite authors, as Melinda picked it up with reverent hands. "I can't start it until after chores, so I've promised myself I won't even crack the cover until then."

"Oh, there's nothing like a new book. Aren't they the best? Of course, sometimes, they aren't what you'd hoped for." Nancy pushed the strands of her dark bob behind her right ear, and her brown eyes turned dreamy behind her chic glasses. "But other times, it's not just good; it's far more than you expected. And when that happens, it's just ... magical, I guess." She stared out at the dreary day with an absentminded expression that Melinda couldn't quite read.

"Yeah," Melinda finally said, when Nancy didn't say more. "New books are always thrilling, even when they're not a thriller."

Nancy suddenly snapped back to reality, the flush on her cheeks so subtle Melinda could have almost missed it. "Oh, by the way, I meant to tell you."

She pushed her chair back with a sudden burst of energy and came around the desk. "We have our first booking for the community center! A woman from Eagle River's Red Hat Society called just this morning, asking when the place is going to be ready. I told her late April, if we're lucky. They've been meeting in Charles City, but are eager to find a spot closer to home."

"Do you think they'll make this a regular thing?" Melinda's spirits soared as she followed Nancy through the cased opening that connected the two city buildings. "And once word gets out, other groups will surely sign up."

"I'm glad the council followed Jerry's suggestion on the rates." Nancy went behind city hall's counter and tapped the computer's keyboard. Even the monitor had fallen asleep on this gloomy day. "Keeping the rental costs low, especially for events where they don't need to use the kitchen or have city volunteers help out, will be really important. That alone will help spread the word."

Nancy motioned for Melinda to join her at the computer. "These are the newest options for the window treatments. What do you think?"

The combination of bad weather, and quick progress on many of the former bank's repairs, meant the community center's steering committee hadn't met for almost a month. Richard Everton, a local contractor, had generously offered to oversee most of the mechanical upgrades using at-cost materials and volunteer labor from his crew, so it had been easy for Nancy to steer the ship with just Jerry's guidance.

The lack of committee gatherings had also kept Delores Eklund, the center's financial benefactress and self-appointed decorator, out of Nancy and Jerry's hair. Most of the time.

"All of the blinds are ... very beige." Melinda frowned.

"You are correct. What about the valances?" Nancy tried, and failed, to keep an edge of irritation out of her voice.

"Well, they are a shade darker than beige. Maybe tan? I know we want to keep things neutral, but this is a historic building. It's Craftsman, an era that made good use of earth tones. Is there any way to make it less ... boring?"

"Delores insisted the valances be covered with fabric." Nancy pulled up her notes. "Oh, yes, here: 'linen-like but synthetic to stand up to wear and tear. The blinds need to be vertical, not horizontal. Everything must be in shades of ivory or beige, but not white. This is not a college dorm.'"

"Is that all?"

"Oh, I hope so, since we're getting down to the final design choices. She's past eighty, you know; I'd hoped we'd have tired her out by now." And then Nancy laughed. "And here I thought Jake was going to be the thorn in my side."

Jake Newcastle was the youngest member of Prosper's city council, as well as its most opinionated. A teacher at the regional high school in Swanton, he'd also challenged Jerry for the mayoral post back in November.

"Well, Jake's pretty simple to sort out." Melinda tried to encourage her friend. "He always wants to do the opposite of whatever Jerry does."

"And Frank always backs up Jerry, and Emmett Beck shrugs and won't offer an opinion until his wife makes him." Nancy rested her chin in one hand. "I wish we had a fairy godmother to sweep in and wave her wand. Then, 'poof!' we'd be done."

The furnace upgrades were completed last week when Richard's crew was between regular customers. With the building's internal temperature now easier to regulate, painting could begin in earnest. The two bathrooms' fixtures were adequate, but the small kitchen that had once been the bank's break room had been a sorry sight.

Delores, who was as tight with her money as she was free with her opinions, insisted the appliances stay and the kitchen cabinets simply be freshened with paint. But the cracked countertop needed to be replaced, as cheaply as possible. There was just enough money left for new lights in the front room, where most activities would take place, and Melinda was scouring websites to find affordable vintage-style fixtures with Edison bulbs. The blinds' design might be a lost cause, but she was determined to restore any period elements she could.

"We're getting close, at least," she reminded Nancy. "Frank said just this morning he might have a lead on the kitchen counters."

"If you can find me an eighteen-foot section, cheap yet indestructible, I'm all ears. Two pieces at eleven and seven are what we really need, but Richard can cut down whatever we get." Nancy looked over her list. "And then, there's the critter issue. The bug guy is coming next week, and the bat guys a few weeks after that."

The former bank had been vacant for ten years, and a colony of bats had taken over the second floor. Since they were a protected species, a specialist from Mason City had to be contacted to fix the problem. Someday, when there was more time and money available, the upstairs could be converted into additional meeting rooms or much-needed storage space for the city.

Prosper's city hall was on the historic national register, but its grand exterior concealed a maze of hallways and partitioned rooms, and its second floor was only accessible by an out-of-code stairway.

Other than the library, and now the community center, the town's only other piece of real estate was the metal shed behind city hall. And it was near capacity with the on-call fire department's two vehicles.

Prosper was so small, it didn't even own a snowplow. The town relied on Hartland County to provide those services, as well as law enforcement.

A cyclone of papers and binders blanketed Jerry's desk just a few steps away, but the mayor was out.

"Jerry was full of news this morning," she told Nancy. "Says the water tower needs to be repainted this summer, and then there's a property he might have to foreclose on."

Nancy closed the files for the community center, eager to set that project aside. "I think he's secretly excited about the water tower. It's one small way he can leave his mark on this town. We'll probably just end up with a different shade of municipal green, but you never know. He left about an hour ago for an errand in Swanton, but I wouldn't be surprised if he pops in at the paint store and comes back with samples in hand."

"Sounds like it could be a fun project." Melinda's creativity started to flow, even though the work was still several months out. "Some towns have a slogan on the water tower, or a unique logo."

"Well, it might help him keep his mind off that property down the street. Especially because ..."

Nancy stopped, and Melinda understood. Even among friends, some things were off limits.

"I get it. It's an intriguing situation, but none of my business. Auggie, however, is already on the hunt."

Nancy sighed. "Thanks for the heads up. I'm sure he'll come sniffing around as soon as he can get away."

A woman appeared in city hall's vestibule, then paused to shake the melted snow off her coat. The time for confidences was over, at least for now.

"We'll deal with things as they come," Nancy told Melinda in a low voice. "I hope you get a chance to crack open that novel tonight. Let me know if it's any good; I might have to put myself on the hold list."

✳ 3 ✳

The barn door latched behind Melinda with a satisfying *click*, and it was a relief to be sheltered from the raw northwest wind that pushed a cold mist across the still-barren fields.

"I'm glad I shut you girls inside this morning. March really came in like a lion, huh?" The eight sheep across the aisle fence were quick to voice their opinions, but Melinda knew those probably had nothing to do with the weather. It was suppertime, and her ewes were impatient for their hay and grain.

Hobo was also happy to be in the cozy barn, and took off on some unknown adventure while Melinda paused to acknowledge the impatient meows of her barn cats, Sunny and Stormy. They had stationed themselves on top of the sheep's grain barrels so as not to be overlooked.

"I know, I know, you boys like to eat first." Melinda pulled off her damp chore gloves and gave Sunny's fluffy orange coat a few pets. Stormy, his gray-tabby tail twitching with impatience, allowed only one chin scratch before he ran for the grain room's half-open door. Sunny soon followed, and Melinda and the cats' food bucket brought up the rear.

"Let me get the lid off, OK?" The aroma of warmed-over chicken gravy soon filled the small space. "Here, I'll dump it over part of the kibble, and leave the rest of your snacks dry. I'll refresh your water, then I need to keep moving."

Getting back into a standing position wasn't as easy as it sounded, given all her bulky layers. On a night like tonight, it hardly seemed possible that in another month she could spend less time getting dressed for chores and more time enjoying her animals and her farm.

The ewes, of course, were rather tired of waiting their turn. Melinda could barely get the grain scoop aimed square at the troughs for all the black noses crowded around.

"Good thing the hens are already cared for, since I'm running out of time." Next came the slabs of hay. "I still need to shower and change, and Josh is going to be here sooner than I'd like."

Annie, the most-vocal ewe, let out a loud bellow of what might have been skepticism.

"OK, you're right! I do have to hurry, but the truth is, it feels like he never gets here soon enough." A smile spread across her chilled cheeks. "Yeah, I'm pretty crazy about Josh. He's got the tall, dark and handsome thing down pat. And he's smart, too."

Annie gave a grunt of approval.

"The word on the street is, half the single women of a certain age in this county are jealous of your mama. Guess I'm the lucky one, huh? What do you say, Clover?"

One of last year's lambs had moved to the end of the line, where she could catch Melinda's eye through the gate's metal panel. Clover wasn't shy, but she knew better than to try to steal the spotlight from Annie.

"Don't worry, Josh isn't coming out to the barn tonight." Melinda reached through the wire grid to scratch Clover's forehead. "No one needs a shot, or other medicine, or anything of that sort."

Now that supper was over, Stormy was at her feet, demanding attention. She picked him up, and he leaned against her shoulder.

"Look at you, my little baby," Melinda cooed. "Wanting to snuggle! I can't believe how you and Sunny have changed since my first week here. Remember when Horace left that open bag of cat food on the floor, so you could feed yourselves until I moved in? You had only been here a few days before he left, and he knew you'd be afraid of Ed and Mabel."

The Bauers were retired from farming, except for a few beef cattle Ed kept as a hobby. While they'd been happy to handle chores between Horace's departure and Melinda's arrival, the two skittish stray cats wouldn't have welcomed affection from anyone.

Hobo's paws soon sounded on the bare boards of the haymow's stairs, and he nose-bumped the leg of her jeans in greeting.

"Anything new going on up there? I don't know how you do it, sniffing around with no lights on." Melinda had been surprised at how quickly she'd adjusted to living alone in the country, but she still didn't like to visit the shadowy corners of the barn loft after sundown.

With her chores finally completed, she snapped off the lights and followed Hobo across the farmyard's frozen mud toward the house. It felt good to get inside the enclosed back porch. She kicked off her boots, peeled off her coat and sweatshirt, and followed Hobo into the bright, warm kitchen.

"Smells good, huh?" There was a creamy chicken pasta dish simmering in the slow cooker, but Hobo was more intent on visiting his water bowl.

Grace and Hazel soon appeared from the doorway into the dining room, curious to sniff Melinda's clothes for any hints of the mysteries that only existed outside. The young cats had never taken an interest in exploring it for themselves, and Melinda was relieved. It was enough that Hobo ran in and out, and Sunny and Stormy seemed to find mischief wherever they went. Hazel and Grace had a luxurious life indoors. What more did they need?

She texted Josh to just let himself in the back door, which was only locked overnight or when she was away from home. As she hurried through the dining room and the living room on her way to the stairwell, Melinda gave the downstairs an appraising glance.

It was neat enough. The throw blankets were folded on the back of the couch, and the wood for a welcome fire was stacked behind the living room's grate. The tops of both built-in bookcases, and the dining room's built-in buffet, were mostly free of clutter. The downstairs bedroom, which now was mostly Hobo and the cats' domain, also passed her quick inspection. As charming as the farmhouse was, it was still drafty this time of year. She paused to pull the fleece curtains across the picture window behind the couch.

She came downstairs fifteen minutes later, her hair still wet and wearing a clean pair of jeans and a different sweatshirt, to the welcome sight of Josh bustling around her kitchen. She paused for just a second in the dining room, and noticed how at ease he was as he set the plates on the table and found the glasses and silverware without missing a beat. Hobo followed him everywhere. Even the girls, who had each chosen a chair for their current perches, seemed charmed by his presence.

Melinda felt the same. It filled her with joy, but she was also a bit cautious. Everything had seemed to fall into place with Josh. But Melinda's heart, which had been battered one-too-many times in the past, sometimes questioned if everything was just too easy.

But then Josh looked her way, and his warm smile erased her uncertainties.

"Hey," was all he said as he reached for her hand.

They kissed, and then kissed again, and only Hobo's sudden barks to stop Grace from jumping on the table caused them to break apart.

"Do you ever get a meal in peace around here?" Josh's brown eyes danced with laughter.

"Charlie now does so well with 'sit' and 'stay' that I guess I've forgotten how this can go."

"Hobo rarely obeys commands. But for some reason, he's an angel at mealtime. I think he and Horace had an understanding. Hobo got his supper first, and all was well. It's the girls that can't resist getting their paws into everything."

Even clearing the table wasn't a chore with Josh around. They stood side-by-side at the sink and shared tidbits of their respective days while she washed and he dried. When they moved to the couch, Hobo sprawled across Josh's lap and left Melinda and the cats to fit in wherever they could. They were just about to turn on a movie when the wind began to whistle around the corners of the farmhouse.

"The rain's really coming down now." Melinda gently set Grace aside and went into the dining room to attempt to see outside. Her view was cloaked in darkness, since the glow of the farmyard's light only advanced so far, but the soft *splat, splat* on the storm windows told her the moisture was still liquid. But she shivered and crossed her arms as she remembered last winter's series of blizzards and ice storms that nearly caused her to give up her dream of country life.

Josh was apparently thinking the same. "Don't worry. As long as it's only rain, we're good," he called from the living room. "Let me check my phone. Hmm. No watches or warnings, at least. Hey, while you're up, I'll take a beer if there's one in the fridge."

Melinda could hear Hobo getting more comfortable, then Josh's answering laugh. "I'd get my own, but I think I'm stuck where I am."

"Sure. I was going there next." Melinda pressed her face to the glass again, and blinked. What was that, just up the road? A flash of white light, and then several more, as something moved down from the north. And then red ones, too, as a vehicle flew past the end of her lane with alarming speed.

"Oh, no! An ambulance!" She glanced at the wall clock, the one that had chimed in Grandma and Grandpa Foster's house for decades. "It's just after seven, not too late, but this can't be good."

In Minneapolis, it had been common to see emergency vehicles speeding past her apartment at all hours of the day and night. She might have given them a passing thought, or said a quick prayer for the first responders and those in need, then went back to whatever she was doing. But out here, it was almost a certainty the ambulance was for someone she knew.

Josh joined her at the window. "Which way?"

"They were headed south." The crew would have turned off the blacktop, which meant they had already passed Ed and Mabel's place as well as the corner to Angie and Nathan Hensley's farm. Melinda felt a wave of relief for her close friends, but it was short-lived. Someone in her neighborhood was in trouble.

Before she could call the Bauers, Mabel rang her phone. "Melinda! Oh, I'm so glad you answered. I hoped you were tucked in at home on a night like this."

"Yes, thankfully. Josh is here, too."

"It's Bart, he fell outside in this terrible weather." Melinda could make out Ed's baritone in the background, and Mabel faded out for a second before coming back on the line. "We're getting our coats, Ed's going down there to help. Mind if I stay with you for a bit?"

A stone of worry settled in Melinda's stomach. Bart and Marge Wildwood lived south of her farm, just through the mile. She didn't know Bart well, but considered herself lucky. He was a difficult person, prone to anger with a drinking problem to match. Marge had memory issues, and they were both in their eighties.

Josh's hand on her arm brought her back to the present.

"Sure, come on down," she told Mabel. "You can sit with us. I'll get the coffee on."

While Melinda busied herself in the kitchen, her plans for a quiet evening long forgotten, Josh stood at the double windows by the table. Hobo soon joined him, and they watched for Ed and Mabel to arrive. "I'm going to go with Ed," Josh finally said. "Maybe they could use another set of hands."

Melinda nodded her agreement, although she knew Josh wasn't looking for her permission. He was a veterinarian, not a physician, but would never sit idle while someone was in need. It was the same reason why Doc was a longtime member of Prosper's emergency department.

Hobo slipped through his doggie door into the back porch as soon as Ed's truck pulled in the drive. Melinda soon went out, too, and her sock-covered toes quickly turned to ice on the painted floor of the unheated room. Josh pulled on his boots and his coat, and Melinda reached for Hobo's collar when she saw Mabel under the yard light.

"No, you have to stay in here with me. Ed's not coming to the house, at least not now. Someone needs help."

By the time Mabel made it up the concrete steps, Ed and Josh were already halfway down the drive. Mabel settled on the porch's bench with a heavy sigh and wriggled out of her soaked coat. Her white curls were disheveled from her hood and the damp.

"Oh, my dear, thanks for letting me come by. It would be so hard to wait it out alone at home, and I'm afraid the news won't be good." Mabel set aside her gloves and reached down to greet Hobo. "How's my second-favorite neighbor? Let me get these boots off," she told Melinda, "and I'll tell you everything I know."

✳ 4 ✳

Once they were settled at the kitchen table, coffee cups and cookies in hand, Mabel brought Melinda up to speed.

Bart had called Clarence Murphy, who lived at the other end of the Wildwoods' mile, that afternoon and asked to borrow a skill saw. Bart's was apparently on its last round, and he was trying to finish some project in the house. The Wildwoods' home was one of the oldest in the township, and always in need of repair. Clarence had agreed to bring the saw over after supper, but wasn't prepared for what he discovered when he came up his neighbors' lane.

"The side door on the house was wide open." Mabel shook her head as Melinda listened, her chin in her hands. "Clarence couldn't figure it out, at first. Their lane is long, and those thick trees block the house from the road, as you know. But then he pulled up in the yard, and saw a big lump there by the sidewalk."

It was Bart, half-frozen and, according to Clarence, completely drunk. He'd come out to get a tool from the shed, Bart babbled to Clarence, and tripped over a rock. There was nothing around Bart but the snow-covered lawn, but Clarence didn't question Bart's story. How long Bart had been out there was hard to tell, and Bart couldn't, or wouldn't, say.

But his ankle was purple and swollen, and his ears and face covered in a terrible bloom of red and white. For various reasons, Bart was unable to get on his feet. So Clarence called 911, then ran to his truck for the stack of blankets everyone carried around this time of the year.

"Bart started to shake once he was covered up. Clarence hated to leave him there, but there wasn't anything more he could do at the moment. He was on his way to the house, to look for Marge, when he called Ed."

"Was she there?"

"We don't know. Clarence had to hang up, he wanted to keep his line clear in case dispatch called him back." Mabel wiped her cheeks with the back of her hand. "Marge is so forgetful these days. Every time I've seen her, she ... oh, I should go over there more often! We're not close friends, you see, but between Bart's temper, and ..."

"It's not your fault." Melinda put a hand over her friend's, which was trembling now. "No one can look after them, all the time. They refuse to move to town, I know, and even their kids can't talk any sense into them, from what you've said."

"I've always been afraid of this very thing." Mabel lowered her voice until it was nearly a whisper. "You know, Ed and I were talking about them, just the other day. Someday, something's going to go wrong with them. Really wrong. And it's going to be tragic, and terrible, and there isn't going to be anything anyone can do to stop it."

Melinda thought of the Schermann brothers, of how long they managed to stay out here before Wilbur, and then Horace, had to move to Scenic Vista. Stubbornness and denial could only take people so far, especially when they were elderly. The call the Wildwoods' grown children would receive tonight was the very one Ada and Kevin had feared for years.

"Well, it's in God's hands now." Melinda searched for something comforting to say. Hobo was at her feet, his brown head leaned against her jeans in a show of support. "I know I'm biased, but the Prosper emergency crew really knows their stuff."

"I pray this will turn out alright, somehow. Maybe this is the wake-up call Bart needs, that they both need. It's not even forty out there, and this terrible rain! They almost made it through another winter, thank goodness; but they cannot stay out here much longer. If it's not this, something else ..."

Mabel's phone buzzed, and they both jumped.

"Yes?" Mabel's shoulders dropped, and Melinda wondered if it was from relief or despair. "Oh, honey, that's terrible! But she's OK, at least? No, no, you and Josh should stay and help, if you can. Yes. Sure. I think there's a phone list, there on the wall by the sink. The kids should be at the top." A small smile crossed Mabel's weary face. "OK, I'll tell her. We'll be ready."

"What happened?"

"Marge was in the house still, thank God. She was upstairs, which they hardly use at all now, curled up in the hallway. Said she went up there to get warm."

The downstairs was freezing cold, and rain had blown in all over the kitchen floor. Marge had no idea what was going on. She told Ed and Josh that Bart had "gone to town," but couldn't say which one, or when he'd left.

Bart's ankle might be broken, and he was in shock from hypothermia. The ambulance had just left to take him to the hospital in Swanton.

Josh tried to talk Marge into putting on a coat and shoes, but she didn't know him and became belligerent. Clarence was still there, and seemed to have more luck getting through to Marge. He had volunteered to take her to Swanton, under the guise of simply going to see Bart. But the first responders had called ahead, and a doctor was going to give Marge her own evaluation.

"What about their kids?"

"Ed's going to call the daughter, she lives closest. He and Josh are going to mop the kitchen floor and tidy up before they come back. And Ed said he hopes your cookie jar is stocked. He'd sure appreciate a few, and a hot cup of coffee, when he gets done."

Hazel padded into the kitchen and made a beeline for Mabel's lap. Not to be outdone, Grace soon planted herself in

Melinda's and they all waited, more patiently now, for Ed and Josh to return. The rain still fell in sheets outside, and the wind rattled the farmhouse's metal storm windows.

"There they are," Mabel finally said. She leaned over to peer out into the dark. "Oh, I hope they've found out more. I can't imagine Bart or Marge is going to be able to come home anytime soon. Thank goodness they don't have any animals to tend to, haven't for years."

"I was wondering about that." The other emotion Melinda felt was guilt. She knew how desperate things were at the Wildwoods' place, but had made excuses to not reach out. "I didn't think so, but I would have been glad to help with chores if they did."

Hobo rushed out of the kitchen and this time, Melinda let him go. He and Ed soon appeared in the doorway, and Josh was right behind. Ed's lined face was weary as he pulled off his gloves and coat. "Bart's lucky to be alive, he could have frozen to death. And Marge?" He shook his head. "She didn't know up from down. If she'd done the opposite, and wandered out into the rain and dark, I don't know how we ever could have found her."

Josh tossed his soaked knit cap on the floor register, and joined them at the table. "Bart, at least, had put on his coat and boots before he started for the shed. Marge would have been outside with no protection at all."

He answered the question in Melinda's eyes. "The hospital promised to call in someone from social services to talk to Marge, not just a doctor. You know Bart. Once he comes around, he's going to play it off like nothing's wrong."

"She may never come home," Mabel said quietly.

"Don't see how." Ed rubbed his chapped hands together. "Man, I'm stiff from the cold." He shook his head. "The house was a wreck, too. We cleaned up as best as we could."

Melinda added a plate of cookies to the table. "Did you get ahold of their daughter?"

"She was upset, of course, but angry, too. Told me there's no power of attorney, no health care directive, nothing. Bart keeps refusing to set anything up. And Marge can't, or won't, stand up to him. Their son's almost stopped talking to them, because of how things are. It's going to be difficult to get them the help they need. The paperwork alone's going to be a nightmare."

"Can't someone do something?" Melinda was incredulous. "This is insane!"

"It may take a judge." Josh wrapped his hands around his mug. "It's the only way to get them help."

"Well, I guess we've done all we can for tonight." Mabel sat back in her chair, and hugged Hazel to her chest. "As for moving to town ..." Her voice faltered with tears. "I guess that day comes for all of us."

Ed looked away, and a melancholy tension seeped across the table. Josh's face was full of questions, but Melinda's answering look implored him to stay silent. Last fall, Ed suggested the Bauers should start to look for a buyer for their acreage. Mabel didn't want to go, no matter which town they might land in. They were in their early seventies, a good ten years' younger than the Wildwoods, but Ed worried that country life was getting to be too much for both of them.

"You know, I've been thinking," Ed said now, "I know we're not getting any younger. Or more flexible, for that matter." He rubbed his right knee. "But seeing Bart and Marge, well, maybe we're much better off than I thought."

Mabel's head snapped up, a light of hope in her eyes. She was known for speaking her mind, but wisely kept silent for now. If Ed was having a change of heart, he needed to come to that conclusion on his own.

"Well, there's no magic age when it's time to hang it up." Josh kept his tone casual and light, and once again, Melinda was glad he was there. She was in Mabel's camp, and Ed knew it. Josh had an outsider's perspective that kept him neutral. "Even if you give it another year or two, you can always change your mind later."

Melinda reached for Mabel's hand, and smiled at Ed. "Things out here wouldn't be the same without either of you."

"I don't really want to go," Ed admitted. "Of course I'd love to live out here forever. But I just wanted to do what's best for us."

"You remind me so much of Grandpa Shrader," Melinda told him. "He tried to retire from the store when he was about your age. But then, his purpose was gone. He was so depressed and always underfoot, and Grandma insisted he go back for a few hours each day. And he lived well into his nineties."

"See?" Mabel raised an eyebrow at her husband. "Retirement can be deadly. And dear, I don't want to have to kick you out of the house to save my sanity."

"You're a better cook than I am." Ed smiled at his wife. "I'd starve on my own. I guess we could stick it out for a while, at least." Then he yawned. "Look at the time, it's already after nine! We should head home."

"Let me know when you hear more." Melinda found a plastic container in the cabinet. "Please take some of these cookies. We shouldn't eat them all."

It felt nice to say 'we,' she thought as she glanced at Josh. On a different night, not so long ago, Ed and Mabel would have left together and she would have been alone. Hobo and the cats were her family, of course, but it was such a comfort to have Josh there.

Josh walked Mabel and Ed to the back door. "The temperature's dropped some more," he reported when he returned to the kitchen. "I think it's going to get icy. Good thing they left when they did."

There was a question in his gaze that made Melinda's heart flutter. She could play it coy, make a joke, or wait for Josh to say more. The evening had been a rollercoaster of emotions, and she was suddenly tired and exhausted. She had no energy left for anything but the truth.

"I know it's only a ten-minute drive normally, but the roads will get bad. Do you think you should head home?"

He squeezed her hand. "Do you want me to stay?"

"Yes. Yes, I do."

He leaned in and kissed her. "That would be a first. Of course, I don't have to spend the night for us to, well, do what we've been doing for a few weeks already."

"Oh, I know." She pressed her forehead against his cheek. "I don't mind living alone, even way out here. But I just ..."

The thought of lying there alone, on a night like this, without Josh at her side, made her feel terribly lonely. The idea of him staying over was just the opposite: a wonderful feeling, even if it was a little scary. Because it was clear she needed him more than she wanted to admit, even to herself.

Josh seemed to understand. "Then I'll stay." He shrugged and squeezed her hand again, then went to Horace's ancient refrigerator and pulled down its stainless-steel handle. "Charlie has plenty of food and water, and he can get out to the backyard if he needs to." He reached in for two beers, then gave her a quick kiss on the cheek as he passed by. "Seems like we were going to watch a movie. I'll see if Hobo will let me have my spot back."

Melinda looked out at the darkness and the rain, and Bart and Marge's struggles weighed on her mind. Her neighbors were safe and warm for the night, but their troubles were far from over. And then, she glanced around her kitchen, and she felt blessed. She didn't see the outdated appliances and tired linoleum. She saw her home, warm and bright, and felt the comfort of being with someone she loved.

* * *

The Watering Hole's parking lot was nearly full, and it was only four in the afternoon. But Melinda wasn't surprised. This was the third warm day in a row, the sun was shining, and people were eager to be out and about.

She was so glad to find a parking spot, she didn't mind that it was almost in the alley. Anything would be closer than carrying the totes of vegetable scraps across the street to Prosper Hardware. While Jessie would let her out the kitchen door later, Melinda knew it was locked, so she started for the sidewalk that would take her to the restaurant's entrance.

Prosper Hardware had been a beehive of activity all day, as well, and Melinda was tired. But it was a content sort of tired. And the thought of how excited her sheep and chickens would be for a fresh batch of Jessie's food scraps made her smile as she rounded the corner.

What a difference a few days could make, both in town and in the country. Bart and Marge's situation, while not ideal, had at least improved. Marge had secured a short-term stay at a Swanton senior-living facility while she waited for a room to open up at a memory-care unit in Charles City. And Bart? He was as stubborn as ever, and had insisted on returning home as soon as he was discharged from the hospital the following day. But the good news was his ankle had only been sprained, not broken, and their daughter was trying to arrange for a home health aide to come to the farm a few times a week. It remained to be seen if Bart would welcome such a visitor, but it was a step forward.

Jessie and Doug Kirkpatrick had done their best to brighten the Watering Hole's interior since they took the business over a few years ago. The dark-paneled walls had been coated in cream paint, and light-blue curtains now hung at the front windows. But the place still carried the usual small-town tavern aroma of French fries and beer, and a wave of animated conversation mixed with country tunes from the jukebox greeted Melinda when she opened the door.

Jessie had started saving the restaurant's vegetable scraps for Melinda during last summer's drought, and pickup was now twice a week. While the rest of Prosper didn't seem aware of Melinda and Jessie's little arrangement, Doug simply nodded and pointed toward the kitchen. "She's in the back, getting ready for the evening rush."

"Thanks." But as Melinda passed the bar, she saw a sight that nearly stopped her in her tracks. There was Bart, perched on the third stool down, elbow-deep in debate with the man to his right and a full mug of beer before him on the counter.

The surprise must have shown on her face when she slipped through the door.

"Yep, he's back." Jessie pushed a strand of dark, curly hair out of her eyes. The neat knot at the nape of her neck, however, was still trying to hold on. "Came waltzing in here yesterday, like nothing ever happened. I think a buddy gave him a ride, at least. I can't imagine he should be driving with his ankle like that. Doug's keeping an eye on him, for sure."

"What did he say? Anything?"

"Oh, you know Bart. He loves to talk about everyone, and everything, but what matters. The fact that word's already spread about what happened doesn't faze him. All he said was that they've been sick, and Marge's still a bit under the weather, but he's back to his old self." Jessie rolled her eyes. "I think we all could do with less of that, Bart included."

"They won't let Marge come back home, and it's not just her dementia." Melinda leaned against the wall as Jessie reached into one of the industrial refrigerators and pulled out two bins. "The house is in such bad shape, there's no handrail on those steep stairs. She's on the wait list for a memory-care unit, at least. I don't know where that leaves Bart."

"Right out there, I'd say." Jessie jerked her chin toward the bar. "But we've been having a good week, one of our best. We had a record crowd for Friday night's fish fry. With Lent going on for a few weeks yet, I expect that's going to continue."

"Glad to hear it! And thanks again for the greens, as always. I have some empties out in the trunk, but I forgot to bring them in." She looked up, surprised by the sudden flash of worry on Jessie's face. "What is it? Is something wrong?"

"No. I mean, not really. Not here," she added quickly. "Doug and I are fine." She pulled off her plastic gloves, tossed them in the nearby trash bin, then leaned on the stainless-steel counter.

"Do you remember when I started saving the scraps for you? You wanted to pay me, but ..."

"Oh, please, let me do that! I know it would just go in the compost bin, but you always take the time to pick out the best, fresh stuff. I really appreciate it."

"Oh, no, I'm happy to do it." There was a faint smile, then Jessie took a deep breath. "I did say, back then, that I'd just ask for a favor in return sometime. And, well, something's come up."

"Sure." Melinda shrugged. "Whatever it is, I'm glad to help."

Jessie cracked the door that opened into the back hallway, and made sure no one was loitering nearby. "Good. Too many sets of ears in this town." She latched it tight, then crossed her arms. "It's my cousin, Lauren. She's in trouble, and she needs a place to stay."

"In trouble? How?"

"I hate to ask." Jessie seemed nervous. "I don't want to impose, and I don't mean she has to stay with you. It's just, I don't know what to do. She called me last night, crying. Her husband, he's ... well, he's what they call 'difficult,' I guess."

"Difficult like selfish, or ..." Melinda's eyes slid toward the door. "Like Bart?"

"Both." Jessie frowned. "Last night, he was out drinking with his buddies, *again*, and they got in a terrible fight when he got home. She told him she wants him to move out, and he shoved her against the wall, said the house is as much his as it is hers, and he's not going anywhere."

Jessie looked down, then answered the question Melinda was about to ask.

"He hasn't actually hit her, not yet. But you know he will. And to top it off, she thinks he's cheating, too. Everything seemed fine while they were dating but, I don't know, it's like he started to change once the ring was on her finger. She's decided to file for divorce, but she needs time to come up with a plan. She wants to get away, at least for a little while."

Now that the story was out, Jessie relaxed a bit. "She lives up in Minnesota, in a little town west of Rochester. Everyone knows everyone, we have a lot of family around there."

Melinda picked up the idea. "But if she leaves the state, he won't know where to look, and it'll buy her some time. Does he know you and Doug?"

"Not enough to suspect anything. And that's part of the reason why she reached out to me. I only met him once, when they were first dating, at a family reunion. Haven't seen either of them since. I had the flu really bad when they got married last year, so we didn't go. We somehow keep missing them at Christmas, with everyone having so many places to visit in just a few days."

Tears sprang into Jessie's eyes. "We were so close, growing up. I've missed seeing her. But now, I think there's a reason why it happened like it did."

Melinda rubbed her forehead and tried to think this through. Lauren couldn't stay with Jessie and Doug in Prosper, at least not right away; there was always a chance her husband would figure out where she went. And while the locals meant well, a new face in town would raise a lot of questions. The last thing Lauren needed was scrutiny from strangers.

Jessie hadn't asked her to take Lauren in, but it was clear the woman needed somewhere to go. What must it be like, to feel cornered and afraid? Even with her family's support, Lauren had a long road ahead of her. Melinda wanted to help. But the situation wasn't just precarious for Lauren; it could quickly turn dangerous for everyone involved.

Melinda's farmhouse was remote, for sure; and while she and Jessie were friendly, they weren't close enough that Melinda would be singled out as an obvious accomplice to such a plan. She thought again of Marge, and even Bart, of how bad she felt about turning a blind eye to their troubles when it would have cost her so little to be a better neighbor.

But this? She didn't know if she should do this.

"I know what you must be thinking," Jessie finally said. "And I can't ask you to do that. No, no, it's fine. It's too risky. But I need to find her a safe place to go. I've already checked around, there are no women's shelters anywhere near here. Even if there were, Lauren would want to bring her dog, and I don't know if that's even possible. I'm running out of places to look."

"Now, that I can help with." Melinda squeezed her friend's arm. "I'll start digging around. She may have to go to Mason City or Waterloo. But it'll be better than where she is now."

"What if there's a waitlist? What if she gets a chance to get away, but she can't ..."

"We'll cross that bridge when we come to it. When does she plan to leave?"

"She's not sure yet. Might be a week, even two. She may only get one chance to do this safely, so the timing has to be right. She went to her mom and dad's again last night. Alec will give her some space for a few days, say he's sorry, the usual. But it won't fix things."

There wasn't anything either of them could do, not right now. Melinda stacked one bin on top of the other, and started for the back door. "We'll figure something out. There has to be a way to help her."

Jessie held the door open with one hand and wiped her eyes again with the other. "Just knowing someone else cares gives me hope. I'm going to give you free veggie scraps for the next thirty years, but even that won't be enough to make this even."

∗ 5 ∗

A trip to Horace and Wilbur's apartment always started with a scavenger hunt to see what Melinda could share from the farm. This time, she'd packed two kinds of cookies along with the antique pocket watch and the ledger.

Josh leaned against the kitchen counter and stuffed his hands into his jacket's pockets, as if he already felt like he was in the way. "Are you sure this is a good idea? I mean, I'm not family."

"Of course it is." Melinda gave him a quick kiss on the cheek, then reached for her purse and canvas totes. "And neither am I, if we're being technical. Besides, Horace has asked a thousand questions about you. He wants answers."

"Just how often do you talk to him?" Josh's brown eyes danced with humor. "I mean, I didn't know I was being discussed at length."

This visit might go smoothly, after all. And she was so excited about the ledger and the pocket watch, she couldn't wait to get in the car.

"You know Horace, he's nosy in his own quiet way. Or, I should say, you're about to find out. He prides himself on keeping up with what's happening in the outside world. And that includes everything in my life, and here at the farm. And don't worry, you won't be the only non-family member at this gathering. Kevin's bringing Jack, his boyfriend."

"What about Ada?"

"She has a dentist appointment." Melinda was sorry to miss a chance to spend time with Horace's baby sister, who was now in her early seventies. "But Kevin told her about the pocket watch and the ledger, showed her the photos I sent him."

She reached for Josh's hand, which was a feat considering how full her arms were, and gave it a squeeze. "But don't worry about Ada. I've told her all about you already, several times over."

"Buddy, I envy you." Josh rubbed Hobo's ears. "You get to stay home and nap while I'm summoned before the judge." He had a thought. "Hey. Sounds like their apartment's not that big. Are you sure we'll all fit?"

"Nice try. The nursing home has dozens of folding chairs ready for situations like this. Let's go."

Scenic Vista was in Elm Springs, about ten miles north and west of the farm. The senior-living facility sat on the edge of town, as close to country living as the Schermann brothers could get these days. But the facility was clean and well-staffed, and Horace and Wilbur had a one-bedroom apartment that looked out over the spacious back yard, where gravel paths meandered among the trees and scores of birds bellied up to the feeders.

"Nice place," Josh said as they pulled into a parking space. "I've heard good things about it. One of my clients moved here in the fall, they let her bring her little dog."

Melinda laughed. "I'm sure 'little' was the key word there. Hobo would never fit in here, no matter how much he and Horace care for each other. I guess I got to be the lucky one, so I can't complain."

Jack and Kevin were waiting in the community room just off the entrance. Kevin's blue eyes, so like those of his great uncles', shined with excitement behind his glasses. He eagerly shook Josh's hand, then turned to Melinda.

"I can't wait to see this watch. Or the ledger. And cookies! Mom sent some, too, so they aren't going to starve."

Jack held up a canvas bag. "And Easter decorations. Their apartment's been kind of bare since the Christmas stuff came down."

Horace was just outside the apartment's entrance, pretending to study the large activity calendar posted in the hallway. But Melinda could tell by the set of his shoulders that he'd been eagerly awaiting their arrival.

He wasn't big on hugs, so Melinda simply patted his arm and introduced Josh. "Well, now, I'm glad to meet you." Horace offered his hand, and Melinda saw Josh relax. Horace had a calm, easygoing way that made people feel at ease. "So you're a vet, huh? Melinda's done well with the farm, but I'm sure she could use someone to help keep Annie in line."

"Yes, sir. I'll do my best." It was clear Josh was in good with Horace, and it had only taken a few minutes to get there. "I'm based in Swanton, took over a practice last spring."

"And you're helping Melinda and Karen with the cats." Horace nodded his approval. "That's good work you're doing. I have a soft spot for them, but there's too many strays and barn critters as it is."

"The spay clinics start up again next week," Melinda told Horace. "And we hope to go to twice a month starting in May. The wait list is already filling up."

Kevin motioned them to come into the apartment, where Wilbur was settled in his lift chair by the picture window.

"Should I say hello to Wilbur?" Josh whispered to Melinda as they found their seats. Jack had already set up folding chairs in a loose circle around the main room, which had a small kitchenette on one side. "Or will it just confuse him?"

"I just smile and wave. He doesn't know me, never really did. Horace can read his brother like a book. If he feels like Wilbur can absorb introductions today, he'll bring it up."

Jack set out a basket of plastic colored eggs next to the television and pulled a stuffed toy rabbit out of his tote. He was about to place it next to the eggs, but Wilbur's eyes lit up with interest and he held out one feeble hand.

"Go ahead." Horace nodded his approval. "He likes things like that."

Wilbur cradled the soft rabbit in his arms, a gesture so gentle that a lump formed in Melinda's throat. He'd been robust and daring back in the day, from what Horace and Ada had said. It was sad to see him reduced to this state, but for someone in his late nineties, his situation could have been much worse.

The cookies were shared, and Kevin came back from the facility's kitchen with a pot of coffee. "Everyone settled? Good. Melinda, I can't wait one minute more. Show us what you brought!"

Out came the ledger, and Horace laughed with delight when it passed into his weathered hands. "My stars! You found that, in the front bedroom?"

"Well, under the front bedroom. Grace and Hazel wanted to help me pull it from its hiding place, but Mom and Aunt Miriam kept them back."

The yellowed ledger was handed around and carefully examined. Horace said he'd never seen this one, which raised eyebrows around the room. So there had been more?

It made sense, Melinda realized. But, where were they? Probably lost to time.

Horace recognized his grandpa's handwriting, even after all these years, and hazarded a few guesses regarding some of the initials listed in the book's timeworn pages.

Unfortunately, none of them rang a bell with Melinda. Jack and Kevin pressed for details, but Horace waved them off.

"Oh, now, it's been so long; I couldn't say for sure. None of them are around, anymore. And their families either don't know a thing, or don't want to remember. It might have been just a little booze, you see, but it was still breaking the law."

"I guess we'll have to fill in the blanks with our imaginations." Josh leaned over Horace's arm for a better look. It made Melinda smile to see the two of them, side by side, enjoying the mysteries of the ledger.

Kevin caught her eye and gave her a wink. There had never been much doubt in her heart, but it was gratifying to see it made official: Josh was in.

"And there's something else." She reached back into the tote and pulled out a small, wrapped parcel. "Horace, this is for you."

"Now, wait. What's this?"

She gently pressed the package into his hand. Horace always refused anything that smacked of charity. "I didn't buy it, I found it. So you have to take it."

Gasps echoed around the room when Horace lifted the pocket watch from its nest. He raised it by its delicate chain, which had been repaired, then thought better of it and cradled the disk in his hand for support. "Well, I'll be. Haven't seen this in, oh, forty years."

"It was with the ledger, in the box under the floorboards," Melinda explained. "Do you know who it belonged to?"

Horace knew what he was looking for, and gently turned over the watch. "W.E.S. Oh, that was grandpa's father, William Ernst Schermann. He came from Germany when he was a young man, traveled weeks on an overcrowded ship to get to New York. He came through Chicago, then came out here." He turned to Melinda with pride in his eyes. "He was a Civil War veteran, to boot. He and his wife are buried in the church cemetery."

The Schermanns were founding members of First Lutheran, two miles' south of the farm. Between Kevin and Ada's visits, Melinda kept an eye on the family's plots. "Oh, yes! I think I've seen him. Or, well, you know."

"Do you think it's platinum?" Jack wanted to know. "Is there a serial number on the back? I saw some once on one of those antique shows. Some of the watches were very valuable, worth thousands of dollars. Not that it matters in the end. It's the sentimental value that counts."

Melinda said the jewelry store in Swanton had confirmed Jack's hunch. She pointed at the large-numbered clock on the wall. "See? The watch still keeps perfect time."

Horace gave her a wary look. "I thought you said this didn't cost you anything."

"I said I found it." She grinned. "Don't worry about it. Consider it a very early birthday present." That made Horace laugh, as his special day didn't come around until late in the year.

Ada had heard stories about an antique watch in the family, but Kevin said his mom didn't know the details. "It apparently went missing at some point," he told Horace, "which we now know to be true. Do you know what happened?"

"Well, it passed to Grandpa Jacob. He wore it every Sunday," Horace said softly. "To church, of course, then kept it on all through dinner. Wore it to town, sometimes. He said it made him feel like a real gentleman, a timepiece like that. When I was a boy, he and grandma lived two miles east from the farm. Down the road from Angie and Nathan's place. Big, square house."

Josh shook his head. "What a find. I wonder how it got in the cubbyhole?"

Horace thought for a moment. "I remember Father had it, once Grandpa passed. These were out of fashion by then, so he didn't wear it. But it was kept in the bottom of Mother's jewelry box. He pulled it out from time to time, cleaned it and checked the mechanism."

He looked over at his brother, who had the stuffed rabbit in one hand and a cookie in the other. Wilbur stared out the window, but Melinda wasn't sure if he really noticed the birds chattering at the feeder.

"Father was saving it for Wilbur, was going to give it to him as a wedding gift. First-born son and all."

Josh raised an eyebrow, but Melinda shook her head. She'd fill in the rest of Wilbur's story for him on the way home.

"And Father had dementia, there at the end. He didn't know where he was, or who he was." Melinda thought about how hard it must have been for Horace and Wilbur to tend to both their parents in their later years. And then, for Horace to care for Wilbur as long as he did. She hoped he might say more, but he turned his focus back to the watch. "No one knew where Father had put it. I guess I figured it was just gone."

Melinda would have torn the house apart trying to find something so special, so memorable. But apparently, Horace had approached the watch's disappearance with the pragmatism he'd leaned on all of his life. He'd accepted something he couldn't change, and then let it go.

"Well, it's back now." The watch had come full circle, and Melinda pressed it into Horace's palm. "You keep it. Maybe Wilbur would enjoy looking at it, from time to time. The past is more real to him these days than the present."

"It feels pretty real to me today, too." Kevin opened the ledger again, as if a new clue might have appeared inside in the past ten minutes. "I can see why Great-Grandpa Jacob hid this under the floorboards like he did. That's how they got Capone, you know. Tax evasion."

Horace laughed. "Oh, I don't know about that. It wasn't that big of an operation, from what I heard." Melinda thought Horace knew more than he would admit, but she let it slide.

"I think you should keep the ledger," Horace told Kevin. "You're so interested in it, and we don't have much room here. Besides, Dave got what was left of the still."

"I'd be honored to take it." Kevin looked at Melinda. "Now, if we just had a recipe for the hooch."

"I'll keep an eye out," she promised. "Maybe I need to check the floors in the other closets for secret compartments. Horace, I wanted to ask you ... George Freitag remembers there being a speakeasy west of town in the forties, if not before. Do you remember where it was?"

"Oh, I didn't go to those, myself." Horace thought for a moment. "Let's see. Oh, yes, of course. It was at Hawk Hollow."

"Are you sure?" Melinda could hardly contain her excitement. Hawk Hollow, which was only a few miles from

Melinda's farm, had once included a creamery, post office, and small store.

"That's the place. Old Mr. Peabody, the one that built that grand house, just north of the bridge? He operated it out of a shed way back in that field, down by the creek. It was gone long before the house burned in the sixties. But back in the day, it was a rough and rowdy place." Horace's tone indicated that, in his opinion, that wasn't a great selling point.

"Sounds like a good time to me." Kevin laughed. "Well, Mr. Peabody just might be one of the buyers in this ledger. Mom has a cousin in Nebraska who claims to be a family historian. It's a long shot, but I'll see what I can find out."

* 6 *

Balancing a tray of seedlings in both hands while climbing the basement stairs was bad enough, but the two curious kitties circling her shoes made it almost dangerous.

"Hazel, look out!" A meow answered from below. "I can't see where you are, even if you're a step or two ahead of me. I don't want to drop these tomato plants. Not only will there be a mess to clean up, but I'll have to start over."

The garden's soil wouldn't be warm enough for transplants until early May, but Melinda was determined to get a jump on things. So, apparently, was Grace.

"How did you know?" The fluffy calico waited in front of the dining room's built-in buffet, anxious to supervise the young plants' arrival. "And no, I don't need your help."

A spread of old towels already covered the top of the cabinet, and Melinda set down the tray of biodegradable cups with a sigh of relief. Her tomatoes had arrived at their next home, and she hadn't lost one yet. Thankfully, Horace's grandpa built the buffet just high enough that a cat couldn't make the full leap from the floor. Hazel, however, eyed the distance with a gleam in her eye.

"Can't quite do it, huh? Yeah, that's why the chairs are pushed in tight around the table." The south-facing windows above the buffet gave the starter plants some of the best light in the house, and Melinda could feel the warmth on her face as she arranged the tiny pots in efficient rows. Her garden was never as robust as the one Horace and Wilbur planned each year, but since her move to the country, Melinda had been bit by the canning bug and spoiled by the unbeatable taste of homegrown vegetables.

A few more young plants could enjoy the single southern window in Wilbur's old upstairs bedroom, where the always-closed door would keep them safe from Hobo and the cats' curious paws. But the other light-filled spaces in the house were either filled with houseplants, or in high-traffic areas. If she did it right, there'd be room on the buffet for the rest of the tomatoes, and most of the peppers, too.

"It's hard to find this variety in stores," she reminded Hobo, who'd left his nest on the couch in the adjoining room to check her progress. "I can't just run somewhere and pick up more German Pinks if these don't make it. You have to start them from seed, you see. They've outgrown those lights in the canning room; they need a chance to thrive."

As she headed back through the kitchen, she checked the blueberry muffins baking in the oven. Despite the comforting aroma, her mind remained restless as she retrieved more young plants from the basement's canning room.

Jessie's cousin also needed a chance to put down new roots. And while Melinda had never been in Lauren's situation, she remembered how it felt to be unsure of what next week would bring. How it felt to have your life turned upside down and realize the things you'd always assumed would be steadfast and true had fallen away.

Shouldn't she take this opportunity to give someone the support they needed? Melinda had made some calls to women's shelters in the region, and only one of them took pets. It was a possibility, but there was always the question of whether they would have an opening when Lauren needed it.

One option would be for someone to take in Peanut, Lauren's Corgi, while she stayed at one of the other shelters. But all of them were so far away from Prosper. It would be ideal if Lauren could find a place close to Jessie and Doug.

"I don't know." Melinda sighed as she reached for the second tray of tomato plants. "I don't know what I should do. I owe Jessie, for all she's done for the sheep and the chickens, as well as her friendship. And I have a spare bedroom," she reminded herself for what had to be the tenth time in the past few days. "I live in the middle of nowhere. Hobo makes friends with every dog he comes across. Maybe I could step up, for a few days, at least, if there was no other way."

She paused as she passed the kitchen sink, and stared out its west-facing window. Beyond the farm's windbreak, still-brown fields rolled toward the horizon in every direction. Her closest neighbors were a half-mile away, and her farm lane was long. No one had to know, really. And if she decided to tell Ed and Mabel, or Angie and Nathan, she could count on her friends to keep it quiet.

But the remoteness of her farm also had one serious drawback: If trouble came, it would take several minutes for any help to reach them.

The sight of Horace's old landline phone, which still clung defiantly to the narrow wall between the end of the cabinets and the porch door, gave Melinda an idea. She dispatched the tomatoes to the buffet, then reached for her smartphone.

"Hey, Adelaide. How's it going? I'm trying to make a decision about something. If you have a few minutes, I'd like to run it past you."

* * *

Lizzie growled in protest as she turned up the Beauforts' lane, but the first muddy splash from the gravel driveway's ruts made Melinda glad she'd fired up Horace's old truck.

"Easy, girl." She patted the dash's cracked vinyl, but quickly got both hands firmly back on the wheel. The lane was a wreck from freezing and thawing, far worse than the road. Or even Melinda's driveway.

"I thought you'd like to get out for a spin. I just hope we don't end up with you spinning your tires. Mason might have to get the tractor and pull us out."

Adelaide's husband was on the sunny side of the stately farmhouse's wraparound porch, his carpentry tools scattered across a makeshift sawhorse-and-plywood table that kept everything out of the muck hiding in the still-dormant grass. Renovation of the historic home, which sported a mix of Victorian and Queen-Anne elements, had been a work in progress since the retired couple purchased the property a few years ago. They had lived for years in the Madison, Wisconsin, area, but Mason had grown up near Swanton.

His considerable carpentry skills had been put to use inside during the winter months, but he'd obviously been working outside part of the last few weeks. Several of the porch railing's spindles showed the soft tan of fresh wood, and two of the front parlor's windows looked to be new.

One of the Beauforts' black labs sniffed the dried remains of last year's garden. The other lounged on the now-sturdy porch steps, one eye on the chickens free-ranging under an ancient oak and the other on Mason's current project. Both dogs began to bark when they spotted Lizzie in their yard.

"Hello there!" Mason pulled the pencil from behind his ear and raised it in salute as Melinda hopped down from Lizzie's rusted fender. "How's it going?"

"Busy at the store, busy at the farm." Melinda picked her way across the soft soil of the yard, then stopped to slide her shoes across the boot-scraper that jutted up next to the sidewalk. Mason laughed as he reached for his tape measure.

"Oh, don't worry about it. Just take them off at the door. We've lowered our expectations to trying to keep the mud in the mudroom, if you know what I mean."

"Don't I ever." She gave closest dog a pat on the head, and was rewarded with a happy tail wag. "But it's a sign that spring is almost here."

"Can't come too soon. I have a few things I want to get done."

Melinda stifled a laugh at Mason's announcement, as his to-do list was one of the longest she'd ever encountered: finish painting the last sides of the house in a lavender-themed color scheme, replace the rest of the dozens of windows, and repair the fish-scale details under the historic home's gables. Countless more projects waited inside, as the couple hoped to one day turn their charming acreage into a working-farm retreat. And then, there was the animal menagerie to care for, which included two stubborn goats, a rescue pig, several chickens, the dogs and cats, and whatever else might have arrived since Melinda's last visit.

"What are you working on today?" She pointed at the stack of trim boards leaned against the home's narrow clapboard siding.

"Scales for the gables." Mason rubbed his short gray beard and glanced skyward. "They're unique. I looked everywhere, even online, to see if I could order what I needed. But, like just about everything else around here, we have to go custom." The lilt in his voice told Melinda that suited Mason just fine. After years of working desk jobs, he relished the chance to use his mathematical skills to put this grand lady back the way she used to be.

"Are you going to install them yourself? It's a long way up there." With two full stories and a steep-pitched attic, the home certainly stood out among the standard farmhouses that dotted Fulton Township.

"You bet." Mason answered her concerned look with a hearty laugh. "When you've spent twenty years as a paid-on-call firefighter, scaling a ladder is as easy as climbing the stairs."

Adelaide met Melinda at the back door, which opened into a small vestibule off the kitchen. Her long gray hair was wound in a simple braid that hung down the back of her flannel shirt. "He's determined to do it himself," she said in answer to Melinda's question. "I told him, fine, but we're going to rent that scaffolding again and he needs to get at least one guy over here to be his spotter. Extension ladder's not good enough. So, what will it be? Coffee or tea?"

"Tea, I think." Melinda slipped into one of the comfortably worn oak chairs at the round kitchen table.

"Good, because the kettle's on and the only coffee I have is that instant stuff, for social emergencies."

While she loved the cozy comfort of her own farmhouse, the Beauforts' home always made Melinda feel at ease. As soon as she was settled, a large black cat with a white patch on its chest dashed in from the dining room and jumped into her lap.

"Panther, be nice!" Adelaide rolled her eyes. "Give a meow of greeting, at least, before you move in."

"Oh, I don't mind." Melinda scratched Panther under his chin. "Is he new?"

"Yep. Last week." Adelaide set a plate of sugar cookies on the table and reached for the kettle.

"Showed up on the front porch one morning, crying so loud that the dogs went crazy. Wouldn't stop until Mason let him in. I called around, but ..."

Adelaide's shrug told Melinda all she needed to know. Outdoor cats were a dime a dozen in the country, and many roamed from here to there without too much concern shown by their owners. Panther seemed unfazed by his recent change in address, and his purr was so loud that he nearly vibrated with contentment.

"The first cat clinic of the spring is Thursday," Melinda said. "That one's full, but should we put him on the list?"

"I was going to ask about that. Yes, the sooner he gets in, the better. All my girl cats are fixed, and my two other boys as well. But I don't want Panther roaming around the township, or fighting with any males that may show up here."

She took the chair across from Melinda, and leaned in. "So, you said there's a dilemma. Why don't you start at the beginning?"

Melinda did, and Adelaide listened intently without interrupting.

"Oh, dear. I see. Yes, Lauren needs to get out of her situation, the sooner the better." She gave a rueful laugh. "I bet when you told Jessie you'd be happy to return the favor, you had no idea it would be something like this."

"Yeah. And I know, Jessie's not asking me to take her in, but I do want to help. You and Mason have been in the area longer than I have. Any ideas?"

Adelaide looked into her tea, as if reading something in its depths. Melinda wondered what was bothering her, but decided to wait and see what Adelaide was willing to share.

"I can understand what she's going through," Adelaide finally said. "There was this one boyfriend, back in college. Everything started out wonderful; too wonderful, in fact. Then it all went south." She waved it away with one hand. "I saw it for what it was, saw him for who he was, and I found the strength to say goodbye."

"I'm so sorry, I didn't know. I hope talking about this doesn't upset you."

"Not really. That was decades ago, and it feels like someone else's life." She looked out the window, and a tiny smile appeared when Mason walked past.

And then it was gone. "I hope that if Lauren can get away, she stays away. I have to say, it took more than one breakup for me to really mean it. He'd call, or come by my apartment, all sorry and upset, and I'd take him back. But things never got better. And then, they got worse."

Melinda swallowed her questions and sipped her tea. "As much as I want to help, I'm not sure if it's safe to get too involved. And I feel terrible about that. A shelter would be best, but if that doesn't fall into place ... I just don't know."

An idea flashed in Adelaide's green eyes. "You know what? Maybe there's a better solution."

"What's that?"

"Mason and I have this whole house to ourselves. Oh, the kids visit from time to time, but otherwise it's just us, knocking around with our projects and our menagerie." She pointed at Panther, who was still purring in Melinda's lap. "You know I want to start a B-and-B, eventually. This would be the perfect trial run. Our first guest! Non-paying, of course."

"Really? Do you think Mason would go for that?"

"Oh, I think he could be persuaded. We have plenty of room, and if Lauren brings her dog, I'm sure everyone will be able to get acquainted. There's plenty to do around here. We could use an extra set of hands."

"That's a great idea." Melinda broke off part of her cookie. "And if there's things to help with, she won't feel like a charity case. She can earn her keep, won't feel like a burden. But, aren't you worried about her husband? What if he finds out where she went, before she's ready to tell him? You don't know what he might do."

Adelaide crossed her arms, as if fighting off a chill. Then, she raised her chin. "He won't know it, but I'll always be one step ahead of him. Some of these guys act like they're so tough. But you'd be surprised how fast they fold when they feel outnumbered. And Mason? Stuff like that doesn't faze him, either."

Her husband was good friends with a few of the sheriff's deputies, Adelaide said, and had decided to join either Prosper's or Swanton's volunteer emergency crew sometime soon. He missed serving the community, as he did in Madison. And, while Mason didn't talk about it much, he had extensive firearms training.

"I can't imagine it would come to that." Adelaide stirred her tea as she thought through her plan. "But between the two of us, we're more able to give Lauren a safe place to land than about anyone else around here. Let me talk to him tonight, and see what he says."

"If it works out, this is more than we could have hoped for." A weight lifted off Melinda's shoulders. "You know, it was strange. I was coming through the kitchen, worrying about what to do, when all of the sudden, I felt like I should call you."

"Of course you did." Adelaide smiled and squeezed Melinda's hand. "I learned a long time ago to always go with your instincts. They won't steer you wrong." She pushed back her chair. "Now, if Panther will set you free, I'd like to get your opinion on some wallpaper samples before you go."

* 7 *

Although it was a sunny morning, and there was more than a hint of warmth in the air, Frank's attire still brought the coffee group's chatter to a halt.

"What is that?" Auggie sneered as Frank unzipped his sweatshirt. "It's a nice day, but it isn't warm enough for golf."

"Golf?" Doc wrinkled his nose. "Look, I don't play as much as I used to, but I've never seen anyone over at the Swanton course dressed like, well ..."

"Like they're on some old-geezer cruise in the Bahamas." Jerry turned in his chair and stared at Frank's shirt. "I get the palm fronds, maybe, but is that a toucan?"

"Dunno." Frank glanced down at the blindingly bright design. "It's some kind of tropical bird. Melinda?"

She widened her eyes over her coffee mug and only shrugged. Frank's Hawaiian shirt was gaudy enough to leave people speechless. And besides, she'd promised not to say a word about her aunt and uncle's plans until they did. Miriam had booked their vacation two days ago, and Melinda wondered when it would be announced. Apparently, today was the day.

"Well, Jerry, you're right about the tropical part." Frank headed straight for the coffeepot. "Miriam and I are going somewhere warm. But not the Bahamas. Nope, two weeks from tomorrow, we ship out for Hawaii."

This was met with stunned silence from the group.

"No way." Bill frowned. "You two never go anywhere."

"That's exactly why they should go," George told him. "Get crazy, I say. Do it while you're young."

Bill, who at thirty-seven was only a few years younger than Melinda, caught her eye and stifled a laugh. Youth was a relative term around here.

But Auggie wasn't amused. "You know about this?" He gave Melinda a searching look.

"She was told to stay quiet," Frank said as he took his usual seat. "We had to decide for sure where we wanted to go, and when. Two weeks of fun and sun! I suppose I should clarify. When I say 'ship out,' I mean 'fly out,' as in, from Minneapolis. No time at sea, unless we get a whim to take one of those day jaunts. We're leaving things pretty open once we get there."

He pointed at his shirt. "Free as a bird."

"Are you sure about that?" Jerry looked up from his phone. No one would know it from the sprawl of papers littering his desk across the street, but Jerry secretly loved structure and order. "You're just going to wing it?"

"Sure am."

"Who's going to run the store?" George wanted to know.

"Who do you think?" Frank chuckled. "Melinda and Bill. They're more than capable."

Melinda wished she felt as strongly about that as Frank did. "My mom and dad are around, they're going to help out."

"We'll be fine." Bill finished his coffee with a punctuating gulp and got to his feet. "It'll be fine. Frank and Miriam are going to fill us in on everything before they leave. No big deal." And with that, Bill adjusted his faded ball cap and ambled back to the wood shop.

No one said anything. Melinda tried to smile away her worries.

"Bill's right," Doc finally said. "Why, Diane grew up in this store, just like Miriam did. Not that it will be the same," he said quickly. "But they'll manage."

"Well, I hope you have a great time." Auggie sipped his brew. "Jane and I have been saying for years that we should get away, take a real vacation. But you know, I always worry about the co-op when I'm not around. And then, there's the weather station to consider. Sure, Dan's very capable, but you never know what might happen."

Melinda saw a chance to recruit some backup, just in case. "Auggie, I may need your help, too. You worked here during high school, and you run your own business."

"Well, I'd be happy to step up." His grin said he'd like nothing more. "Your grandpa and grandma taught me well, that's for sure."

"Careful, Melinda." Doc laughed. "You might get more than you bargained for with an offer like that. Why, with Auggie's hand in things, you and Bill might as well take off, too."

* * *

Hobo was eager to jump into Lizzie's passenger seat, but Melinda dashed his hopes for a drive. "Sorry, we aren't really going anywhere." The old truck's engine protested for a second, then kicked into gear. "Only backing her out and putting her next to the shed. Someone else needs to park their vehicle in here, at least for tonight."

Melinda put the truck into reverse and focused all her attention on backing out of the rolled-open door. She checked all her mirrors, then looked over her shoulder to be sure Sunny and Stormy weren't behind the truck.

"Good." Sunny was perched in an oak in the nearby windbreak, and Stormy was busy sniffing its base. "Free and clear."

Hobo looked around in surprise when the truck lurched to a stop, but still gave a faint wag of his fluffy tail. "No, I'm serious; this is as far as we're going."

She jumped down from the cab, and went around to open Hobo's door. "We need to get the chores done and get back inside, make sure we're ready for our guests."

Hobo was once again upbeat as they made their way to the barn. Sunny and Stormy ran ahead, and teased each other with playful swats and leaps as if this evening were like any other. Only Melinda knew better. Lauren was expected to arrive by seven, with Peanut in tow.

A week had passed since Jessie asked Melinda for help. Lauren returned home, as her husband expected, and then gratefully accepted the Beauforts' offer of a place to stay. The waiting ended yesterday when Alec was tapped for a last-minute business trip to Chicago. He left this morning, and the women quickly put their plan into action.

The only hitch was that Mason and Adelaide had just left to visit their son in the Quad Cities, and wouldn't arrive home until very late tonight. Melinda and Jessie had discussed whether Lauren should wait until tomorrow, since her husband wasn't due home for three days. But they'd agreed Lauren needed to leave as soon as she could, before she lost her nerve.

"I wish I still had mine," Melinda told the sheep as she dished out their grain. "But I'm not sorry I offered to let her stay here until tomorrow morning. Besides, her husband's already gone. There's no way he can be in two places at once."

Annie let out a bellow and demanded some attention.

"Well, Annie, I'm glad you're around. That means I have two watchdogs. Tell you what. You keep an eye out from the front pasture, and if you see anything or anyone that doesn't belong around here, you sound the alarm."

Hobo padded out of the grain room, where Sunny and Stormy were enjoying their supper. "Into the cat food again? Never mind, I'm not going to scold you for it." Melinda wrapped her arms around his neck. "I'm so glad you're here. Every day, of course, but especially now."

Melinda checked the barn door was securely latched, although it didn't make one bit of difference. She tended to the chickens, then returned to the house with refreshed resolve and determination. It was done. She'd already agreed to help, and there was no turning back now.

"This farm gave me the fresh start I needed," she told Grace, who bounded into Melinda's lap as soon as she sat on the back porch's bench to remove her muddy boots. "And Lauren needs one far more than I did. This will be her first step forward, and we'll help in any way we can."

Melinda made one last pass through Wilbur's old room. It was the smallest bedroom by far, and there wasn't much space beyond the full-size bed nestled into one corner. A nightstand was wedged in nearby, and a narrow dresser sat near the single window that looked out over the barn.

The tray of plant seedlings had moved to the basement canning room for the night, so as not to tempt Peanut. The sheets were freshly washed, as were a cozy stack of quilts. An old pillow covered with a clean towel was packed into a low-sided cardboard box to serve as a makeshift dog bed.

Her phone buzzed in her pocket, and Melinda jumped. It was Jessie; Lauren had stopped for gas when she turned off the interstate, and should be at the farm within the half hour. Jessie was leaving the Watering Hole now, so she was sure to be at Melinda's long before her cousin turned up the drive.

As soon as Melinda saw Jessie, the last of her reservations melted away. They were soon replaced with the great sense of satisfaction that comes with stepping up.

"I can't thank you enough." Jessie gave her a hug. Hobo danced at their feet, but his eyes were still trained on the drive, as if he knew more visitors were on the way. "Are you sure you don't want me to spend the night? Or Doug could come out, if you're feeling unsure. The restaurant's open until eleven, but our staff can get by if needed. And if you change your mind later, please, just call."

"No, we'll be fine," Melinda said, then realized she meant it. "It would raise questions if you or Doug were suddenly absent. Adelaide and Mason will be on their way home soon; and they're only two miles away. Josh offered to stay, too, but I told him not to worry about us."

Jessie let out a big sigh of relief when a car appeared by the creek. "Oh, there she is."

Lauren's dark-blonde hair was as curly as her cousin's. She cried tears of joy at the sight of Jessie, who wiped at her own cheeks more than once as they hugged for the first time in years. Melinda caught sight of Peanut in the back seat, as the pet harness and her short Corgi legs gave her just enough leeway to look out the window. Hobo saw her, too, and let out a short bark.

"You'll be a good boy," Melinda whispered to him as she held his leash steady. "Let's give them a second before I introduce you."

"Jessie told me about your dog." Lauren's weary face broke into a smile. "Peanut is good at making friends, so I hope this goes well."

"His name is Hobo. And I have cats, too." Sunny popped through the small opening on the front of the barn, and Stormy was at his heels. "Here come two of them now, and there's two more in the house."

"There's sheep, and chickens, too," Jessie told her cousin. "Maybe you can visit them in the morning."

The ewes had come outside to see what they could see. "Look at them! I've always loved animals." Lauren turned back to Melinda. "Peanut's crate is in the trunk. It makes her feel safe. I think I might get her settled first, before supper."

"I'll get Hobo somewhere so he's out of the way for now, then I can set the crate up in your room. The two of you will have your own space."

Sunny had already approached Lauren, and she paused to pet his fluffy orange coat. Stormy, true to his more-cautious nature, studied their visitors from his post on the picnic table.

Melinda was suddenly glad for all the animals milling about, as they provided a much-needed conversation starter. One could almost forget the real reason for Lauren's visit, and maybe that was the best way to approach the situation. A few hours to unwind, a hot meal, and a soft bed for a safe night's sleep were just what she needed.

"I'm so glad you're here," was all Melinda said, then gestured toward the back porch. "Come inside, supper's almost ready. Let's get Peanut settled and then, we can put your car in the machine shed. It'll frost tonight for sure, and that way you won't have to scrape your windows in the morning."

Lauren caught the real meaning of this offer right away. "That's a good idea. I'd like that."

Jessie had Peanut by the lead, and a duffel bag in her other hand. Peanut gave a curious bark, then approached Hobo to get an introductory sniff. He graciously allowed it, then she returned the favor.

"Well, looks like everyone might get along after all," Jessie said brightly. "I'll stay for supper before I go back to work. Melinda's quite the cook," she told her cousin. "And I'm starving. Let's go inside."

The three of them gathered around the small table in the kitchen, and Jessie left after a round of hugs. Lauren helped clear the table, then reached for a dish towel. "I'm happy to dry, but I'll let you put things away. Everyone likes their stuff where they can find it again."

"Don't worry about the dishes, you've had a long day. There's plenty of towels upstairs, everything you need if you want to take a shower. Please, make yourself at home."

"Thanks, I'll do that. Are you sure you don't want me to help finish up?"

"Go on, I can get it."

It was long past dark now, and the wind was stronger than before. Now that she was alone in the kitchen, Melinda could hear it whistle and moan as it shifted around the corners of the house. The constant murmur would make it harder to hear any other outside noises, any hint of someone approaching the house. She shivered, even though the old furnace hummed along in the basement, and decided to start a fire in the hearth.

The cheerful flames and comforting warmth soon drew Hobo and the cats to the nearby rug, and their contented expressions eased her concerns. It wouldn't be long before the evenings felt too warm for a fire, so they might as well enjoy one tonight. But she left the picture window's curtains open and chose her reading chair over the couch, so she could keep an eye on the darkness that stretched down to the gravel road.

She was trying to focus on a magazine when Lauren returned, her hair washed and her clothes changed.

"Feel better?"

"Oh, yes." Lauren settled on the couch. "Peanut's snoring away in her crate. Thank you so much for letting us stay here, I know it was last-minute, but it was our best chance." She let out a deep sigh. "Day One is done. I don't know what to think about Day Two."

"Then don't," Melinda said gently. "Do you want anything, maybe some tea? I was about to get some, myself."

They sat in silence, and sipped their tea while the wind hummed and the fire popped. Melinda propped her feet on the ottoman, and Grace demanded a seat in her lap. Hobo apparently didn't want to give up his prime place before the fire, and Hazel had already made herself at home with their guest.

"I love your place." Lauren studied the farmhouse's wide woodwork, built-ins and hardwood floors. "It's so beautiful, look at all the details! And so well cared for."

"The Schermann family owned it for over a hundred years before I came along. Horace, that last one who lived here? He hated to give it up and go to the nursing home. But later, he told me maybe he was just hanging on until the right person came along. I guess that was me." Melinda then recounted the changes that had brought her to this place in life.

"That was a big step for you, moving back here like you did," Lauren said. "Did you ... are you ever sorry that you did it?"

"No. Well, not now. There were times, early on, when I wondered if I was crazy and needed to just go back to the city, back to the way things used to be. But it was too late. I'd already changed, and I think for the better."

"And you've been single, all this time." Lauren's voice held no trace of pity. In fact, it carried the opposite. "You've handled things here on your own, just fine."

That made Melinda laugh. "Oh, I can hardly say that. I've had plenty of help. My family, friends, and especially my neighbors, they've all helped me get through. And I'm seeing someone." She couldn't help but smile. "He's a veterinarian, actually."

"Oh, really?" Lauren raised an eyebrow, and smiled. "How handy is that? Sounds like he's perfect for you."

"Well, maybe." Melinda took a sip of her tea. "We'll have to see. It's only been about three months."

"But you don't need him." Lauren sat up straighter, and Hazel didn't mind. "I mean, you care for him, sure, but you'd be alright if things didn't work out. Why, you'd just go on, on your own, no matter what."

Melinda wanted to believe that was true. She was pretty sure that it was. But yet, the thought of losing Josh was like a sudden weight on her chest.

"Oh, sure," she said, more confidently than she really felt. "I certainly would."

"That's how I want to be." Lauren stroked Hazel's thick coat. "I used to be that way, actually. And then Alec came along." She blinked back sudden tears. "I used to be so many things, before ..."

"And you can. You can do it again."

"Yes, I will." Lauren wiped her face with the back of one hand. "I have to. I used to be a nurse, you know; I loved my job. But I was laid off last month, when the clinic I worked at closed. My job meant so much to me, it's like I don't know who I am without it."

Melinda knew exactly what that was like. "Once you get settled somewhere, I'm sure you'll find something. There's always a need for nurses." Her phone buzzed, and she frowned at her screen. "Sorry, I'll be right back."

She went into the kitchen, where Lauren wouldn't be able to read the irritation on her face. It was Josh.

Just finished a call for Doc out your way. I'll come by.

No, please don't, she typed. *Everything's fine.*

*I know you told me not to, but I think I should. I brought
my overnight bag along. You shouldn't be out there alone
like this!*

Melinda thought of the wind howling outside, and how far
it was to her nearest neighbors. But she set her mouth in a
firm line and tapped away.

We are doing just fine.

*I need to know that for myself. I'm two miles out. Be
there in about five.*

Melinda dropped her phone on the counter and crossed
her arms. How many times had she told Josh to stay out of
this? He was worried, sure; but he'd only be in the way. She
thought for a moment, and went back into the living room.

"My boyfriend's coming by, just for a second, on his way
home from a call," she said in a voice far more cheerful than
she felt. "Just wanted you to know, if you see headlights
coming up the drive."

"Oh, yes. Thanks for telling me." She reached around
Hazel to the coffee table, and picked up the latest edition of
the Swanton newspaper. It came only twice a week, but was
packed with news from a three-county area. "Don't mind me,
I'll just be catching up on what's happening in this corner of
the world."

Melinda found it hard to sit still. She went into the
kitchen and shuffled from the refrigerator to the stove and
back again, her frustration mounting with every step. Hobo
soon joined her, then ran to the south-facing windows and let
out a short bark.

"Yeah, he's here," she said through gritted teeth. "But he's
not staying. Not tonight."

* 8 *

The back porch was unheated, and Melinda almost reached for a second sweatshirt to pull over the one she already had on. But no matter; she didn't plan to be out here long. Hobo had already dashed through his doggie door and was out by the steps, greeting his friend.

Josh came in with a sheepish smile. "Hey there." His dark hair was plastered against his forehead when he swiped off his knit cap, and the concern in his eyes almost caused Melinda to change her stance. And then, she noticed the duffel bag over his arm.

"I thought I was clear." She bit off her words. "No one here needs to be saved tonight. There's no bogeyman hiding in the windbreak. I told you, her husband's in Chicago."

"So you think." The duffel dropped to the painted floorboards with a soft thud. "But you don't know that for sure. What if someone's already told him? What if someone saw her packing the car?"

"She was careful, OK? Really careful. Her parents know, that's it. And they won't ..."

"And again, you don't really know that. I'm sure they're good people, they care about their daughter. But if this guy is dangerous, and it sounds like he might be ..."

"Adelaide and Mason will be home around eleven. I'll call them if I need to. But I won't."

"Yeah, and they've been driving and driving, and they'll be exhausted. Starting tomorrow, they'll be responsible for Lauren, and it's great how they stepped up. But that's not tonight." He held up his phone. "It's just past eight; by my count, you're in charge for at least another twelve hours."

Melinda knew he had a point. But she'd faced many challenges here long before they'd met, and managed just fine on her own. She thought of what she and Lauren had been talking about, just minutes before, about taking care of yourself and being independent.

"And just what message do you think your staying here is going to send?" She kept her voice low, even though the kitchen door was closed. Hobo had padded back in and now waited at Josh's feet. "I've been telling Lauren how I do things for myself, and how good it feels. She used to be that way, she says, and wants to again."

Josh laughed, but there was a note of something in it that made Melinda's blood boil.

"So, that's it." He narrowed his eyes at her. "This is about your ego, or something? Being strong and all that? No, see, you have it all backwards. Having someone else here will show her you're taking this seriously. This isn't a game!"

Melinda crossed her arms. "Look, I know you spend your days and nights saving the day, but I don't know if this is in your wheelhouse. Let's say something happens, he does show up here tonight. Which he won't. But what if he did? What exactly are you going to do, other than call for help? Which I can handle on my own, just fine."

Josh didn't answer her at first, and she could hear the wind whistling around the thin frames of the back porch's windows. Despite the chill, Melinda's face turned warm. And then, her cheeks were on fire.

"I was just trying to help." Josh sighed. "The more people here, the better. And I know that no one else knows." He took a step toward her, as if he was about to take her hand, but she pulled back. "It's a secret, right? Ed and Mabel are in the dark, and the Olsons, and Angie and Nathan."

Melinda shook her head again. "Lauren doesn't know you. She's already in a strange place, she's had a long day, but she's finally getting a chance to unwind. The last thing she needs is someone else hanging around."

"Please don't put this on her. It's all on you, Melinda. No, I'm right, and you know it. Look at you." He shook his head. "There you stand, your arms crossed, literally guarding the kitchen door. Like I'm some intruder, someone you don't dare let in!"

"Now you're just being dramatic." She rolled her eyes. "That's not ..."

"Yes. Yes, it is. Why can't you just let me in?" There was something else now in his eyes, a flash of hurt. Melinda bit her lip.

"That's all I want." He crossed his arms. "For you to let me in, in every way you can. I'm doing the same for you. Or I'm trying, at least."

"Well, so am I." She raised her chin. "You know I am. I mean, we're already ..."

"That's not what I mean, and you know it. Sometimes, that's the easy part, right?"

She looked away. Josh waited, then sighed.

"Fine." He reached for his duffel bag. "I'm going home. I hope things stay quiet out here tonight. But if they don't, well, you can always call. I'll come out, you know I will."

"I know," she said softly, the tears pricking at the corners of her eyes. "And I appreciate it, I do." Part of her wanted to take it all back, ask him to stay. Or at least, take those last few steps and kiss him before he left. But she couldn't seem to get her feet to move, even though they were turning to ice on the cold floor.

Josh gave Hobo a pat and reached for the doorknob. "I'll check on you in the morning."

Melinda hurried back into the warmth of the kitchen, and stood at the windows with Hobo, where they watched Josh's taillights disappear down the drive. "We have company," she whispered to Hobo. "Let's go back in there, huh?"

Hobo's arrival was met by a smile from Lauren, but her face turned pale when Melinda returned. "What happened?"

"Oh, it's fine." Melinda waved it all away as she returned to her reading chair. It was a relief to pick up Grace and snuggle her close. "He's on his way home, had to drop something off, is all."

Lauren was quiet, but Melinda's could feel the weight of her gaze. "Melinda, please. I know that look. I've felt it on my own face more times than I care to admit."

Melinda looked down. "I'm so sorry, I don't want you to worry. It's not like that. Sometimes he wants to give me more than what I think I deserve. Josh is a good man, and he cares. I do, too, but ... I guess I've been independent for so long, it's hard to let him help."

Lauren smiled. "You're so lucky to have him." She turned to peer out the picture window, which showed nothing but the dark. But Melinda noticed the slight quiver in her shoulders as she looked again, just to be sure.

"I know I am. He's one of the best things that's ever happened to me." Melinda rubbed Grace's ears. "You've had a long day. I'm tired, myself. I think I'll say good night soon."

As Melinda had suspected, this was the cue Lauren was looking for. She was drained, for sure, but didn't want to seem like a rude guest. "Sounds like a good idea. I think I'll turn in, too."

After Lauren went upstairs, Melinda extinguished the fire, put away the last few dishes waiting in the kitchen sink and wiped the counters, then straightened the stack of magazines on the coffee table. She looked around her home, and took comfort that everything was in order. Inside, at least.

She made one last check of the doors' locks and scanned the yard from every direction, aided only by the feeble glow from the yard light by the garage, before she finally turned out most of the lights and headed for the stairs.

Grace and Hazel were already on the bed, taking up one of the pillows. It was the one Josh used, and Melinda looked away as she turned down the comforter and blankets. "It's pretty wild out there tonight, isn't it?" Grace didn't even look up, but Hazel stretched out one front paw and flexed her toes as if she didn't have a care in the world. Melinda wished she felt the same. "Where's Hobo?"

He was at the other end of the hall, sprawled out in front of Wilbur's old room. The door was closed, but a faint beam of light shone through the crack above the floor. On her way to the bathroom, Melinda stopped long enough to pat his back. "I'm glad you get along with Peanut," she whispered. "She's in there, protecting her family, so you don't have to spend the night out here."

But she knew he would, and brought him his favorite blanket from the foot of her bed.

* * *

Melinda finally fell into a deep sleep, and it was with great relief that she pulled back the curtains to greet the new day. Mason and Adelaide would be there in about an hour, but she hoped to get chores done and see Lauren off with a hot breakfast. A little lie to Aunt Miriam about a non-existent doctor appointment meant Melinda wasn't expected at Prosper Hardware until ten.

Hobo was happy to accompany her outdoors, where the last of the frost still clung to the brown grass. They were on their way back from the chicken house when Melinda spied a car, vintage but still familiar, rolling slowly down the gravel.

"Harriet?" She frowned. "I thought she was coming this evening to get her eggs." Melinda glanced at the house; thankfully, the curtains in Wilbur's old bedroom were still drawn. "She always wants to come inside. Hobo, we have to head her off, somehow."

Harriet Van Buren, a widow who lived north of the blacktop, never drove her old Cadillac much farther than Prosper or Swanton. But she loved to come to Melinda's farm to stock up on eggs and neighborhood chatter. The hens had recently increased their production and, as promised, Harriet had been Melinda's first call.

Melinda, with a smile plastered on her face, kept hold of Hobo's collar and waited by the picnic table for Harriet to guide her maroon beast into a spot in front of the garage. Harriet might be in her eighties, but her mind was still as sharp as a tack. She missed nothing.

"Well, hello!" Harriet lifted herself out of the car. "Sorry to be so early, but it's such a nice morning and I thought, well, time for a drive! Guess I have a case of spring fever."

Her keen eyes swept the yard. "This has always been such a lovely farm. Anna and Henry kept it up impeccably over the years and, well, Horace and Wilbur did their best. I was so glad when you decided to stay."

Melinda normally enjoyed Harriet's company but today, she couldn't get her out of there fast enough. "Well, I have big plans for this year. I'm going to get the roof replaced and paint the house, too."

"Oh, my, that's a big project." Harriet gazed up at the peak above the kitchen, then carefully leaned down to pet Hobo. "Why, it'll be beautiful! Anna would have loved that."

"Sorry I'm in such a rush." Melinda blocked the sidewalk before Harriet could even start for the door. "I'm on my way into work soon. How about you just wait out here with Hobo? I'll run in and get your cartons. Just have a seat at the picnic table, that will keep you out of the wind. Hobo's been a little lonely, as we haven't had company for days."

Hobo, of course, didn't give anything away. Sunny and Stormy's feline senses had alerted them to their visitor, and they were now on the run from the barn, tails up with curiosity and welcome.

Harriet, who had three cats of her own, began to coo when they approached. "There's my special boys. How are you today?"

Sunny jumped on the picnic table, and Harriet couldn't resist stroking his fluffy coat. Stormy, not to be outdone, rubbed his gray cheek against Harriet's polyester slacks.

Melinda saw her chance, and tried not to run as she made a break for the back porch. In desperation, she snapped the lock behind her. Surely Harriet wouldn't try to follow her inside, but just in case ...

"I could say the door sticks," Melinda whispered to Grace, as the calico was thankfully the only one in the kitchen. Melinda listened carefully for a moment, and was glad to not hear any movement upstairs. "Tell one lie, and it's so easy to tell another. But this is too important to mess it up."

Melinda reached for the stack of cardboard cartons kept in the cabinet next to the landline phone, filled two with eggs from the refrigerator, and hurried back outside. Hobo and the barn cats still had Harriet occupied, and Melinda made a mental note to offer a generous round of treats once their neighbor departed.

"Sorry I don't have time to chat," she told Harriet. "How about I call you tomorrow? Maybe you can come over later in the week for coffee?"

"Oh, that would be lovely."

"Here, I'll put the eggs in the car for you." Melinda started toward the garage, hoping that would be Harriet's cue to follow. And she did. But she stopped short before she reached the driver's-side door.

"I see you have Lizzie out of the shed." Harriet's tone was as friendly as ever, but there was a flicker of curiosity in the older woman's eyes. She hitched her purse squarely over her shoulder, and studied the yard more closely. "Horace always fussed over his truck, I'm sure you know. He said the best way to make sure Lizzie started up when he needed her was to keep her inside."

"Yeah, he sure did." Melinda smiled as she tried to think of something to say. "I do the same. Most of the time. But, well, spring cleaning and all. I got her out first thing this morning, figured I'd sweep out the bed and wipe the inside down, at least. It's still too cold to wash her, for sure."

"Oh, we'll get there. Warmer and better days to come." Harriet opened the car door, then stopped again.

Melinda felt as if she might scream from frustration. What now?

"Do you have any carriers I can borrow? For my babies."

"Oh, yes, of course." Back before Christmas, Melinda had promised to transport Harriet's kitties to one of the first spay clinics of the season. "I have two crates, but Karen and Doc have extras. I'll get a spare and clean them all up, then bring them over so we can set them up in the garage and let the cats get used to them for a few days."

"I'm so glad they can go." Harriet blinked rapidly, and her gratitude touched Melinda's heart. "You don't know what it means to me. And if you're sure there's no charge ..."

"Nope, none at all. It's covered." Harriet could barely afford the eggs. Karen and Josh had quickly agreed to cover the cats' at-cost fees out of the nonprofit's grant funds.

At long last, Harriet got behind the wheel. She turned the key and the big old car roared to life. After the Cadillac was carefully backed around, Harriet put it in park long enough to wave to Melinda and Hobo, then started her cautious roll down the driveway.

Once Harriet reached the road, the farmhouse nearly out of her sight, Melinda dropped to the picnic table's closest bench with a sigh of relief. "I never thought I'd say this about Harriet. But boy, am I glad she's gone."

Sunny and Stormy meowed and paced, eager for their breakfast. Melinda had to kick it into gear. But as she took a moment to gather her thoughts, she realized she was exhausted. Despite the cheerful morning, her nerves were still stretched tight. And then, her fight with Josh ...

He'd only been trying to help; she shouldn't have snapped at him like that. And while he'd promised to call that morning, Melinda didn't want to wait.

"Am I ever going to learn?" she asked Hobo, who leaned his head against her knee as she reached for her phone.

"Why can't I just let him in ... all the way in? What am I so afraid of?"

✳ 9 ✳

"I've marked the Easter candy to fifty percent off." Esther dropped the stack of stickers on the counter. "What about the winter boots? Are those next?" Every approaching holiday was Esther's favorite, and today's pink sweatshirt was screen-printed with the slogan "Have a Hoppy Easter" and a rabbit clutching a basket of eggs.

Melinda glanced over at the Prosper Feed Co. calendar tacked up next to the refrigerated case. The calendars were always oversized and hard to ignore, just like Auggie, with numbers to match. Which meant the dates were visible from the counter.

"Well, tomorrow's the first day of spring. But we'd better not test Mother Nature quite yet."

"The curse of the winter discount." Esther chuckled. "There's not many pairs left, I don't think we'll have trouble getting rid of them, no matter the price. Besides, I hear there's snow coming tomorrow."

"That's what Auggie said." Melinda looked out at Main Street, where there was no sunshine to be found. Dirty slush clung to the curbs and huddled along the buildings' foundations, but a patch of muddy grass was visible here and there. "And I saw it on the news this morning, too. But if he's in agreement, I'd say it's a shoo-in. You know he prides himself on being right."

"Yeah, that's for sure. And not just about the forecast, but everything else, too."

Melinda's phone rang in the pocket of her green apron. "Hey, Nancy, what's going on?"

Esther looked up from across the aisle, as she'd moved on to straightening the store's display of garden seeds. Miriam kept them near the register, allegedly to tempt people waiting in the checkout line, but Melinda suspected they were really placed there to raise the spirits of whoever worked behind the counter. Enjoying the cheerful illustrations of peppers and peas and flowers had made it easier for Melinda to get through the dreary winter months.

"Oh, really?" Melinda couldn't see the community center, kitty-corner from the post office, from where she stood behind the register. Even so, she craned her neck to look in that direction. "Are you serious? Well, there's not much going on in town today, not that there usually is. Yeah, I can get away for a few minutes; Esther's here and Bill's in the back. Sure, I'll head down and play traffic cop."

Esther was almost holding her breath. "What is it? Is something happening?" The glint in her eyes made Melinda want to laugh. Every day in Prosper was a slow news day.

"Well, sort of. Nancy says the bat guys are here, and they're drawing a crowd."

"Of bats?" Esther grimaced. "We had some in our attic a few years ago, and when you see one, you have a dozen."

"I wish it were only the bats." Melinda reached for her jacket. "Prosper's human residents are gathering on the sidewalk out front, and Nancy's worried the gawkers are going to get in the way. She's trying to get the documents together for the next council meeting. Can you watch the register for a bit?"

"Sure can." Esther was already on the move. "I ask just one favor in return."

"What's that?"

"Tell me every single detail when you get back."

"Will do."

Melinda allowed herself a secret smile of triumph as soon as she was safely outside Prosper Hardware's front door. Esther was so curious about the bat crew, and eager for any bit of gossip that would provide a much-needed distraction during what had been an uneventful week.

Little did she, or anyone else in Prosper, know what Jessie, Melinda and the Beauforts had accomplished during that time.

Lauren and Peanut were still staying with Adelaide and Mason, and had been invited to remain as long as they liked. After consulting with her parents as well as the Beauforts, Lauren had called her husband and told him what she'd done, and what she planned to do next. By not waiting for him to come home to an empty house, she'd been able to diffuse some of his outrage and show him she was taking charge of her situation.

There had been tense words, of course, and Alec even made a veiled threat to drive the two hours to the Beauforts' and force Lauren to come home with him. But he quickly changed his mind after a verbal dressing-down from Mason.

Alec called again the next day, still wounded but already angling to turn what was left of his marriage to his advantage. He told Lauren he was already seeing someone else, which she'd suspected all along, and what he really wanted was the house. They didn't have much equity in the home, so would she take a cash payout of her share?

Lauren was relieved, of course, but her emotional wounds would still take time to heal. She had settled in at the Beauforts' farm faster than anyone expected, and seemed invigorated by the country air and caring for the animals. There was always some task that needed tending to, which kept her mind distracted as well as her hands. And Peanut had quickly made friends at the farm as well.

Lauren was talking about finding a part-time job in Swanton, and letting the rest of her life evolve from there.

Jessie had been out to the Beauforts' to visit her cousin several times, which meant Lauren's unfamiliar face had yet to appear in Prosper. And judging by the commotion created by the bat guys' arrival, it had been the right move to keep Lauren out of town for now, and out of the spotlight.

Nine people were already gathered at the base of the community center's corner steps, and more were making their way to the scene. The bat crew's van was at the curb, and the poor guys were trying to unload their gear and simultaneously fend off the gawkers' questions. Both men wore brown, cotton-canvas jumpsuits, which were surely practical for working in dusty attics and crawlspaces.

Richard was already there, trying to keep things moving. He was tall and broad-shouldered, so when he motioned for people to move away from the back of the van, they complied.

"Nancy sent me over to help," Melinda told him. "I'm glad you could make it. Especially since this group's about to grow."

"It's like a circus sideshow. Except I doubt these bats are trained."

"They sure aren't, so it's a good thing we are." One of the wranglers extended a hand to Richard and Melinda. "They're timid critters, really. Good folk, if you know what I mean. You respect them, and they'll return the favor. They keep to themselves and try to stay out of trouble."

"Then they're easier to manage than some of the people in this town," Richard muttered to Melinda, then jerked his chin down the street. Auggie's work truck had just come through the intersection and, in what was a rare challenge in Prosper, he was searching for a place to park.

Melinda made sure to be waiting, arms crossed, when he opened the truck's door. "Slow day at the co-op? Did you bring the bats some farewell snacks?"

"Now, you know I cater to a wide variety of animals." Auggie was so excited, he missed the barb in her first question. Or chose to ignore it. "But these guys? Nah. Want to see the show, though."

"I don't think it's going to be very exciting," Melinda said in a voice loud enough to carry through the growing crowd.

"They're going to go in, go upstairs, make some changes, then drive away. That's it."

"But exactly how are they going to do that?" one bystander wanted to know.

His friend also had questions. "Will they fly right into the cages, or will they have to tackle them?"

Melinda sighed. No wonder there were so many gawkers. They expected a dramatic battle that resulted in immediate capture, with dozens of bats hauled out in cages and deposited in the back of the van, where they could be examined up close. That's not how this worked, though, and the truth would be much-less entertaining.

Bats were a protected species in Iowa, and had to be approached with the utmost care. They couldn't be killed or poisoned, of course, but the rules went far beyond that. This was more of a defensive game than an offensive one.

The crew would survey the second floor, and the attic crawl space above it, to determine all the locations the bats used to access the building. Some of the spots, such as cracks in the walls, would be sealed, and the others would be fitted with tiny one-way doors that allowed the bats to fly out, but not get back in. It wouldn't happen overnight, but the bats would eventually vacate the premises on their own. Today's other task was the disgusting one: feces removal.

Before Melinda could begin to explain the process, a woman had another question.

"How many are there, anyway?" She glanced around nervously, as if hundreds of bats might suddenly burst through the community center's entrance, wing their way around Prosper, and attack residents right in their own yards.

"Now, Wanda, don't you worry." Melinda heard a familiar voice over her shoulder. "It's not gonna be like in that Hitchcock movie. No one's in danger."

"Glenn!" Melinda frowned at him. "Who's watching the counter?"

"Pete's in, he's on his break." Glenn Hanson, the town's postmaster, crossed his arms. "I wasn't about to miss this.

Looks like I'm just in time, too. What are they going to do with that? Is the roof leaking?"

The two men were back at the van, pulling out sheets of plastic.

"Protective gear," Auggie announced to the crowd. "And they're going to need it, too. There are many kinds of manure in this world, but bat poop? It's as nasty as it comes."

"And there's nothing wrong with the center's roof," Melinda quickly added. "It passed inspection, everything's fine."

Then she elbowed Glenn. "The last thing we need is more rumors, especially wrong ones. And Auggie, how are you such an expert on bat dung?"

"Oh, we've had a few in the co-op from time to time," he answered with the casual air of someone with the upper hand, which apparently had also been a forgiving one. "I don't go for this sort of thing, you know, chasing them away. They get messy, but they also eat tons of insects. I say, live and let live. Dan and I put up some of those bat houses around on the property. Makes for a nicer place to stay than hanging off some pipes up in a tower."

"Well, maybe some of them will find their way down the street." Melinda stepped back as more people arrived on the sidewalk, eager for whatever they could see. Which was still nothing more than two guys unloading a van.

"They better head out to your end of town." Glenn crossed his arms. "If they show up inside the post office, I'll be forced to take drastic measures."

"You can't do that." Another woman leaned into the conversation. "It's illegal. And you're a public employee, no less!"

That gave another man the prompt he was apparently looking for. "Yeah, Glenn. Maybe if you'd followed through on that retirement threat and were on your way out. But since the post office is staying open, and you're staying, too, you aren't going to be able to get away with that."

Glenn's ruddy face turned red, and not from the brisk

wind. "Listen here. It's my job to keep that post office safe and clean for all who enter to do business, make sure residents have the services they need and that the mail is delivered in a timely, efficient manner."

Melinda and Auggie exchanged raised eyebrows. Glenn obviously had his operations manual memorized.

"And that includes pest control." Glenn pointed at the man, who now listened with a bemused smile. "These bats better stay out of my belfry. And more importantly, out of my hair."

Glenn had very little hair left, and Melinda hoped the debate wouldn't swing in that direction.

"Oh, come on." The woman rolled her eyes. "Bats are harmless. That's an old wives' tale!"

"I've got a tennis racket in the back room of the post office that would tell you otherwise." Glenn launched into a long-winded tale about a long-ago battle that ended with a stunned bat escorted outside to recover. "See? I'm not cruel. But it's my job to protect that piece of public property."

"But that's still not right." She wouldn't let it drop. "What if they don't wake up, at least for a long time? If they're out cold, they're susceptible to predators, like owls."

"The post office has never been open at night," Auggie reminded her. "This would have been during the day. Besides, the owls around here are smart enough to sleep when the sun's up."

Melinda saw a need to change the subject, and quick. "Who's going to the council meeting Monday night?" she asked, a little too brightly. "Should be interesting to see what the council does about that delinquent property, huh?"

"They're going to lower the boom on that guy." Auggie's tone carried a ton of judgement and more than a bit of satisfaction. "We all have to pay our taxes in this town. Just because you live out of state, and the place fell into your lap, doesn't give you a reason to skirt the system."

"That's for sure." Glenn stuffed his hands into his jacket pockets. "Play by the rules or you're out."

Melinda wasn't sure the owner of the vacant storefront was worried about being pushed out of Prosper's tiny circle of commerce. It would probably be a relief to unload something that, given the look of the lonely building two blocks' down, was surely more of a money pit than a moneymaker.

"Turns out, the guy's Clark Whitson's grandson," one man said. "I swear, I never would have expected it from that family. Clark was always on the straight and narrow."

Auggie smirked. "Well, you know the young people these days. They move away, and things around here don't matter anymore. He's out in Chicago, I hear. And you know, not everyone in those kinds of places share our values."

"Or values history, for that matter." Glenn nodded in agreement. "Or family honor, either."

"Gee, thanks," Melinda said sarcastically. "I didn't know I was such a degenerate."

"Oh, you're an exception," Glenn said quickly.

"You came back, though." Auggie's brown eyes twinkled behind his glasses. "And I don't know if you're in the 'young people' category these days."

Melinda didn't mind. She was rather glad to have left her twenties behind. And to think of it, her thirties, too. "So, what I'm wondering is, who might buy the place? What might it become?"

The group considered for a moment.

"Good question." Glenn looked down the street toward the vacant building. "It's been so many things over the years, but empty at least the last thirty."

"Well, it has some nice plate glass there in the front." Auggie had to give the space a little credit. "And that hexagon-tile floor, white with the black, like from the twenties or thirties."

That piqued Melinda's interest. "Plaster or drywall?"

"Oh, I think it's still the plaster. Lots of vintage charm, if someone wanted to put a little elbow grease into it."

"You seem to know a lot about it," another man observed. "Thinking about throwing your hat in the ring?"

"It's not going to be me. I'm too busy figuring out how to expand what I have. Been working on some ideas for those gas pumps, you know."

Everyone waited for Auggie to say more. But it seemed that when it came to his own interests, he preferred to play it close to the vest. At least for now.

"Well, I've got the agenda up there in the post office," Glenn finally said. "From what it says, all that'll happen is the council could open up an application period for potential buyers. People have been talking about it, so I'm sure the property will draw interest from someone."

Glenn's secondary role was manager of the town's bulletin board, where people posted items that ranged from lost pets to church suppers. It was also the place to find official notices from the city, the county and beyond.

Government documents were online these days, but Melinda had been pleasantly surprised to see how many residents still wanted to see public business posted right there in black and white.

"Meadow Lane has been such a success," one woman said to Melinda. "If this other building's that charming inside, maybe we'll get ourselves another gift shop."

"I know, but how much can this area support?" Glenn wasn't sure. "Vicki has that market sewn up, I think. My wife stopped in the other day, and said there's a whole new selection of spring knick-knacks and things. She came home with only a small sack. I was proud of her restraint."

Several minutes had passed and, while the bat guys had yet to return, the crowd didn't seem ready to disperse. It was a pleasant day, by late-March standards, and people were obviously eager for any excuse to congregate outside after several months of ice and snow. Melinda felt the same, but she needed to get back and give Esther a hand.

Just then, Richard appeared at the top of the steps and clapped to get the crowd's attention. "Everybody, the show's over. The guys are upstairs, making the necessary repairs, and it's going to take most of the afternoon."

He explained what the crew would do over the next couple hours, and a groan of disappointment slipped through the crowd when it became clear that none of the bats would make an appearance.

"That's it?" someone shouted.

"I'm afraid so. They'll figure it out on their own. Whether you like them or not, bats are highly intelligent and creatures of habit." Richard flashed a smile. "Of course, there's plenty of dung up there to haul out. If anyone happens to have a respirator mask at home, and wants to volunteer, it would be much appreciated."

That did the trick. Auggie fished his truck's keys out of his pocket. "Melinda, how are you doing on that special food the princess kittens like so much? Got a shipment in today."

Grace and Hazel's insistence on getting the royal treatment, even at mealtime, had become a running joke between Melinda and Auggie. She always let it slide that Auggie's felines were just as picky. And just as spoiled.

"I have half a bag left. But thanks for letting me know, I'll come down. It'll save me a trip to Mason City."

"Good!" He waved as he got in the truck. "Remember to shop local!"

"He's in a good mood," Glenn observed. "But then, a little excitement around here is enough to raise anyone's spirits. Especially this time of year." And then he chuckled.

"What?"

"I had a little chat with Jerry yesterday, about the plans for the Easter egg hunt. He's sick of being the bunny, but he has his replacement all figured out."

Glenn pointed down Main Street at the receding bumper of Auggie's truck.

"The rabbit-on-deck just doesn't know it yet."

* 10 *

"Jessie gave me four little buckets of ranch." Melinda set the lunch sacks on the break room table, then eagerly reached for her own. It was noon, and she was starving. "Between the sandwiches and fries, that should be more than enough for everyone."

"I'll stick to ketchup, thanks." Uncle Frank reached for the paper bag closest to his elbow and peeked inside, his face lit up like it was Christmas morning. "Oh, smell that! It's been ages since I've had a burger."

"And it'll be several more until the next one," Aunt Miriam reminded him. "So honey, I hope you savor it."

Since Frank's heart attack, his diet was rather restricted. Or at least, it was when his wife was around. Melinda suspected the rules changed when she wasn't.

"Don't worry, I'll use up your share." Melinda's dad reached for one of the ranch packets before he even unwrapped his sandwich. "And Melinda, tell Jessie thanks the next time you see her. She must be a really good friend to load us up like this."

Melinda smiled, but said nothing as she arranged her fries and chicken sandwich on the wrapper.

Roger wasn't the only lunch guest. Diane had joined them, as had Bill. He wasn't a relative, of course, but when it came to Prosper Hardware, he was like family. And despite the sounds of contentment as everyone tucked into their lunches, there was serious business to discuss.

Esther, due to her part-time status and, bless her heart, her tendency to gossip, was downstairs watching the counter.

"OK, I suppose we should get started." Miriam wiped her hands on a paper napkin and took another sip from her straw. "Let's go over some things quick. That was delicious, but I'm soon going to feel like a big slug. I want to be home, napping on the couch, within the hour."

"The recliner's mine." Frank leaned back and rubbed his stomach. "Well, dear, let's see if we can compress our combined wisdom into what these folks need to know while we're gone."

Frank and Miriam were leaving in a week. Melinda was very happy for them, and a little terrified for Bill and herself. She was grateful her parents had time to help out, as her mom's experience with the family's business would be an invaluable resource over the coming weeks. Even so, Melinda had a fresh notebook in front of her, and was ready to absorb everything she could.

"First off, I don't want you to worry about payroll." Miriam smiled at Bill and Melinda. "It's all taken care of. And as promised, those bonuses will come in next week's check; Esther's, too. Roger and Diane, keep track of your time and we'll make it right when we return."

"Oh, you don't have to do that," Diane said quickly. "It's been years since I've worked here, and I'm really looking forward to it."

Roger was also accommodating, but a bit less eager. If nothing else, he knew Frank and Miriam's pride was at stake. "We can talk about it later, but I'd say a nice steak dinner just might take care of it."

"And the monthly tax filings are coming up, too," Miriam continued. "But don't worry, I called the bank and those are ready to go."

Melinda nodded. Tax filings? Of course those would be needed, but she'd never given them a thought. There was so much she didn't know. Frank's and Miriam's absence might pass quickly, with little drama. At the same time, the waters could easily turn choppy and fill with sharks.

Bill crossed his arms but tried to smile, and she wondered if he was thinking the same. "I'd feel better if we had an emergency call list," he said. "I mean, if a pipe bursts or the roof leaks, or, something else goes wrong."

"Oh, I'm sure there's lots of things that could." Frank's chuckle brought raised eyebrows around the table. He'd been hesitant when Miriam first suggested they take this much-needed vacation, but Melinda had noticed how cheerful her uncle had become over the past few weeks. He was usually in a good mood, of course, but his rosier outlook hinted that managing this business might be far-more stressful than Melinda had imagined it would be.

Miriam pulled a sheet of paper out of the file folder in her lap. "Everything's right here. All our contacts, the suppliers, our attorney, you name it."

"The truck comes on Wednesdays, right?" Roger asked. "Seems that's what I remember."

"Well, yes and no." Frank shrugged. "General merchandise is that day, but the hardware shipments are separate. That guy used to come on Wednesdays, but he's switched to Thursdays the last few months."

"Truth is, we're never sure exactly when he'll show up," Miriam admitted. "We're trying to get to the bottom of that one. Oh, but it's small stuff, mostly. Packets of screws, tools, that sort of thing."

"I thought it was odd that he started showing up a day late." Bill frowned. "That one time, it was Friday. And the refrigerated stuff's drop-off keeps changing, too."

"They showed up on Monday this week," Melinda told her parents. "But sometimes, it's Tuesday."

Roger seemed worried. "Doesn't that make things difficult? Isn't that one of the most-popular departments?"

"Yes, but we're such a small account for them," Miriam explained. "It all depends on their overall customer route, since everything is perishable. We have to take it when we can get it."

Diane and Roger lived fifteen minutes' away in Swanton. Not that far, but far enough if a truck showed up and there weren't extra hands to help unload. But maybe, Melinda decided, this was an opportunity to let Bill take the spotlight. She'd learned the hard way that Bill yearned to provide direction for Prosper Hardware's future in addition to serving as its expert craftsman.

"Do you have any friends that work here in town, that have some flexibility in their schedules?" she asked Bill. "It would be great to have some people lined up we could call on in a pinch."

Bill thought for a moment, then nodded. "Yeah, actually. I can think of two off the top of my head, and there might be more. Of course, my Dad's retired, he and Mom are over on Oak Street."

"That's a great idea." Miriam was pleased. "Bill, if you can round up some substitutes, I'd be happy to pay them if they need to come by."

"Oh, some pizza and beer might do it."

Miriam checked her list, then took off her reading glasses for a moment and rubbed her eyes. "Now, here's something else I want to make you all aware of. Bill and Melinda know we have issues at times with people questioning our sale ads and coupons. They know to hold firm on those. But sometimes, people don't like the answers."

Bill sighed. "Yeah, when they get really cranky, we normally hand them off to you or Frank."

Frank lowered his voice, even though there wasn't anyone else around, and turned to Roger and Diane. "There's a list for that, too. It's not written down, but we want you to be prepared. There's not too many, so you can memorize them."

It went without saying that, given how few people lived in the area, Diane and Roger would probably recognize some of the names.

"What about Esther?" Diane wanted to know.

"She's a dear, but, well." Miriam shrugged.

"We'll handle them. We'll take care of it." Bill looked at Melinda, and she nodded her agreement.

With his fries down to their last bites, Frank began to gather up his lunch trash. "Here's the deal. Some people around here assume that since this store's been in Miriam's family for over a hundred years, and the doors are still open, that we're, well ... rich."

Diane burst out laughing. "Some things never change."

"They think we owe them." Frank threw his hands up in frustration. "I mean we do, in a way, owe everyone for their continued support of this store when so many small businesses have failed. But some people think they should get special treatment."

"In other words, the customer is usually right." The twinkle was back in Miriam's eye. "But not as often as some of them like to think."

Miriam ran through the rest of her to-do list with renewed energy, and Melinda could almost see the weight lifting off her aunt's shoulders. Maybe this wouldn't be so hard. If they all worked together, they could find a way to muddle through.

Just before they wrapped up, Bill raised his hand. "Everyone, I have some news." His wide grin brought the chatter around the table to an abrupt halt.

"And?" Miriam leaned in. "Don't keep us in suspense."

"I'm pregnant!"

Roger spit soda all over the table.

"Sorry, no, I mean, we're pregnant." Bill was so excited, he found it hard to stay in his chair. "Emily is, you know. We confirmed it yesterday."

"That makes three." Frank clapped him on the back. "Are you going to stop there?"

"Frank, really." Miriam rolled her eyes. "That's not our business."

"Oh, yeah, I think that'll be enough. We don't know yet if it's a boy or girl."

Roger helped Frank tidy up the office while Diane and Miriam discussed the Langes' impending purchase of their friends' ranch house on Third Street. Diane had been authorized to handle any paperwork while they were gone, and they still planned to close in early May.

Clearing out their rambling Victorian on Cherry Street, and putting it on the market, was a task that would have to wait until summer.

"You know, I think we've got this," Bill said to Melinda before he went back to work. No wonder he was so positive about this upcoming challenge, given what was going on at home. "Really, it shouldn't be too bad."

"We'll just have to stay on top of things, and do the best we can. They'll be gone and back before we know it. And, wow! Congratulations again!"

Melinda walked her parents to the front door. "Bill's going to be a key player, in the near future as well as later," Roger said. "But he's more than fit for the job. And with another little one on the way ..."

Diane agreed. "He loves this store as much as our family does. And Melinda, if you let him take the reins now and then, give him some input, I think he'll make the perfect business partner one day."

"That's exactly what I plan to do. I can't run this place alone." She hugged them each in turn. "Even with good help."

Roger had one more question. "This store is Frank and Miriam's baby. How are they ever going to shift gears enough to really enjoy this vacation?"

"I guess it's a good thing they'll be thousands of miles away," Diane said. "It will force them to unwind."

* * *

Several cars were already parked in the nature preserve's gravel lot when Josh and Melinda arrived. "There's Karen and Eric." Melinda pointed out their friends, and Karen waved back. "I'm so glad we decided to do this. Fresh air, a walk in the woods, a bonfire. Doesn't get any better than that."

Weary of being stuck indoors during winter and drawn by the promise of a new activity, the couples signed up for an evening hike through the conservation area just west of Eagle River.

March was almost gone, and the woods were dotted with only small clumps of snow. It was a beautiful night, not too cold, and the event was perfectly timed to take advantage of both the impending sunset and the emerging full moon.

"I'll admit, I was skeptical at first." But Josh grinned as he pulled on his knit cap. "You know I love nature, but wandering around in the dark? Didn't sound very safe."

"Well, I'm sure the conservation board will be glad there's at least two doctors in the group, just in case. Even if you and Karen are usually helping animals, not people."

"Who knows?" Josh locked his truck and pocketed the keys. "If we come across a rabbit or owl in need of assistance, we might have to stop."

Karen and Eric, who taught at Prosper's elementary school, waited for Josh and Melinda to catch up before they joined the rest of the group. While the dozen participants couldn't use flashlights, as they would disrupt the preserve's wildlife, the two organizers carried them in case of an emergency. The participants ranged in age from children to senior citizens, which told Melinda their walk wasn't exactly going to be on the wild side. One of the leaders quickly confirmed her assumption.

"The gravel path is four feet wide." The woman's bright-orange parka glowed in the dimming light as she pointed toward the trail entrance. "There's a few small rises, but nothing steep to worry about. There are several tributary paths that wander off from our route, but please, do not leave the main trail at any time."

"It's also important we don't tromp through any of the grasses along the way," the man explained. "Even under all of those trees, there are several species of native plants that need to be protected. Not to mention, animals that'll be making their usual rounds."

"What kind of animals?" one little girl wanted to know.

"We haven't done one of these night walks since October, so the residents along the trail may have changed a bit," the woman said. "But keep your eyes peeled for rabbits, deer, opossums and the like. Owls are likely to be found up in the canopy, although many of their bird friends are probably tucked in for the night. Even so, we might spot a hawk that's still feeding at dusk."

"There's a place where the trail follows the riverbank," the man added. "The beavers have started a dam and, if we're really lucky, we might see one or two of them finishing up their day's work."

That brought a chorus of ooohs and aaahs from the crowd, as did the promise of hot dogs and s'mores around a campfire at the end of the walk.

Josh elbowed Melinda. "What about the mountain lion?" He kept his voice low, but there was more than a hint of humor in it. "I want to see him, too."

"They're not very social, you know," she whispered back. "Besides, the DNR always says they don't actually live in Iowa. One just passes through, now and then."

She shivered. The evening was damp from the ongoing thaw, but that wasn't what gave her a chill. "Those tracks I saw at the farm, the winter before last? I hope to never see them again. Or whatever it was that made them."

"You never know." Eric leaned in as the group started for the woods. "They can travel several miles a day. And just look at these woods and meadows. The perfect habitat, a reliable water source, and lots of small animals for snacks."

"Stop it." Karen told her boyfriend, but included Josh in her gaze. "Melinda doesn't want to hear that, and neither do I. Besides, look at how excited those kids are. They're here to see cute critters, not predators."

The group lined up in pairs once they got to the trail, and Josh wrapped an arm around Melinda's shoulders. "I think you should stay close to me," he whispered. "You never know what's in these woods." Then he sneaked a kiss.

"I promise." She reached for his hand.

The group fell silent, just as the conservationists requested. The only sound was their boots and shoes crunching on the gravel trail. As the sun slipped toward the glowing horizon and the woods fell into shadow, Melinda's sense of hearing became more acute. Soon, she could pick out slight rustlings in the still-yellow grasses along the sides of the trail, and the faint click of squirrels' claws on the bare branches above.

Even in the dim light, the forest felt more ethereal than foreboding. There was a sense of the coming spring, the promise of infinite shades of green washing over the nature preserve in the weeks to come. In a few spots, so small they could easily be missed, the tender shoots of very-early wildflowers heralded the arrival of a new season.

There was a slight, cool breeze, but the air was invigorating. Melinda's layers kept her warm, as did keeping close to Josh. Even in the gathering darkness, glancing at him took her breath away almost as much as the stunning scenery.

Karen and Eric were just ahead of them, walking hand in hand. Suddenly, Eric pointed into an approaching oak.

"Is that an owl?" Josh leaned closer to Melinda. "Yes. Wow, look!"

The magnificent creature had its large, searching eyes trained on the travelers below. It was incredibly still, but Melinda imagined how it would lift its powerful wings and soar into the deepening sky in a second's notice. A sudden ray of sunset light burst into the woods, then slipped away as fast as it arrived.

Melinda took in the beauty around her, and tears formed in her eyes. In Minneapolis, in her old life, she'd loved to walk the trail around the lake in her Uptown neighborhood. But there was nothing like this, nothing there that could compare to this. She looked at Josh again, and he smiled at her, and she knew: This was where she was supposed to be.

The woods slowly gave way to a dormant meadow, and someone behind them let out a small gasp. There, hidden in the tall grass maybe fifteen feet from the trail, a pair of eyes glowed in the low light. Just in time, Melinda saw the swish of a bushy tail as the fox scurried away from the unexpected visitors.

As the dark was about to settle in and stay, Melinda turned her focus to what was under her feet and right in front of her. Eric and Karen walked in tandem, their shoulders touching, and Melinda thought about how happy they were. She was glad Karen had met someone so compatible in a rural area where there were so few available men. That she had done the same with Josh seemed almost too good to be true. Karen said last week that she and Eric were talking about moving in together, and Melinda wondered if a ring would be next. She couldn't see that far ahead with Josh. Not yet.

The group soon came to the bend in the river where the beavers were at work. Even though there was no sign of the critters, the outline of their in-progress dam was just visible in the dim light. The moon was robust, and its glow led them back into the woods and, much later, out into a clearing near the parking lot where an in-ground fire pit surrounded with sand offered lengths of logs for seating.

Once they were out of the preserve and less likely to disturb the wildlife, the hikers shared exclamations and started conversations about what they'd experienced. As the logs had already been stacked for the fire, a cheerful blaze soon added light, as well as warmth, to the rapidly cooling air. Josh and Melinda found a spot on one log, and Karen and Eric squeezed in at another space around the bend.

As the flames rose higher into the clear sky, the group's once-meditative mood soared, too.

"That was so much fun." Melinda stacked two marshmallows on a metal stick and leaned toward the fire. "We should come back this summer, when the preserve is at its peak. And I can just imagine how beautiful it is in the fall."

"I've lived around here for a year now, and didn't even know this place existed." Josh had a paper plate of graham crackers and chocolate squares in his lap, ready for when the marshmallows were just brown enough. "And it's only fifteen minutes from Prosper. I say we come back several times. Night, day, the season doesn't matter."

"It's a deal."

A package of hot dogs came around, and Josh took one before he handed the sleeve to the man on his right. "You know I enjoy going out for dinner or drinks. And of course, hanging out alone at home, regardless of whose house it is, is always a good time." He winked at her, and the heat of the blaze made a good cover for the blush that crept into her cheeks. She was elated with the direction their relationship had taken, but there were strangers all around who could be listening in. Including the wide-eyed kids on her left.

"Hey!" she whispered, cutting her eyes at Josh, and then at the boy and girl.

He laughed and elbowed her. "Oh, don't worry, I doubt they picked up on that. Anyway, as I was saying, let's look for more activities like this. It's easy to go to the same places all the time. Just because there aren't all the options you'd find in an urban area, doesn't mean there aren't gems like this place to explore."

"I was thinking the same thing. I'm going to start asking around, see what else we're missing out on."

Karen passed by on her way to the parking lot. "I'm going to get a blanket out of the car. You two need anything?"

"No, we're good." Melinda smiled at Josh. "Perfect, actually."

The s'mores were soon ready, and the first bite was even better than Melinda remembered. It had been years since she'd enjoyed one, and the fresh air and the company only added to its sweetness. Josh focused on roasting his hot dog, and it smelled so good as he slipped it into a bun that Melinda decided she wanted one of those, too.

"You know, I've been thinking." Josh took a bite of his hot dog and chewed carefully. "This isn't a place for us to go but, well, it's something I think we should do."

"Yeah? What is it?"

He smiled at her, but there was a hesitation on his face that cracked Melinda's reverie just a bit. Whatever it was ... was he worried she might say no?"

"I just think, I mean, if you're up for it." He took a deep breath. "I'd like you to meet Aiden."

Josh's son lived in Elkton with his mom, a two-hour drive away. Melinda had seen endless photos of the five-year-old and listened to his proud dad share the little boy's accomplishments, but she hadn't felt it was appropriate to become part of Aiden's life. Not yet.

"Really?" was all she was able to say at first. "I guess I wasn't sure if that was a good idea. I mean, right now."

"Why not?" Josh shrugged, clearly relieved she hadn't entirely shut down the idea. "I didn't want to do it right away, of course, but maybe that's the next step." When she didn't respond, he frowned. "If you don't want to, I guess ..."

"No. Oh, no, I'd love to meet him." And she meant it. "I just wonder if he's going to have a lot of questions that might be hard for you to answer. I mean, he's only five." She thought for a moment. "So, what do you think you'll tell him? Am I just a friend?"

"Sure. See, Amber's dating someone, has been for several months." Josh's words now came out in a rush. "He lives there in Elkton, so he's been to the house several times."

Melinda widened her eyes, and Josh knew her thoughts well enough that she didn't have to say more.

"He only stays over when Aiden is spending the night at a friend's, or visiting Grandma and Grandpa. There haven't been any awkward questions, in that way, and Amber and I agreed there won't be, for quite some time. It'd be the same thing, here. I just would like you to get to know him, is all. And for him to know you."

He reached for her hand, and Melinda was glad she had one free to give him.

"It'd mean a lot to me," Josh said softly. "Some weekend, when he comes to visit. Maybe we meet for lunch, go to the park. Nothing too elaborate, or for too long."

His searching eyes pleaded with her to say yes. The idea of meeting Josh's son was a bit intimidating, but Melinda couldn't tell him no.

"Of course." She squeezed his hand. "When?"

"Oh, maybe in a few weeks. Let's wait for the weather to get really good, so we can have as much fun at the park as possible. That'll help break the ice, right?"

Melinda had to agree. It made her spirits soar that Josh was so eager to introduce her to his son. As much as she cared for Josh, Melinda was no fool. This was a package deal. Everyone had to get along, or things wouldn't work out.

Josh was now deep in conversation with the couple on the other end of the log. But as Melinda finished her s'more, she thought again of what Josh said about his ex.

Was Josh really that ready to have her meet Aiden? Or was this all motivated by Amber's new relationship?

The divorce had been rather amicable, or so Josh had said. But still, bitterness and hard feelings couldn't help but be part of the equation. As could a little competition. A need, even if a subconscious one, to appear as if your new life was just as advanced, just as evolved, as your ex's.

Josh wasn't petty. He loved her, had told her so; and she had done the same. But as she stared into the fire, her emotions darting around like the flames dancing in the cool breeze, Melinda wasn't sure what to think.

✳ 11 ✳

Karen popped in Prosper Hardware's front door a little before noon. "Got my morning rounds done just in time. I'm so excited to go out for lunch." She set her things on the end of the counter and adjusted her ponytail. "Even if it's just taking my sandwich over to Meadow Lane."

"When Vicki suggested we get together, I figured we'd go to the Watering Hole." Melinda took off her apron and hung it on the peg behind the counter. Aunt Miriam would take over the register, and was overjoyed to do so. It was one of the last days before she and Frank shipped out for Hawaii, and Miriam was nearly giddy about their impending vacation.

"Why aren't you going there?" Miriam asked. "It smelled wonderful down the street, as always, when I came in."

Karen and Melinda exchanged raised eyebrows. "Oh, I don't know." Melinda smiled. "Vicki has some new sales going on, and you know Mom's birthday is coming up. I plan to do a little shopping."

"We'll have the place to ourselves, with Meadow Lane closed on Mondays." Karen was in a hurry to leave, as Miriam was studying them closely. But finally, she waved them on.

"Enjoy yourselves, girls," she trilled. "Melinda, don't be in a rush, take your time. You'll be swamped soon enough."

Once they were out the door, Karen let out a gasp of relief. "She asked a lot of questions. I'm glad we got out of there when we did. Maybe I'm being dramatic for nothing, but Vicki was so mysterious about this. Do you think it's a huge deal?"

Melinda pulled her jacket hood up against the breeze, even though Meadow Lane was next door. "Vicki only said she had something exciting to share with us. I tried to get it out of her, but she wouldn't budge."

Vicki was adjusting a spring-themed display in one of her shop's front windows, which had been crisscrossed with trim to give the modest storefront a cottage feel. Melinda knocked on the door, and Vicki's eyes were full of mischief when she unlocked it.

"It's like a speakeasy," Karen laughed, "coming in like this when the shop is closed. Is there a special password?"

"Nope, you two are on the list. Come in! We'll enjoy our lunch and then, as I said, I have a special surprise!"

Francesca, Vicki's Pomeranian, danced at her feet. The little dog was always dressed just so, which today meant a pastel-blue sweater with a wreath of flowers stitched along the neckline.

And even though this was Vicki's downtime, she was just as stylish. Her tan, cowl-neck sweater looked to be cashmere, and her black yoga pants were perfectly tailored for her petite frame.

Melinda glanced down at her own khakis and knit top, and over at Karen's faded jeans and "Prosper Veterinary Services" polo shirt, but didn't feel any judgement from their fashionable friend. Vicki had the kind of cash that made it easy to look good, but she was far from the posh snob some people assumed her to be.

The once-vacant storefront's transformation into a quaint, upscale gift shop was finally complete. While most of the work had been done in time for the store's fall grand opening and the holiday shopping rush, the final touches were now in place: perfectly pleated valances over the front windows, a fully stocked coffee and tea bar, and built-in racks to display prepackaged sweet treats crafted by Angie Hensley, Melinda's neighbor.

As they made their way through the grouped displays of candles, housewares and antiques, Melinda stopped short. "Are those baskets new?"

"Just came in last week. Everyone wants to get organized in the spring, so they're selling well. There's round ones there on top, and some squares and rectangles on the bottom shelf. Are you interested?"

"Yes, in fact. Mom's birthday is next week. She's always saying how quickly the house fills up with books and magazines. A few of these would be perfect."

"Well, you get the special-friend discount." Vicki beamed. "An extra twenty percent off."

"Really, are you sure? Well, I'll probably take three, then."

Vicki pointed to a small display of Easter-themed items. "If any of these tempt you, I'd just about give them away rather than store them until next year."

Easter had been yesterday and, true to Glenn's prediction, Jerry had persuaded Auggie to suit up as the big bunny for the town's egg hunt in the park. It was hard to tell, since the bunny's face always wore a sunny expression, but Melinda sensed Auggie had secretly enjoyed being in costume and interacting with the kids.

"I'm going to load up on some of these treats." Karen eyed the selection of wrapped cookies, bars and muffins. "Angie's snacks are so good! And I haven't had any time to bake lately. I'll keep a few in the truck for emergencies."

They settled at one of the coffee bar's round tables with their lunches, and Vicki kept up a stream of conversation as if nothing had changed.

Whatever it was, Francesca wasn't the least bit concerned, as the little dog jumped on the extra chair and enjoyed her own meal from a small stainless-steel bowl on the wooden seat.

When they were almost finished, Vicki hurried over to the store's antique counter and disappeared behind its molding-encased top. She soon reappeared with two books, then paused for a dramatic moment before returning to her chair.

"Ladies, I've come across something wonderful over at the library." She set one of the titles aside and opened the other. "This is a Hartland County history book, with details on all the communities and when they formed." She opened the embossed burgundy cover and turned to the first bookmark. "Prosper incorporated in 1890, as you may know, but the area was a settlement several years before that. Everything is in here: how the railroad caused the town to grow, the first businesses, even short bios on the families."

Karen's eyes lit up with interest and Melinda leaned over the table, the rest of her sandwich suddenly forgotten. She loved local history and, while she'd read a bit on Prosper's beginnings, these new details had her full attention. "Wow, look at those pictures! Family photos, not just ones of Main Street."

"This other book has more personal info on people from the county's early days." Vicki tipped her head at the smaller volume. "Between the two, and what I hear is available at the county historical society's archive, I think there's a story here. Several, in fact."

"I'm sure there are." Karen studied the photos. "What are you thinking of doing with them?"

Vicki slid her chair back a bit so Francesca could leap into her lap. "Prosper's birthday is coming up, and I think we need to celebrate! What about a Founders Day festival? With a play? It doesn't have to be long, or very elaborate." But given Vicki's excitement and penchant for over-achievement, Melinda suspected it might be.

"I've already talked to Nancy, she thinks it's a great idea. I'll ask Amy and Shelby to talk to the elementary-school principal. I'm sure some of the kids would love to play the parts. Maybe we can incorporate songs, too."

Karen and Melinda widened their eyes in surprise. Vicki laughed.

"Oh, no, let me explain. I'm not going to compose any music, or ask anyone else to. Just some traditional tunes, whatever fits best. But I think I can pull enough from these sources to write some simple scenes portraying Prosper's beginnings."

Karen nodded slowly. "I like the idea! When exactly is the anniversary?"

"May eighteenth. But that's a Thursday, so we can move it to Saturday. Close enough." Vicki waved away the facts with a manicured hand. "Besides, we'll want to do this right, so it has to be on a weekend. Have some activities in the park, the merchants can offer special sales, food, music, the whole bit. I know, it's not a milestone year this time around, but why wait? This could be the start of something big!"

Melinda found Vicki's enthusiasm contagious.

"Well, it's true Prosper doesn't have much going on that time of year. We have the Fourth of July, then the fall festival and the holiday celebration. It would be a nice kick-off to summer and ... hey, isn't that the Saturday the farmers' market is supposed to start?"

Vicki clapped her hands. "Perfect timing, isn't it?"

Melinda loved Vicki's vision, but even good ideas took a lot of work. "So I guess the next question is: What do we have to do?"

"Absolutely nothing," Vicki promised. "I mean, not yet. I need to get cracking on this play, start digging into the town's founders." She gestured out the windows. "They started all this, built it with their own hands, all out of a swatch of sweeping prairie."

Karen grinned at Melinda. Some actor surely would deliver that line on stage.

"Once I get their personalities down, and compile a few incidents that were key to the founding of the town, it'll be a snap." Vicki took a satisfied sip of her green tea. "And I know the community center will be ready by then, but I think we'll put on the play at the school. They have a full stage, there in the gym. And it'll make it easier for rehearsals, too."

"Sounds like you have it all figured out." Melinda wondered how Vicki would pull this project off. But she had to admit, it was an interesting idea.

"When you get further along, let me know what I can do to help."

"Thanks. It'll be awhile, and that works out perfectly, since I know you'll be swamped for several weeks while Frank and Miriam are out of town."

"Yeah, I'll have my hands full. But I'll have plenty of help. I'm hoping things don't get too crazy. Besides, this will be a trial run for Bill and I. Frank and Miriam will retire eventually, of course, although I think they're a long way off from that."

"Retire?" Karen laughed. "I can't see either of them doing anything else. Besides, Frank's already reduced his workload, since you came back, and it suits him just fine. I don't think you have to worry about that happening anytime soon."

"I know, and I'm so relieved. But still, it's going to be interesting."

Vicki frowned. "What are you worried about, exactly? You have the perfect skills to take over the store one day. Bill does, too. Running a business can be difficult, for sure, but where there's a will, there's a way."

"Oh, I think we can handle the operations and decisions, with more mentoring from Frank and Miriam." Melinda looked down at the table, then around at Meadow Lane's understated elegance. "It's money that I'm worried about."

She quickly answered the question in her friends' eyes. "The store's doing fine. I just wonder, in the coming decades, if that will continue to be the case. This area's not growing, as you know, and with online shopping ..."

"I wouldn't worry." Vicki spoke with a confidence Melinda wished she felt. "Prosper Hardware has a niche in the market; I can only hope that Meadow Lane will do the same. So far, so good." Then she gave a knowing smile. "Besides, I think you're going to end up with Josh."

"Well, maybe."

"No, I'm serious. I have a good feeling about this, always have. And he's got quite the successful practice going. I don't think you're going to have to worry about money."

Francesca, still snuggled in her mom's lap, added a bark of agreement.

Melinda felt a pinprick of irritation. It was no secret Arthur made excellent money managing one of the banks in Swanton, and many residents assumed it was his salary that made Meadow Lane possible.

Josh's practice was doing well, from what little Melinda knew, but she had deliberately not asked too many questions so far. They weren't married, far from it; and his money was his business. As was hers. And, even if they did end up together, Melinda was determined to make her own way in life. She always had before; why should this be any different?

Karen gave her a look that said, *be careful what you say.*

"Well, that's a long way off." Melinda gathered up her things. "Look at the time! I better get back to the store. Miriam was happy to watch the counter for me, but I'm sure she needs to get home. She and Frank haven't even started packing yet."

* * *

The eastern sky was rosy with promise that morning, and the ground under Melinda's chore boots was softer than it had been the week before. Spring was really on the way now, with only a few days to go before April arrived. She was in a hurry, but paused long enough to admire the tender green shoots lined up along the south side of the house. The daffodils would soon be in full bloom, and they were a welcome hint of everything wonderful to come.

But first, Melinda had to get through the next few weeks. More exactly, sixteen days. Frank and Miriam drove to Minneapolis last night because their early-morning flight left at, well, any moment now. She scanned the heavens, tossed up a quick prayer for them to have a wonderful vacation, then looked down to find Sunny glaring at her.

"I know. You eat first. At least Stormy is polite enough to wait by the barn door." With his morning inspection of the still-sleeping garden complete, Hobo joined the procession.

"If only I had just the store to contend with while they're gone. But that's not the half of it."

The first spay clinic of the season had gone off without a hitch, thank goodness, but they'd scrambled to schedule an in-between event due to the overwhelming number of cats on the wait list. With kitten season already ramping up, it seemed reckless to hold off until later in April. And, as Karen had pointed out, if they didn't double the schedule now, they'd never clear the backlog that built up over winter.

Harriet's kitties had received a short reprieve, but were now on deck for next week's clinic. Melinda would have to get the carriers over there a few days in advance, set them up so the cats could become familiar with them, then transport the cats that morning and still get to the store by seven. No, earlier would be better. Because starting today, she was determined to beat Auggie in Prosper Hardware's door. Even an extra twenty minutes would let her burn through some small tasks before the day's craziness took hold.

The cat clinics would continue to be held in the council chambers for now, since the community center was a barely controlled mess of last-minute projects. Check-in usually didn't start until seven-thirty. But if she could get a key from Nancy or Jerry ...

"Well, I guess I should be grateful Mabel offered to host the township club's meeting tomorrow night." The morning was serene but still cool, and she put down the cats' food bucket to rub the frost off the barn door's iron latch. "My house is sort of a mess, but no one other than Josh is likely to see it over the next few weeks. I can't imagine having a dozen people come over, much less prepping all that food."

After much discussion and moving of dates, the local ladies hatched a plan to resurrect the Fulton Friendship Circle. For once, all Melinda had to do was show up. She just hoped to be alert enough to enjoy it.

Her churning thoughts were soon interrupted by the ewes' morning greetings. "Hello, ladies! I'll be back in a minute. You know how bossy the boys can be."

She went into the grain room, expecting to see both cats standing guard over their dishes. But instead, they were distracted by something in one of the corners, and Hobo was, too. Even when Melinda opened the cats' food bucket, the three of them couldn't be bothered to look up.

Her stomach dropped. "What's going on over there? Do I even want to know?"

Just before she reached the group, Sunny turned and let out a loud, triumphant meow. A second later, Melinda answered with a groan of disgust.

It was a dead rat. Not too large, but still bigger than Melinda ever wanted to see again. And nearby, behind a dusty wooden crate, she spotted a second, smaller corpse.

Sunny was still meowing, and Stormy joined in. They seemed pleased with themselves. Melinda didn't want to take a second look, but when she did, she could see the bite marks on both rats' necks.

"You two did this?" Stormy rubbed his cheek against the leg of her jeans, then ambled over to the smaller rat and picked it up in his jaws.

"No, that's OK. You don't have to present it to me." She took a quick step back when Stormy didn't halt his advance. "Put that nasty thing down!" He looked a bit disappointed, but complied. "Thank goodness you both have your rabies shots. You too, Hobo."

So much for getting to the store early. But this couldn't wait. Melinda gave the cats their real breakfast, found an old paper feed sack and a discarded pair of chore gloves, then reached for a shovel.

"Stay back, Hobo! Don't touch them, OK? Let me do it." She shooed him out of the grain room and shut the door. With their moment of show-and-tell over, and fresh kibble and warm gravy available, Sunny and Stormy quickly lost interest in their trophies.

It wasn't too hard to get a dead rat on a shovel, if she used the blade to slide the carcass against the crate, but it made a sickening plop as it dropped into the bag. When both were pocketed, she started for the windbreak with the offensive sack gripped in an outstretched hand.

It was just as well the ground was still frozen not far from the surface. She couldn't bury the dead rats deep enough to keep wild animals from finding them, so it would save her several minutes to not have to try. As for Hobo, well, she just had to hope he had some sense.

"Ugh!" The dead rats flew out when she gave the bag a shake, and she turned away as quickly as she could. Then she took the long way around the machine shed and stuffed the sack in the old iron incinerator. She'd need to burn trash in a few days, and the nasty bag would go up in smoke. At the last second, she tossed in the ratty cotton gloves.

"That's the old-school version of disposable gloves, I guess," she muttered as she hurried back to the barn. "Now I see why Horace and Wilbur never threw anything away. Use everything until it's worn out, then give it one last go."

Pansy shared several squawks of disapproval when Melinda appeared in the chicken house, disheveled and stressed. Melinda rushed through those chores and passed a quick hand through the nesting boxes. There were more eggs than she expected, which was good, but no time to prepare them to take to the store. Maybe tomorrow ...

Diane's car was already in the gravel parking lot behind Prosper Hardware when Melinda finally made it to town, only ten minutes' late. Settled in Frank's usual chair, Diane peppered Auggie with questions about his plans to add gas pumps to the co-op's lot.

"I filled up yesterday, of course." She paused long enough to wave at her daughter. "It's not even ten miles to Swanton, so that'll get me back and forth for quite some time. But how wonderful it will be to have gas in Prosper again!" The tiny town's last gas station closed shortly after the farm crisis of the nineteen-eighties.

"You're not the only one who's excited about it." Auggie beamed with pride as he filled the coffee pot. "But this is a big project. It'll take time to get it just right."

Melinda set her things behind the counter and tried to gather her racing thoughts. Despite her best intentions, the day was already getting away from her. But she noticed the oak showcase's surface was already clear, and glowed from a fresh rub of lemon oil.

Diane had joined her at the counter, and now leaned over. "Honey, what is it? You seem frazzled. I tidied up a bit when I got here, so we're ready to go. Did I do something wrong, put something in the wrong spot?"

"Oh, it's not that." Melinda sighed. "Thank you. I don't know what I'd do if you weren't here. No, I found two dead rats in the barn this morning, and their furry killers were very proud of themselves. Had to make a trip to the windbreak for a sort-of funeral, which meant I spent more time in the shower than I'd planned."

Auggie now stood at the window, watching for his friends to arrive. And to see whatever else he could see. Melinda lowered her voice.

"But if you're worried about stepping on any toes, I can tell you this: Frank's role in the coffee group is usually to listen, he doesn't ask too many questions. But he'll back Jerry on city issues when needed, of course."

"I see." Diane nodded. "Thanks for the tip. I'll be silent as a mouse, then."

"Oh, but if Auggie says anything witty, and he usually does, he'll expect you to laugh, for sure. But don't worry, he doesn't get a free pass around here. The other guys hold his feet to the fire when needed."

"Look who's here!" George came in the front door. "A new face in the circle. Or should I say, an old one."

"Hey!" Diane warned him, but she was laughing.

"You know what I mean." George added his jacket to the hall tree by the refrigerated case. "You're right back where you started! As for actually being old, well, I'm the geezer around here. Why, I remember you and Miriam running the aisles when you were girls. And later, working behind the counter."

"Melinda promises there's a cute apron for me when the store opens. We didn't have fancy branded ones back in the day." Diane helped herself to Auggie's brew. She took a sip from her mug, and coughed.

"Watch it," George cautioned. "It's strong."

"Strong?" Diane's eyes watered. "I'd say so. Strong enough to strip paint off wood."

"It has a little octane." Auggie's first gulp went down without a blink. "You'll get used to it."

"Used to what?" Doc came in the door, with Jerry right behind him.

"The coffee," Melinda said. "Mom's tastes run to something a little more, well, palatable."

"I'll be right back." Diane started for the stairs. "If I cut it with water, maybe I can get it down to my level with some cream and sugar."

"What's new this morning?" Auggie asked Doc. "Do you think you'll get down to the co-op today to check on the ducks?"

Doc hid a smile. "Uh, yeah. Or maybe Karen can come by sometime. What did you say was wrong with them, again?"

"Nothing, really. It's just that they've been gone all winter. Only showed up a few days ago. Maybe give them a look over, make sure they're healthy?"

Jerry chuckled. "Auggie, they're ducks. If they're flying around and waddling and gobbling corn, then they should be OK."

The co-op's vast lot was mostly gravel, but there was a large swath of grass on its east and south sides, along with some bushes and a few trees. While there was no real pond on the property, the largest low spot tended to collect rainwater and snowmelt in the spring. A few years ago, a pair of Mallards decided it made a nice pit stop on their travels. The kernels of corn scattered across the lot, of course, added to the spot's appeal.

"Lucy and Desi are the co-op's ambassadors." Auggie raised his chin. "I just want to be sure they're OK."

Before Diane could ask, Melinda filled her in. "They're named after the comedy team. Lucy is actually pretty chill, and Desi fusses over her. They're really cute."

"I thought Mr. Checkers and Pebbles were the faces of Prosper Feed Company." With his coffee cup in hand, Jerry took his usual seat. "Unless you're going to bring Lucy and Desi inside, and have them nest on the counter, I'd say the cats are still in charge."

"How's that working?" George asked. "Don't the cats bother the ducks?"

Auggie chuckled. "Goodness, no. It's quite a hike out to the duck pond. The kitties are too fat and lazy to wander far. Although they both love to take the stairs up to the weather lab with me when I do my reports." He turned to Diane. "It's important work, you know. They like to be part of it."

"You sure?" Jerry was skeptical. "I think it might be those fancy cat trees you installed in that room. There's quite a view, too."

Auggie looked as if he was about to argue, and Melinda jumped in.

"So, Jerry, since that property's fallen into the city's hands, do you have any leads on a buyer?"

Jerry's nod quickly caught Auggie's attention. "Oh, there's been a few calls. But we'll see. If they can cover the back taxes, they can have it."

"Who's *they*?" Auggie wanted to know.

"Now, Auggie, you know he can't say anything yet." Doc crossed his arms. "The city has to accept proposals, have it inspected, the whole bit."

"We'll find out when it's time." George settled into his chair. "No sooner, no later. Auggie, I suggest you find a way to reign in that nose of yours. You'll find, as you get older, it's best to just go with the flow."

"Hrumph."

"See, Melinda." Doc offered a sympathetic smile. "Someday, when Frank and Miriam retire, you'll be fielding all this gossip on your own."

"Oh, no, I won't." She shook her head. "I think I'll let Bill handle it."

"Bill has the right idea." George pointed over his shoulder as Bill came through the shop door. "He joins us sometimes. But when the clock strikes eight, he gets to work and keeps his mind busy with other things the rest of the day." George stared at Auggie.

"Yeah, I know what you're thinking." Auggie frowned. "OK, I guess you're right."

George laughed. "Well, now. Someone write this down. A day for the history books."

"Speaking of history." Jerry turned to Melinda. "What's Vicki up to? Nancy said something about a play."

Eyebrows shot up around the circle.

"I'm not doing it." Bill was adamant. "Don't ask me. One musical, freshman year of high school, was enough."

"Who will?" Auggie perked up. "Maybe I could ..."

"There's no play." Melinda held up a hand. "Not yet. Vicki found some interesting local-history tidbits at the library, and the anniversary of the town's incorporation is in mid-May. She'd like to pull something together by then." She then turned to Auggie. "Nothing too elaborate. Because the actors are going to be kids from the elementary school."

"I think that sounds wonderful!" Diane beamed. "And I'm glad Vicki is taking charge of the idea, like she usually does. That means it shouldn't end up on Nancy's plate. She has far too much to do."

George looked toward the city's buildings. "At least the community center's nearly complete. I was in the library the other day and, well, she didn't seem like herself. Oh, she was helpful as always," he added quickly. "But ..."

"Is everything OK?" Diane was worried.

"It was funny," George mused as he took another sip of coffee. "She seemed a little tired and distracted but, well, not discouraged or upset. Kind of the opposite, actually."

The men thought on this for a moment. No one looked directly at Melinda, seeking an answer, but she wouldn't have

minded if they did. Truth be told, she'd noticed the same
about her friend, but had no idea what was behind it. There
hadn't been a good time to ask Nancy how she was doing, at
least not without other ears around.

"Well, it's been a long time since I've been here at this
hour of the day." Diane glanced at the clock, and rose from
her chair. "But I have to say, I'm a bit surprised by the topics
of discussion. I didn't know people's personal lives were such
a source of fascination."

"Get used to it." Melinda told her mom, then looked at
each of the men in turn. "As for Nancy, let's cut her some
slack. Ryan is a senior this year, remember? Between
finalizing his college plans and getting ready for the
graduation party, she has her hands full."

"Melinda's right." Jerry drained his cup. "It's none of our
business. Diane, I'm proud to welcome you to the coffee club.
And Melinda and Bill, hang in there. Frank and Miriam will
be back before you know it."

* 12 *

The clock on the nightstand told Melinda she was running late. But then, she'd been running behind for a few days now.

"I just have to pick something." She pushed her hair out of her face and studied the skirts, pants and cardigans displayed on the bed. Or rather, they had been nicely arranged fifteen minutes ago. That was before Hazel and Grace arrived to play stylist. "What did I wear the last time I had to dress up, even a little? When was that?"

Grace yawned and stretched her fluffy calico paws across a black shirt. "Of course, you like that one. It has the best backdrop to show off your stray hairs. Hazel, what do you have over there?"

The light-blue cardigan and tank looked springy enough. If Melinda dug a necklace out of her jewelry box, she might squeak by with a pair of knit pants but nice shoes. Still, it was a balancing act. Mabel's invitations for the rebooted Fulton Friendship Circle had gently requested "dressy casual" attire.

"Whatever that means. Of course, that's the term Angie and I came up with, to be fair. We thought it conveyed the spirit of the old club, but gave everyone plenty of leeway."

Hobo barely looked up from the sofa when she flew through the living room ten minutes later. His feet were now sor-of-clean after several minutes of tug-of-war in the kitchen, and Melinda was glad she always kept a throw blanket draped over her cream-colored couch. Who would have considered something in that pale hue to be practical? The old Melinda, that's who. The one who lived in the city, and wore skirts and heels on a regular basis.

There was a mirror on the dining-room wall, next to the front door, but she barely gave it a glance. She looked fine, really, and okay would have to be good enough. It was a cool evening, and she grabbed her nicest spring jacket on her way out the back door.

How strange it seemed to be heading to a neighbor's with nothing in her arms but her purse, but Mabel had insisted on preparing all the food for the party.

"That's how it was always done," Mabel reminded Angie and Melinda when they offered to help. "I love a good potluck as much as the next person, but this isn't the time for that. The host does it all, and the rest of the ladies get a break."

Melinda tried to hopscotch around the muddy patches in the new grass between the house and the garage. The gravel road was soft, too, so she tried to keep to the packed-down tracks in the middle of the road. Even so, she was momentarily distracted as she crossed the creek.

One of the eagle parents sat proudly on the nest, which was in a towering oak just east of the bridge. The regal birds were one of the rural neighborhood's worst-kept secrets. Even so, its human residents had agreed to not broadcast the eagles' presence, much less the location of their nest, to give the birds their privacy.

The Bauers' gray, foursquare farmhouse was set off with cream trim, and flanked with welcoming porches. Angie and Adelaide had already arrived, and Melinda pulled in next to their cars with a mix of excitement and trepidation. This was going to be a fun evening, the start of something new, yet a nod to tradition. But first, Melinda had to come up with a plan to get herself from the car to the back door.

Sammy, the Bauers' friendly lab, wagged her tail with welcome by the steps. It was Hector, the overprotective gander, that Melinda had to outsmart.

"Hector, get back!" She swung her purse in a threatening manner as the gigantic goose barreled toward her from the front lawn, his wings wide open. Hector's honks were soon mixed with Sammy's excited barks, and the tranquil early-spring evening was suddenly far from that. The gander's hisses were more for show than anything else, but Melinda wasn't about to take any chances.

Ed popped through the porch door. "Hey, stop that!"

At the sight of his caretaker, Hector suddenly turned docile. Ed often had a little sack of cracked corn in his coat pocket, and besides, he'd given the gander and his two lady friends a home when no one else bid on them at the Eagle River auction barn.

"Where are the girls?" Melinda asked. "I rarely see him without his harem."

"Off behaving themselves, as usual. As for this guy, his manners are improving, but he's hit his limit for tonight." He shook a finger at Hector. "You had your fun, swooping in on Adelaide and Lauren, then Angie, and now Melinda. Three strikes, and you're out. It's off to the barn for you, and your ladies, too."

The kitchen bustled with activity as last-minute preparations were made for the meeting. Mabel's white curls were immaculate, as usual, but it was the frilly apron over her dress slacks that caught Melinda's eye.

"Fancy!" She set her purse on a chair, as the counters were filled with trays of food. "Where did you get that?"

"The grandkids, Christmas last year." Mabel shrugged, but there was a twinkle in her eye. "I never bother with one, otherwise. But I thought, might as well. Mom always wore one when she was hostess."

Angie came in from the living room, where she had been setting up chairs. Her print blouse was pretty, and her auburn curls were caught up in a tasteful bun, but there were lines of fatigue under her eyes.

"I thought I'd never get away," she told Melinda. "Blake has an upset tummy, and the warmer weather has the girls bouncing off the walls. I told Nathan, just get everyone off to bed by whatever means necessary."

"Sounds like you needed a break; tonight couldn't come soon enough. Now I'm really glad Mabel insisted we not help with the food."

Adelaide and Lauren came up from the basement with more folding chairs. "Mabel, how many are coming?" Adelaide asked. "Is twelve enough?"

"Should be." Mabel gave a nod of satisfaction as she closed the oven door. "Good, the ham-and-cheese buns are about ready. Didn't want to leave them in too long."

Lauren offered Melinda a shy smile. "It's good to see you again."

"How are you doing?" Melinda gave Lauren's arm a small squeeze. "I hear you got a job at the coffee shop in Swanton."

"Yes." Lauren's smile was a mixture of pride and relief. "Only part-time for now, but it's a start. Adelaide and Mason keep me busy around the farm, too. Peanut and I love it there."

"Where did you get these?" Adelaide picked up an oval glass plate from the stack on the counter, and admired its floral design. "My mom had a set. But over the years, many of the cups got broken."

Mabel wiped her hands on a towel. "Mom's snack trays were still boxed up on a shelf in the basement. A good scrub and a scalding bath, and they were ready to go. I don't think they're worth much, as they go cheap at the secondhand stores. But they're pretty, and it's one way to link the past and the present."

Club hostesses used to give presentations as well, Mabel said, and she'd wanted to do the same. A selection of everyday household goods, perched on one end of the dining room table, caught Melinda's eye.

"Natural cleaning products." Angie picked up a box of baking soda. "Eco-friendly is all the rage these days, but Mabel says it's nothing new. Her mother had all sorts of tricks and tips."

"That's the perfect way to kick off the new club!" Melinda loved the idea of the township's women sharing their knowledge with their neighbors. But she'd offered to host next month, and now saw she had more to do than plan a menu and clean the house until it sparkled.

Anna Schermann had surely owned a set of snack trays, too, but Melinda thought it was likely they'd been sold at the family's auction. She could always borrow Mabel's, but something else was still missing.

"I just wish we could have found the original club's records. Mom and Miriam and I looked all over in the storage room, and I've checked the basement shelves. How perfect it would have been to bring them to tonight's meeting."

"Maybe they'll turn up yet." Angie wasn't ready to give up hope. "They could be at someone else's house. Let's ask around tonight. You never know." Her eyes lit up. "Besides, you found some other cool stuff that day. Is Kevin having any luck with the ledger?"

"Nope. But he's going to keep trying. He and Jack are obsessed, at this point. They're determined to crack it, and I'm glad. Because I certainly haven't had any time to help them."

"Frank and Miriam will be back before you know it." Mabel passed by with a stack of napkins. And not the paper kind. "It won't be long, and you'll have the first week under your belt."

Angie looked out the dining room's picture window, which faced the driveway. "Here come some more of the ladies. Oh, I'm so excited!"

The house was soon filled with laughter and chatter as the women made their way into the living room. Many of them honored Mabel's request to dress up, if even a little. But Maria Jackson, Angie's neighbor through the mile section, was still in jeans and a tee shirt. She had four children under ten, and considered herself lucky to make it at all.

"Brady spit up on my blouse just as I was about to leave, so I grabbed whatever was clean." Maria set her tote down so she could pull her long, brown hair into a ponytail, then admired Angie's skirt. "It's been so long since I've had a reason to dress up! I was really looking forward to it."

"Well, there's always next month," Angie told her. "Don't worry about it. Oh, there's Donna!"

Melinda turned to see a middle-aged woman with a friendly, if not quite familiar, face. And then, she remembered. She'd stopped at Donna's last summer with an invitation for the Lutheran church's women's luncheon, and almost left with three orange kittens.

"Thanks for letting us know about the spay clinics." Donna gave Melinda an unexpected hug. "We took all the babies when they were old enough, and Mama, too."

"We're trying to halt the population explosion, one cat at a time. Harriet's kitties are next." The old Cadillac had just rolled slowly past the window. Harriet, who took her time getting out of the car, was wearing a lavender cardigan and even a swipe of lipstick.

Helen Emmerson, a longtime friend of Mabel's, came into the dining room with an armful of mixing bowls for the presentation. "I can't remember the last time I saw most of these ladies. It might have been last summer's church luncheon! And that's a shame."

The women found their seats in the living room, and Mabel called the meeting to order. After introductions, the group gathered around the dining-room table for the presentation. As Mabel mixed a homemade window cleaner, Harriet stepped forward to hold the bowl steady for her neighbor. As it turned out, Harriet knew a similar recipe, and soon, she and Mabel were trading suggestions and ideas. Then Helen joined in, and they had the room laughing as they compared notes.

Angie elbowed Melinda. "Look at this! All these years of life experience, and everyone so willing to share what they've learned."

Melinda looked around the circle and saw more than just a dozen women enjoying a reprieve from their usual routine.

Even with modern technology at their fingertips, all of them were eager for a new way to connect. She could see how this club was a lifeline for the township's ladies decades ago.

Mabel's spread of snacks went far beyond the hearty ham-and-cheese buns she pulled from the oven. There were dainty cucumber sandwiches, asparagus spears wrapped in bacon, and a throwback gelatin fruit salad with marshmallows that Mabel's mother served to the former club.

Miniature cupcakes frosted in pastel colors waited at the end of the kitchen counter, along with coffee and punch.

The polite conversation that marked the meeting's beginning had quickly evolved into easy chatter punctuated with plenty of laughter.

"Look at all this!" Donna exclaimed to Melinda as they balanced trays on their laps. "I almost feel underdressed, like I should be wearing a hat and white gloves."

Melinda took a bite of a cucumber square and rolled her eyes with delight. "These dill sprigs are as fresh as can be; no sprinkles from a can. Mabel's set the bar pretty high; who knows if I'll be able to top this next month?"

"You won't have to. Frozen pizza would be enough to bring us together, given how much fun everyone is having."

After the women settled into their snacks, Mabel raised a hand to get everyone's attention. "Ladies, I think this evening has been a great success."

Murmurs of agreement echoed around the room.

"We just need a little bit of business to get things rolling. If we can land on a regular night to meet, and have a few volunteers serve as club leaders, that's good enough for now."

No matter what was suggested, someone had a conflict. Of course, there would never be perfect attendance, but it was important to find the best night for the most members.

"Let's give that some more thought and move on." Mabel rubbed her hands together and gave Melinda a worried look. This was more difficult than they had imagined. "It won't be too much work to be an officer, but it's still a commitment. Who's game?"

Several ladies raised their hands. But again, time was going to be a factor.

What about naming co-chairs? someone asked.

Would the terms be for a full year, or a half year?

Should we set up a social media page to stay in touch, or just use email? Who would take that on?

At this last question, several of the women looked to Melinda, and she knew she couldn't say no. The debate continued for several more minutes, then Adelaide set her tray at her feet and stood up.

"Well, I'm wondering about the best way to proceed. Tonight has been lovely, and I don't see enough of all of you as it is." This was answered with nods of agreement around the room. "But as much as I want to see the women's club resurrected, I'm not sure we can make that happen. Or, more importantly, keep it going if we do."

That last statement was met with silence, then murmurs of resignation.

"I know what you mean." Angie sighed. "I'm booked the way it is. It was hard enough for us to agree on a night for this first meeting. And with the kids ..."

"I hate the thought of letting the idea drop," Helen said. "I've been looking forward to this for weeks! This was so much fun, but maybe times are too different these days."

"How about this?" Adelaide looked around the circle. "What if it wasn't so structured? We set up a group email, for example, and I'd be willing to reach out to the ladies that aren't online." She included Harriet in her gaze. "Maybe we can try for lunch or coffee somewhere once a month, for whoever can make it."

"I like that idea," Melinda said. "The important thing is that we keep in touch."

"I'd still like to find some community projects to get involved in," another woman added. "Nothing that takes too much time, of course."

Adelaide had an idea. "The township trustees are holding a clean-up day later this month at Hawk Hollow cemetery. It's a Sunday afternoon, and they need more volunteers. No pressure. But Mason's on the board, and I can send out a reminder. If you can make it, just show up."

"Easy as pie." Harriet smiled, then held up one of the sweet treats. "Or cake, rather."

"I think that's the way to go." Helen wiped her hands on her cloth napkin. "I was still a member when the club disbanded, and this is exactly why. Everyone's too busy these days to mess with the pomp and circumstance."

Melinda turned to Mabel. "Are you OK with this? I know you were so excited about getting the club going again."

Mabel sighed, but then untied her ruffled apron with two swift turns of her hands. "It's been fun for one night, but I'm beat. The worst part is, Mom's snack trays won't stand up to the dishwasher. They have to be scrubbed by hand."

"I enjoyed dressing up," someone said, "but my yoga pants are calling me."

Laughter erupted around the room, and Maria stifled a yawn. "I don't know when I'd have an excuse to make them, but Mabel, I'd love your recipe for the cucumber sandwiches."

"To be fair, I think we should take a vote." Adelaide looked around the room. "Everyone in favor of rebooting the Fulton Friendship Circle, but not really, raise your hand."

Arms went up all around the room.

"Well, that was easy!" Melinda laughed. "A unanimous decision. And Mabel, don't worry, I can hang back for a bit and help you clean up."

"Me, too." Angie folded her cloth napkin. "I barely made it out of the house. Nathan can spare me for another hour." She looked around. "Hey, I know he can't be in the club, but where'd Ed go?"

"He's out in the kitchen, I think." Mabel rose from her chair. "Probably helping himself to some ham-and-cheese buns."

But they soon heard a rumble on the back porch, and Sammy's bark of distress echoed from the side yard. The kitchen door jerked open, and Ed popped through.

"Honey, change your clothes and come quick! The cows are out! I thought I'd patched that fence good, but they found a way."

Groans of understanding echoed around the room. "I have chore boots in the car," Adelaide told Ed. Mabel had already disappeared upstairs to change. "Let me get them, and I'll meet you at the barn."

"Me, too." Donna set her purse on her chair. "I never go anywhere without a pair. I can watch the gate, at least."

The other women took the trays to the kitchen and folded up the chairs. "Look at all the helping hands," Angie told Melinda. "I'd bet this is what the ladies really had in mind when they started this club, over a hundred years ago."

"Maybe we're not as far off the mark as we thought." Melinda reached for a dish towel. "Let's see if we can get everything cleaned up before Mabel gets back."

* 13 *

The woman leaned her elbows on the counter and glared at Melinda. "I told you, the sign said fifty percent off." She pointed an accusing finger toward the grocery aisle. "Why else would I buy three boxes of instant rice at once? It's just Elmer and I at home now, has been for years."

Melinda opened her mouth to say something, then quickly closed it. And counted to five before she tried again. Prosper Hardware's groceries never had that steep of a discount, as they were some of the store's best sellers. So it was common for customers to stock up on non-perishables when a sale came along. And it had, last week. But the discount had been twenty percent.

"I'm sorry if there was a misunderstanding." She tried to smile. "I'd be happy to refund two of the boxes. But unfortunately, we can't take back the one that's been opened."

Esther, who was straightening the kitchen towels across the main aisle, tried to catch Melinda's eye and offer a look of support. But Melinda did her best to avoid it, no matter how well-meant it was. Her exhaustion meant she'd start laughing; or more likely, start crying; and neither would do.

She scanned her addled brain for the woman's name; it would help smooth this over.

It was a little unique, seemed like. Eloise? Masie? Like so many things these days, she had no idea.

"There's nothing wrong with that rice." The woman crossed her arms. "It's not like we ate any of it. Look, I didn't notice the receipt was wrong, at first. There were so many things on it."

She waved the strip of paper in Melinda's face. The receipt was only a few inches long; the woman hadn't purchased more than eight items that day.

"I'm sorry," Melinda said again. "I can refund two boxes, but not three."

The woman's face turned pink with frustration. "When are Frank and Miriam going to be back? I swear, it's not the same without them."

You're telling me, Melinda thought but didn't say. *They can't get home soon enough.*

Miriam would never take back an open container of food. But she surely knew this woman, and her name, and would have been able to smooth this over far better than Melinda ever could.

"Why hello, Bessie!" Esther suddenly appeared at the woman's elbow. "I didn't see you come in. Are you planning your garden yet? We have quite a few seeds in, you know. And we got a shipment of pretty new garden gloves just yesterday."

Bessie's eyes lit up with interest. "Really? Well, I may have to take a look."

Esther leaned in with a big smile. "I have to say, rice is one of my go-tos when I can't decide what to fix for supper. Why, just cook some chicken and pop the rice in the microwave, then mix it with cream of chicken soup, a little water, veggies. Easy-peasy."

She reached for the pad of paper kept on the end of the counter, and pulled a pen from the flowerpot next to it.

Melinda had wondered about the scratch pad when she'd started working at the store, but soon saw how much use it got. Socializing and connecting were as much the store's stock and trade as the groceries and the tools. Someone always wanted to write down an old friend's phone number, or a recommendation for a doctor or babysitter. Bill even used the tablet to sketch rough designs for wood-shop customers.

"I'll write it down for you." Esther scribbled on the pad. "Chicken, rice, veggies. Oh, and cheese. Everything is better with cheese."

"Oh, I agree! Cheddar, or ..."

"I like that mixed stuff. Melinda, what's it called? Colby jack?"

She only nodded, too tired to make more small talk than what was absolutely necessary.

"And get the shredded." Esther pointed her pen for emphasis. "Not the slices. Just sprinkle it on the top." She tore off the recipe with a flourish and presented it to Bessie, who's mood had markedly improved. Bessie tucked the taped-up box of rice into her tote bag, and Esther saw her chance to close the deal.

"Let's go look at those gloves, huh? Melinda will get your refund ready while we shop."

Melinda found just enough energy for another smile, but couldn't stop the irritated sigh that escaped as soon as Bessie and Esther were out of earshot.

A headache had taken hold in her right temple, and its steady pound soon matched the throb of the wrapped-up finger on her left hand. It was cat-clinic day, on top of everything else, and she'd managed to get all three of Harriet's kitties to city hall on time that morning.

But while Harriet had corralled the cats in their borrowed carriers the night before, Shadow's door hadn't latched tight and he'd spent the wee hours bouncing around the garage, desperately trying to escape whatever fate awaited him at dawn.

Melinda had made the winning tackle, but Shadow extracted his revenge before she got him back in his crate. Harriet started to cry, her tears a mix of relief over getting her kitties the care they needed and her worry about the blood dripping down Melinda's hand. At least Harriet recovered enough to help clean and dress the bite before Melinda started for town. Josh had pronounced the wound as superficial when she arrived at city hall, but the pain in her hand only added to her stress.

Bill had opened the store so Melinda could check in patients at the clinic, but he had to rush back to his stack of cut orders as soon as she arrived. Esther had come in a few hours' early, but Melinda wasn't sure it was going to be enough. Roger had the stomach flu, and Diane had rightfully decided not to come in. She wasn't feeling the best, either, and the last thing any of them needed was for more people to get sick.

Melinda rang up four customers in short succession, then glanced at the clock. It was almost eleven. She'd promised to run across the street on her lunch hour to help with the clinic, as usual. Esther was capable, and Bill would run the register if they got in a bind, but Melinda found herself wishing she had two sets of arms. Or, even better, that she could be in two places at once.

To top it off, they were expecting a shipment that afternoon. Which, of course, meant it could come at any time. Or not show up until tomorrow.

She was grateful Bill's dad and two of his friends were on alert and willing to come back if needed. Their help had certainly been welcome yesterday.

She rubbed her temples and reached for her purse, searched for something to ease her headache. Why couldn't it just go away? And should her finger throb this much? And what would they do with all of those screwdriver sets? The thought of the kits stacked on the floor of the office made her head hurt even more.

Miriam had warned them it might happen, but it was still a shock when yesterday's hardware shipment had a glaring error. Miriam had ordered ten, eight-count bags of screwdrivers to replenish the open-stock bins in the hardware aisle.

Instead, they received eighty screwdriver kits. Each plastic carrying case held a main handle and seven interchangeable heads. Convenient, to be sure, but not what they ordered. Bill and the driver had exchanged words, but the guy said it wasn't his problem and they needed to call the office. With that, he got back in his truck and drove off to his next stop.

This couldn't wait until Miriam got back, so Melinda called the supplier. The company could send the proper replacements, but they wouldn't arrive until next week. As for what was already delivered, well, there were steep restocking fees for whatever Prosper Hardware returned.

Melinda had to be careful, keep the relationship Frank and Miriam had built over the years from being damaged beyond repair. The switch had been a simple mistake, and this company was one of the store's longest-running suppliers. They'd set up the new shipment, but Melinda still had to figure out what to do with what they already had.

"I just wish we could get all our money back," she muttered as she reached for her bottle of water and downed the aspirin.

"What's that?" Bessie had two pairs of brightly colored garden gloves in her hands, and a smile to match.

"Oh, nothing. Those are so pretty!" Melinda silently chided herself for nearly losing her cool with Bessie. She needed to be more patient with people, including herself.

What had Miriam said? *The customer is usually right. But not as often as some of them like to think.* Wasn't that the truth!

"I can apply your refund to this purchase." Melinda reached for the gloves. "You have $3.58 coming back."

"Well, that almost pays for one pair!" Bessie grinned over her good fortune, and wished Esther and Melinda a good day as she started for the door. "I'm going to make that casserole tonight," she trilled. "Esther, I'll let you know how it turns out."

"Oh, please do!" Esther smiled and waved. But she sighed when the front door finally closed. "I suppose that means she'll be back tomorrow."

"Well, if we can sell her a screwdriver set, that would make my week a little better."

Esther reached for the broom. While there was less mud to battle this week, dirt still found its way into the store. And the heavy clouds piling up in the west promised another round of rain. "Look at the time! You'd better get over there. I bet they could use another set of hands."

Melinda spun around a little too fast for her aching head, and slipped her apron over the hook behind the counter. "You're right; I know they can. That vet from Charles City is helping out today. Maybe we shouldn't have offered all those extra slots, since this is her first time, but there was a huge wait list." She reached for her jacket. "I'll be back in an hour. I promise."

It's a good thing the clinic is still across the street, Melinda thought as she waited for a truck to pass by. *I don't know where I'd find an extra five minutes to run down to the community center.*

The former bank's renovations were nearly complete, but it wasn't ready to host any events. Painters' scaffolding stood all around the main room, and buckets and brushes were everywhere. Brown paper covered the hardwood floors. Richard had the new kitchen counter in place, but hadn't had time to hook up the sink.

Nancy looked up as Melinda ran into city hall. "Oh, am I glad to see you! One patient just had a reaction to the anesthetic, and threw up all over the floor. The poor thing!"

"How did that happen? The cats aren't supposed to have breakfast the morning of surgery."

"Who knows? I guess people do whatever they must to get these kitties into carriers. She's wild as can be, Karen said. They're going to try again to put her under, hopefully they can spay her today. Her odds of being caught again aren't good."

The historic city hall, which was even older than Prosper Hardware, had been sliced up over the decades into a series of offices and hallways. "And that's not all," Nancy called over her shoulder as they entered the maze. "Josh's vet tech had to leave, apparently her daughter has the flu. She had to pick her up at school."

"Dad's sick today, too." Melinda hurried after her friend, who was always in motion but now stepped in double-time. "What's with everyone?"

"Who knows? I'd check the calendar to see if there's a full moon, but I haven't had a moment to spare. Water bills are due today, and I've had about ten cranky callers and walk-ins since I got here this morning."

The door into the council chambers was closed, and Nancy paused with her hand on the doorknob. "And that new vet? She's full of ideas."

"If she has any good ones, I'm fresh out."

The council's meeting room was filled with hustle and bustle, but the volume was somewhat muted so as not to frighten the already-scared patients.

Vet technicians and volunteers moved among the surgical stations with careful efficiency, and carriers were lined up under, and on top of, the tables along the far wall. The crates were draped with sheets to give the cats a sense of security as they waited their turn, and privacy to help them rest after surgery.

Josh's table was at the front of the room, and Melinda's heart swelled with pride as she watched him begin a procedure. His generous offer to help get this program off the ground had brought him into her life last spring. He'd soon become an integral part of the nonprofit's team, then a professional partner for Doc and Karen, and now ...

He glanced up, and even his surgical mask couldn't hide how happy he was to see Melinda. Nancy elbowed her. "Caught yourself a good one." She giggled.

"Stop." But Melinda's smile reached from ear to ear.

The new volunteer vet had her makeshift exam space in another corner, and Karen was not far away. Iris Anderson was in her early sixties, according to Karen, and passionate about community spay-and-neuter procedures. She already offered those services to feral and barn cats at a steep discount through her practice, and had been eager to help with Prosper's expanding program.

Auggie and George were again part of the Cuddle Crew, a small group settled in chairs in the last corner. Their only job was to hold the cats, wrapped in towels and fleece blankets, until their body temperatures returned to normal after surgery. That meant these helpers spent most of their time gabbing and gossiping, but the still-sleepy patients didn't mind.

Auggie waved to Melinda, and she was about to start in his direction when Iris' vet technician cut her off at the pass.

"Who are you?" The woman planted her hands on her hips. "I'm sorry, but you can't pick up your cats until at least three."

She raised her chin. "Doctor Anderson and I have been doing this for decades, and we never allow anyone to take a patient home too early."

"Oh, no, sorry. I'm not here for that. I'm Melinda Foster, one of the program's coordinators."

The vet tech glanced at Melinda's jeans and sweatshirt. "Where are your scrubs?"

"I don't help out at the surgical tables, usually." Melinda crossed her arms. "I ferry supplies, set out the lunch, that sort of thing. I work across the street, at Prosper Hardware, my family's business."

That elicited a raised eyebrow, but its full meaning wasn't quite clear. Melinda decided she'd rather not know.

"Well. Carry on, then." The tech stalked off.

"Yes, ma'am," Melinda whispered.

Karen, who had just finished with a patient, widened her eyes at Melinda. "I see you've met Nurse Ratched. I mean, Fran." She pulled off her disposable gloves and tossed them in the wastebasket at her feet. "Did you pass inspection?"

"Barely. Nancy said things aren't going too smoothly today. The new vet ..."

"Isn't our real problem." Karen sighed. "Iris means business, sure, but she's solid. I've watched her out of the corner of my eye, and wow, she's in and out like nobody's business. Fran's going to be the thorn in our side, but they're a package deal."

"Well, if it brings our daily count closer to sixty than forty, I'd say we have ourselves a bargain." Melinda glanced over at the rows of carriers. "We get one fixed, and there's three more waiting in line."

"And spring kitten season is here." Karen groaned as she wiped down her makeshift surgical stand with disinfectant and laid out supplies for the next patient. "There's many more to come."

Auggie was frowning by the time Melinda reached him. "I thought you'd never make it over here." He gently tucked a pink fleece blanket around his current charge. "We have an emergency, and ... what the hell happened to your hand?"

She'd forgotten about the pain in all the rush. "Oh, one of Harriet's got me this morning. Shadow got out of the carrier overnight, and ..."

"What if he's rabid?"

"No, come on." She rolled her eyes. "He's not." Although, the very thought had crossed her mind that morning. Josh assured her that if Shadow had rabies, his behavior would have been far worse. He was scared and defensive, nothing more.

Melinda's exhausted mind circled back to Auggie's complaint. "Wait, so what's going on? What emergency?"

"We're out of cookies already." George shook his head. "I don't know if someone didn't bring enough, or what."

"More like we ate too many," another man said. Melinda didn't remember his name, but he was some buddy of Auggie's. "I don't know what we'll do this afternoon, then."

Melinda closed her eyes for a moment. "But the lunch is here, right? In the kitchen?"

"Oh, yeah," Auggie said. "Jessie brought it over about fifteen minutes ago. I went in and supervised, made sure we had everything." He looked at the floor, and Melinda knew he'd already helped himself to something.

"Well, thanks. No one will starve, then. George, when you have a minute, can you run across the street? We have some cookies in stock. Esther's at the register, just tell her to put them on my account, OK?"

That seemed to calm the group. "I'll go as soon as this little guy's done." George rubbed the cheek of a young cat with a long, gray-tabby coat. "He's a sweet one."

"He's still out cold," Auggie reminded him. "Just wait until he starts to wake up. Be careful, you don't want to end up like Melinda."

No, you sure don't, she thought. *Too many irons in the fire, and no extinguisher to be found.*

Melinda was about to unbox more syringes and distribute them to the exam tables when her phone buzzed in her pocket. It was her mom.

"Hey, honey." Diane's tone was already apologetic. "I hate to ask for a favor, but I think it's safe to say I have what your dad does."

"Oh, no!"

"The Realtor just called. There's some paperwork for Frank and Miriam's house that needs to be picked up at their office. Not right now," she added hastily. "Just by tomorrow morning, but end of today would be best. I would go, but, well, I can hardly sit up, and ..."

"No, I don't want you driving. Or giving that to anyone." Melinda grimaced and looked at the clock. No matter how many times she checked the time, it was always getting away from her. "I can try to, I suppose I could ... what time does the office close?"

"Five. Oh, that would be wonderful! They said they could email something over, and I'd sign it online, but I don't know if I'd do it right."

"Don't worry about it." Melinda knew it would be faster to pick up the papers and leave them on her parents' front porch than to walk her mom through that process. Besides, she was almost out of some things at home, and could stop at the Swanton superstore while she was there.

"Could you fill out the forms tonight? I could pick them up in the morning and return them." Melinda had no idea how to make that work, but she'd have to find a way. "I doubt you'll be well enough by then, if Dad's any indication. Do you need anything from the store?"

"You're a lifesaver!" Diane rattled off a short list and Melinda hustled into the kitchen, hoping to find a scrap of paper and a pen before the items flew out of her short-term memory. "I owe you one. Tell you what. I'll make a big dinner this weekend and ... oh, dear, I have to go." Diane hung up in a hurry.

"Melinda!" One of the volunteers popped into the kitchen. "Karen's out of syringes. Do you know ..."

"Yes, I'm coming. Be right there."

She handed out more supplies and then went back into the kitchen to set out lunch. The volunteers started their rotation for the noon break, but Melinda was too distracted to eat anything. Besides, there was a grim task that needed to be done.

It was common for the cats to relieve themselves in their carriers, especially if they had been cooped up overnight. Every crate needed to be cleaned and sanitized before the patients returned to them after surgery.

Two volunteers had already spent most of the day doing just that, but they were falling behind with so many extra cats at today's event. If Melinda had a minute or two, they'd really appreciate the help ...

She called the store, and thank goodness Esther said they could get by for an extra hour. Melinda was scrubbing away, elbow-deep in vinyl gloves, when one of the vet techs tapped her on the shoulder. "Josh said he needs you."

"Can it wait a few minutes?"

Her face clouded. "Sorry, he said for you to come right away."

She pulled off her gloves and cleaned up at the temporary surgery sink. Josh was in the hallway, and he pulled her into an alcove and then opened the door of one of city hall's storage closets. Exhausted and bewildered, Melinda burst out laughing.

"Honey, I know we haven't seen each other in a few days, but really? We don't have time for ..."

He pulled the door closed and kissed her before he even turned on the light. Her worries melted away for just a moment, but returned. Once the bare bulb in the ceiling snapped on, she could see her worries reflected on his face. "You're right, we don't," he said gently. "But that's not why I dragged you in here."

"What's wrong now?" Tears pricked behind her eyes. "If even one more thing ..."

"That's just it. You can't deal with one more thing, can you?"

She started to cry, and Josh wiped her face with his hand.

It all tumbled out, the irate customer and the messed-up shipment and the bossy vet tech and ...

"I wish I could do more to help," he finally said. "What can I do?"

"I don't know. I don't know what to do. How am I ever going to handle all of this someday when Frank and Miriam retire? Thank God Bill plans to stay on." Her eyes widened. "But what if he left? And Esther? She'll retire someday, too."

"Don't think about that now." He pulled her close, not caring her tears soaked the shoulder of his scrubs. "One day, one thing at a time. What's your most-pressing problem, right at this minute?"

She thought for a moment. "My hand. It's throbbing something terrible. I took some aspirin for my headache, and that's better, but I thought maybe it would help my finger, too."

Josh peeled back the bandage and swore. "That doesn't look good, no wonder it's hurting. It might be infected. Just a little," he assured her. "Or not, just nasty and sore."

"Auggie asked me if Shadow had rabies." She started crying again. "What if he does?"

Josh snorted. "No, he doesn't. Had him on my table a few

hours ago. Like I said, he was just scared." A smile pulled at the corner of his mouth. "Now, tell me the truth: Are you foaming at the mouth, by chance? Disoriented? Screaming for no reason?"

She leaned back against the wall and stared at the cracks in the plaster ceiling. "Not yet." She sighed. "But I can't make any promises. If even one more person asks me to do something for them, I might."

Josh leaned in and pressed his forehead to hers. "Well, it's only noon, Superwoman. Who knows what might happen?"

"I don't know what I'd do without you," she whispered.

"Good, because I feel the same." He touched her hair, and kissed her again. "I didn't tell anyone where we were going, so we wouldn't be bothered. I'm sure we have about two minutes before something else happens."

When they finally broke apart, Josh reached for the door handle. "Feel better? Let's get that finger cleaned up and get you back across the street."

"But the carriers! I'm not done, and ..."

"We'll manage. And be sure to take a sandwich with you. You need to keep up your strength."

14

"Can't Gertrude pick up her cat food this time?" Esther asked Melinda. "I saw her the other day, and she said her back's been much better lately. That physical therapist is really working wonders."

"Maybe she could," Melinda admitted as she gestured for Esther to get the door. The cart held three economy-size bags from the stash in the back room, and her hatchback was parked next to the building. "But I want to go over there. A few minutes in a metal porch chair with four cats on my lap is just what I need."

Esther laughed. "Make that three in your lap, and one around your neck. Watch out for Tiny. He's a sweet boy, but he's far from small. Last time I stopped by, he rode on my shoulders all the way out to the car. Took Gertrude forever to get him to let go."

Once the cat food was loaded in the back, Melinda slid into the driver's seat and let herself yawn. Eyes closed, she leaned against the headrest and felt the warm sun beating through the windshield. It was so quiet, here in this bubble. The opposite of the constant noise and chatter inside Prosper Hardware.

At least her sore finger was on the mend. Melinda had changed the bandage again this morning, and made sure it was on tight before she pulled on her chore gloves. Despite all the hassle, the gratitude on Harriet's face had been worth it. Her cats were happy to be home, and Harriet had called the next morning to report all of them had fully recovered.

Josh had been right about her wound; it wasn't too serious. And he was right about the rest of it, too. Because despite her good intentions, Melinda needed to be on guard. If she spread herself too thin, she wouldn't be able to give any of her projects the effort they deserved.

She was working on it, but it was easier said than done. "Tiny's not the only one having a hard time letting go." And with one more deep breath, she turned the key and rolled out of the gravel parking lot.

Helping someone like Gertrude was never a burden; in fact, it gave Melinda a sense of satisfaction that was hard to find anywhere else. Every time she stopped at the elderly woman's house, which was at the very edge of Prosper's tiny grid of streets, reminders of her efforts were everywhere. There were always several furry faces eyeing visitors from the shaggy grass in the adjacent field, and more of them hurried out from under the open back porch.

Thanks to the community cat clinics, all the members of Gertrude's colony were spayed or neutered. It had been no small task, and had meant taking several cats to every clinic for months before everyone got the medical care they needed. But they were healthy, and no longer reproducing, and received wonderful care and lots of love from Gertrude.

And there she was now, waiting in her driveway.

"Oh, I'm so glad you could bring the kibble over!" Gertrude's stride had indeed improved, but the light in her eyes said she was just as grateful for the company as the free delivery.

Two cats twirled around her feet as she led the way to the garage's walk-in door, but the older woman was as sure-footed as they were.

Once the food was safely stored in the galvanized metal tubs, Gertrude waved Melinda around to the back of the house. "Care to sit a spell? It's such a nice day."

"I would love that." Melinda gave in to the meows of a chubby gray cat and hoisted the feline into her arms before she followed Gertrude down the sidewalk. She wasn't sure of this one's name, but it was obvious it was used to being carried like a baby.

Most of the porch had long ago been commissioned for feeding stations and all-weather shelters, so its two metal chairs had to be content with a cozy spot along one wall. The gray cat quickly took over Melinda's lap, then let out a polite growl when a black-and-white feline showed interest in also claiming a seat.

But when a smaller, orange kitty made the same request, the gray cat didn't mind.

"That's Sheba." Gertrude pointed at the portly feline. "She's bossy, but little Georgie there was one of the last of her babies. She's willing to share with him." Gertrude's lap had already been claimed by three cats.

The house Gertrude shared with her husband was small and a bit shabby, but she took pride in her flower beds and her garden. Their large lot had sweeping views of the adjacent fields, and the green spaces along the nearby railroad tracks would soon fill in with native flowers as well as weeds. In the summer, this place was a haven for butterflies. But for obvious reasons, Gertrude had long ago given up feeding the birds.

Melinda scratched Sheba's chin. "I see your perennials are starting to come up, and the wildflowers, too."

"Oh, yes, spring is on its way. The calendar says March 20 is the first day, but folks around here know better. It comes in little by little, day by day. Then all of the sudden, everything's bursting out all over."

Melinda glanced in the living room's picture window. "How's Edgar doing?" Gertrude's husband was in his lift chair, watching television. He'd beaten a bout of cancer last year, but his health had never fully recovered.

Gertrude suddenly looked down, and Melinda wished she hadn't asked.

"Well, he's hanging in there, I guess. Nothing really changes." She blinked away tears. "We found out this week that Valerie, his home-health care nurse, is retiring at the end of April. She's so good with him, and he can be a pill, sometimes. When Valerie's been on vacation, you should see how he reacts to the subs they send over."

Gertrude shook her head. "Or maybe, you shouldn't. Edgar doesn't like his routine being changed. Once he gets to know someone, that's it. He doesn't want 'those crazy strangers' coming around, as he calls them."

Gertrude and Edgar were high-school sweethearts, and had been married almost fifty years. Two of their children had moved out of the area, but the one daughter was still nearby. She tried to help all she could, but so much of Edgar's care had fallen to Gertrude.

She loved cats, of course, but the companionship of her colony was probably one of the reasons she'd been so devoted to Prosper's strays. Even the skittish ones, in their own ways, showed her unconditional love.

"When might his new nurse be chosen? I'm guessing they have routes around the county, just like a mail carrier. Sounds like the sooner someone is trained to take Valerie's place, the better."

"I don't know." Gertrude sighed. "I called the office in Swanton yesterday, trying to find that out. Turns out, several of the nurses are retiring this spring, so they'll be short-handed for a while, either way. They screen candidates carefully, of course, so it takes time."

Home health care was a tough business, driving from house to house and handling cases without the comforts of a clinic or hospital setting. It took special people to do the work right and perform their tasks with the cheerfulness the patients and their families needed.

Gertrude needed more help, not less. Melinda was trying to slow down to save her sanity, but were there ways she could still step up? Once Frank and Miriam came back, maybe she could drop off a casserole every so often. And while small towns were notorious for gossip, people looked out for each other, too. She'd say something to Esther about all this, see if Esther could find a gentle way to ask friends and neighbors to offer a little extra support to the Millards when they could.

And then, as she shifted her legs to give Sheba the extra room she demanded, Melinda had an idea. Lauren was content working part time at the coffee shop in Swanton, but Melinda knew she was looking for more. Was her nursing certification still current? Would she want to stay in the area, or move away?

Melinda didn't know Lauren very well, but she seemed patient and understanding. She'd known hard times in life, and likely had compassion for others who had seen the same. Between that and her professional skills, she just might be what Edgar, and also Gertrude, needed. Melinda was going to the Watering Hole after work to pick up vegetable scraps, and it was the perfect chance to put in a word with Jessie.

If the home health care office was hiring more than one position, it made Lauren's chances even better.

She almost shared her plan with Gertrude, but didn't. It wouldn't do to get the woman's hopes up.

"I have a feeling it's all going to work out, somehow," was all she said. Then she nodded at the cat shelters stacked in two rows under the living-room windows. "Well, the new totes made it through their first winter. That foam insulation will probably keep the insides cool this summer, too."

"Oh, yes, they're so much better than the wood boxes we had before." Gertrude petted the white cat that insisted on taking up most of her lap. "Don't you agree, Snowball? All the kitties love them. And by the way, I wanted to show you, before you go. We have a new resident. One for now, actually, and more on the way."

"Really?" Melinda was curious, but also a little discouraged. She knew exactly what Gertrude meant.

Gertrude pointed at one tote in the bottom row. "She's way back from the door, the poor, scared thing. Showed up here last week, one night when it took a cold turn. That's always when they find me." Despite the extra mouth to feed, the pride in Gertrude's voice was unmistakable. "She knew this was the place to come to, that she'd be safe here. If you can extricate yourself from Sheba and Georgie, see if she'll let you say hello."

Melinda finally did, and tiptoed over to the shelters. She crouched on the porch floor's rough boards and peeked inside. There, half-hidden in the nest of straw, was a long-haired cat with a brown tabby-and-white coat. She was smaller than Melinda expected, hardly more than a kitten herself.

"Oh, she's pretty! And pretty wild, too." Melinda kept her voice soft, but the cat's eyes still glowed with fear. "How far along do you think she is?"

"Well, she's showing, even with all that fur. Only comes out to eat, at least when I'm around, so I haven't gotten a really good look at her yet. Maybe a few weeks, though, and there'll be babies again." There was a lilt in Gertrude's voice that made Melinda both happy and sad. Kittens were cute, and spring was always full of new life, but it was another reminder the cat clinics would never lack for patients.

Gertrude did the math. "Let's see, I'd say she and the kids will be ready for a trip to city hall sometime in July. So maybe make a note of that."

"Will do." It was clear the cat didn't want to interact, so Melinda stood up. She needed to get back to the store, but this had been the break she'd desperately needed. "Actually, they'll get to go to one of the clinics held at the community center. It should be ready by the end of the month, and we plan to move operations there as soon as we can."

"One more thing to look forward to." Gertrude smiled and rubbed Snowball's back. "I can't wait until the center is finished. It's something our town's needed, for years. And spring's the perfect time for a fresh start."

* * *

A gust of wind blew in with Bev Stewart as she entered the community center.

"Gracious!" She pushed back the hood of her waterproof coat after Melinda took a lidded plastic tote out of her arms. "It's really pouring now. I swear, it kicked in as soon as I left the farm."

"Well, they say April showers bring May flowers." Vicki hovered over the tote, which Melinda had put on the floor, but was too gracious to open it.

"I'm glad you can see the bright side of all this rain." Karen wiped her shoes on the generous mat that protected the refinished hardwood floors. That wasn't going to do the job, so she untied her laces.

"All I see is mud! Mud on my work boots, mud on the truck's mats, mud in every farmyard I visit. Yesterday, I got mud in my hair, my eyes ..."

"Oh, dear." Nancy laughed. "What happened? I think you need to tell us about it."

Nancy had moved the library book club's April meeting to the nearly completed community center. It would serve as a test drive, of sorts, as she knew the members would give honest opinions on the last-minute projects.

Sam Hayward helped himself to the cookies and snack mix next to the coffee pot on the end of the meeting room's lone table. So far, it was the only bit of furniture in the renovated space beyond a scattering of folding chairs. "Yes, Karen, I agree! Tell us the story before we move on to the other story. The one we all read."

Sam's joke was met with bemused glances. But a few of the members looked guilty, as well. "We all read the book, right?" He raised an eyebrow at Shelby Dunlap, the elementary school's music teacher.

"Well, I started it," Shelby insisted. "In February, in fact, right after we picked it. But then the younger grades were asked to put on an Easter program at one of the Swanton nursing homes, and we have the big spring concert coming up later this month."

"Never mind." Nancy waved it all away. "We're all busy to start with, and it's so easy to get distracted."

Vicki raised her hand. "I'll confess next. I didn't finish it, either. Actually, I got through the first fifty pages and, ugh, it was just terrible. Sorry." She gave Amy Westberg an apologetic wince.

"Oh, you're not the only one." Amy stirred her coffee with sharp flicks of her spoon. "I was disappointed, too. Very disappointed. I think I picked a lemon."

"I found it slow-going, myself." Bev heaped a small plate with snacks and eased herself into a chair. Only once she was settled did she pat down her unwieldy hair. It was short, and gray, but had a mind of its own. "But I decided to plow through. When I set my mind to do something, I have to finish it."

"And?" Vicki wanted to know.

"You didn't miss much, honey. If I wasn't so stubborn, I'd have had several hours back to do other things."

"I didn't care for it much," Melinda admitted. "But, I don't know, I love reading so much. I guess I figure it was time well spent."

"Maybe time well wasted, for some of the group," Sam interjected. "Looks like I'm in the minority here but, well, I liked it."

"Really?" Nancy was intrigued. "Now, this I have to hear. But I need everyone to do more tonight than just chat about the book."

She gestured around at the freshly painted walls and gleaming vintage woodwork. Melinda had to admit that the blinds and valances, which had been ordered to Delores' specifications, accented the tall windows perfectly.

"As you can see, the center's coming along nicely," Nancy continued. "But I want to be sure everything's ship-shape for our first rental, which is in less than three weeks. So, as we hang out tonight, think about a few things. The furnace is running, but is it too hot or cold in here? Are the blinds straight? See anywhere we need to touch up the paint? Just take in the ambience, if you will. And please, make a pass through the kitchen, and the bathrooms."

Sam chuckled. "I'll give the men's a tour."

"I hope so." Bev elbowed him. "Now, Karen, you were saying something about mud?"

Karen began her tale, which involved one farmer, two irate cows and three teenage sons who couldn't take instruction from their father or a veterinarian.

The club, as it always eventually did, turned the conversation to the book at hand. Once its shortcomings and frustrations were discussed and laughed about, Sam leaned over to study the plastic tote that still waited by the door. "Bev, what did you bring?"

"Oh." She turned in her chair, her box almost forgotten. "Tomato plants. I started too many again this year, and decided I'd rather share them than toss them out."

Bev was always generous, and Melinda was sure the surplus hadn't happened by accident. Her own German Pink heirloom tomatoes had been a gift from Bev last spring, a gift that kept on giving. Melinda had shared the tomatoes with friends and family, including the Schermanns, and later harvested several dozen seeds to start this year's plants at home.

Bev brought the tote to the table. "I have extra plastic sacks, if anyone wants one to carry home their plants. And please, take as many as you like. I have more."

"If you can't give them away tonight, maybe you can leave them in people's mailboxes," Sam suggested as he inspected the seedlings. Bev was a part-time carrier for the post office in Eagle River.

"Now, that's probably against regulations," Bev pointed out. "But you're on to something. I know just about everyone on my regular routes, and I'm spreading the word about my tomatoes. Those who want them will get some, for sure."

"I'm so excited." Amy carefully added two seedlings to her sack. "I meant to start some earlier, and ran out of time. Last year, I had the opposite problem. Paul and I went overboard, and we had so many tomato and pepper seedlings that we never found homes for them all."

Melinda saw the sudden sparkle in Bev's eyes. Vicki did, too, and her face broke into a grin. "Why, Bev, I think you're thinking what I'm thinking."

"Great minds think alike."

"What?" Shelby wanted to know.

"The holiday decoration swap was a huge success," Vicki said. "Why not a plant exchange? There's one in Swanton every year, and I hear it's well-attended."

"We could hold it during the opening day of the farmers market," Melinda suggested. "Make it one more event for the Founders' Day celebration."

"I'm afraid that might be too late," Nancy cautioned the group. "That's later in May, people will be itching to plant before then. Maybe the first Saturday?"

"People could baby their seedlings at home until the time is right," Bev said. "That way, they'll know what they have to work with, and can get started as soon as the ground's warm enough."

"I felt so terrible last year when our excess landed in the compost pile," Amy said. "That shouldn't have to happen. Why let perfectly good plants go to waste?"

"Oh, this is perfect!" Vicki pulled a notebook from her purse, and Melinda knew what that meant: the ideas were flowing. "The plant swap could be the first community-wide event at the center. What a great way for everyone to see the finished product."

"Oh, no you don't." Nancy crossed her arms. "We just paid a pretty penny to have these floors refinished."

"You mean, Delores did," Bev said with a chuckle.

"Even worse." Nancy sighed. "I can't imagine her reaction when she sails in here and sees clumps of dirt all over the floor. It's a wonderful idea. But it has to be outside."

The community center had a small gravel parking lot in the back. But as the idea grew, the group decided the city park would be the best location. A torrential downpour would cause the event to be rescheduled, but a little shower wouldn't be enough to put a damper on local gardeners' enthusiasm.

Sam disappeared for a few minutes, then returned with a look of concern.

"Oh, no." Bev shook her head. "What is it?"

"The men's room looks nice. But the sink seems to drip a bit. I tried the handle a few times, to be sure."

"If that's all it is, I'm relieved." Nancy's face showed it. "I have a last-minute punch list going. I'll ask Richard to take care of it before our first event." She glanced at the clock. "My, look at the time! I'd better get going."

"I'll lock up," Melinda offered. "I have a key. Frank gave me his before he left."

"Oh, thank you." Nancy smiled as she reached for her jacket. "Well, everyone, have a good week. See you soon!"

Shelby left to inspect the women's restroom, and Bev took the kitchen. Amy gave Vicki and Melinda a questioning glance. "Wonder where Nancy's off to in such a hurry?"

"Oh, probably one of the kids' events," Vicki said. She gathered up the garbage while Amy wiped down the table. "It's a busy time of year."

Melinda reached for her purse. "Bev, what do you think of the kitchen?"

"It's beautiful. Everything seems to be in order."

"Women's bathroom gets two thumbs up," Shelby reported.

"Hmm," Vicki said. "Scratch what I just said about Nancy. If Ryan or Kim had any activities tonight, they would have started long before now." She checked the time. "It's eight-thirty, you know."

Sam let out a sigh of irritation as he reached for his sack of tomato plants. "Well, I for one don't care where Nancy's going or what she's up to. She gives so much to this town, the community ..."

"Oh, of course." Vicki frowned. "I just ..."

"Ladies, I bid you goodbye." Sam raised a hand in salute and started for the door. "My wife's over at a friend's tonight.

Which means as soon as I let Baxter out to do his backyard business, we're going to enjoy us some baseball." He laughed at the blank look on many of the women's faces. "It's the Cubs' season home opener, and I've already missed half the game."

Vicki smirked after Sam left. "Liar."

"No, he's right," Amy said. "Wrigley Field's back in business. Paul was glued to the TV when I left."

"I'm talking about what's up with Nancy." Vicki raised an eyebrow. "And I believe there is something. Sam's as curious as the rest of us. He just doesn't want to admit it."

* 15 *

Melinda lowered herself to the back-porch's bench and reached for her waterproof chore boots. Her impulse purchase from Prosper Hardware's stock last year had served her well. And looking out at the puddles dotting the farmyard, they would be needed again this morning.

The rain that began last night, just before book club, still hadn't stopped. And now, occasional rumbles of thunder could be heard under the constant drumming on the roof. The deluge wasn't going to quit anytime soon, and that had put a damper on Melinda's plans as well as her spirits.

Susan and Cassie, her best friends from Minneapolis, had planned to visit this coming weekend. But with more rain in the forecast, the women postponed their gathering. It wouldn't be fun to traipse through Swanton's outdoor flea market under such soggy skies, and there would be no rambles up the gravel road and along the creek to get a closer look at the eagle family. Ed, who watched over that pasture for its out-of-town owner, said yesterday he'd seen two downy heads popping over the nest's edge.

"I bet Mama and Papa Eagle wish they had an umbrella." Melinda rubbed Hobo's ears. "The trees are just starting to leaf out, so there's not much canopy yet."

Hobo watched the rain with the same resigned expression Melinda knew was on her own face. He loved water, but only in small amounts. A drink from the garden hydrant, a quick splash in a puddle, and he was done.

The rain was falling in sheets, but the chores couldn't wait. She pulled up the hood of her jacket and gave Hobo a questioning look. "Are you coming?"

He curled up on the bench as if ready for a nap, even though it wasn't even seven in the morning.

"I don't blame you, I'd stay in here, too. At least you're not angry at the rain. Grace glares at it like it's a personal insult, even though she never puts one paw outside. I suppose fewer birds congregate at the feeders when it pours like this, so it rains on her parade."

Melinda lowered her head as she trudged toward the chicken house, grateful that Horace's grandpa built his farm on one of the neighborhood's few elevated spots. It was too generous to call it a hill, but in addition to providing sweeping views of the township, the location's higher ground kept the farmhouse's basement dry.

Her arrival inside the coop generated a chorus of agitated clucks and squawks. "Hey, calm down! It's just me." She shoved back her hood to identify herself. Pansy rushed at the vinyl boots, eager to get in a peck or two.

"Yeah, they're not just waterproof." Melinda reached for the feed scoop. "They're Pansyproof, too. So peck away."

One look out the row of low windows, and Melinda knew it was pointless to open the chickens' access to their run. "You all are staying in today, sorry. And the sheep will do the same."

The ewes didn't seem to mind. Despite her wet clothes and weary attitude, Melinda had to admit the snug barn was cozy on days like this. Sunny and Stormy were also taking the damp in stride. They were curled up in the mound of straw in their cubbyhole under the haymow stairs.

"There you are, the most-spoiled cats in Fulton Township." Melinda had yet to put away their heat lamp, as the nights were sometimes still a bit chilly. The cats loved it so much, she might as well leave it up until the weather dried out. "It costs only pennies a day to run your lamp. And it's so cheerful, too. We could all use more of that these days."

The guys at Prosper Hardware were in low spirits that morning, but perked up when Melinda pulled a food cannister out of her tote bag.

"Treats?" George's blue eyes suddenly sparkled. "I'd say it's the perfect morning for something a little extra."

Auggie trailed Melinda to the sideboard. "What's in there?"

"Lemon-poppyseed bread. It sounded good. I found the recipe online."

Doc was eager for a slice. "Well, it's a shame the Fulton Friendship Circle didn't get off the ground. Would've saved you all that time hunting through databases."

Melinda rolled her eyes. "Yeah, I know. That was one idea that ..."

"Fell flat?" Jerry chuckled. "The bread didn't, though. It looks delicious. But seriously, I see why it was too tough to resurrect the club. Sounded like an awful lot of work."

"What's a lot of work?" Roger pulled off his raincoat.

"The women's club," George answered. "You know, the one that's no longer a club."

"Well, it was defunct for over forty years, so I guess it can stay that way." Melinda handed her dad a slice of bread on a paper plate. "Let me guess, it's pouring in Swanton, too?"

"Yeah. Water everywhere, all the fields between here and there are soaked. It's a good thing the farmers haven't started planting yet."

"We do need some moisture this time of year." Auggie settled in his chair. "Dry weather's coming back in a few days, so things will be ship-shape in time for planting. But when it's wet like this, everyone looks for any excuse to get out of the house. For the guys, that means coming to the co-op."

"Been a good week, huh?" Jerry filled his mug.

"Yep, one of the best so far this year."

"I beg to differ." Doc got up for a refill. "I don't think I've been warm and dry for days. Melinda, are those waterproof boots still on sale? I have two pair already, but I keep one at home. My work pair's so muddy, I have to scrub them every time I take them off."

"Get a rotation going," Jerry suggested. "I do that with my socks. Have more pairs than you really need, and you're never left without."

"They're marked down until Monday." Melinda pointed at the rack in the clothing area. "I had mine on this morning, doing chores. Been worth every penny."

"If this rain keeps up, what you're really going to need is an ark," George told Doc. "That stock trailer's not going to get your big patients into town."

"Well, there's no room at the inn, so I probably won't be hauling any critters anytime soon." Doc turned to Roger. "We try to leave everyone at home, they do better in their usual environment. But sometimes they need extra care, and we put them in the shed behind the clinic. Trouble is, we only have two stalls."

"Melinda has a huge barn, if I recall." George tried to be helpful. "The sheep only take up part of the front half, right?"

"Hey." She held up a hand. "I love animals, but I can't take on one more thing. Besides, you all know my veterinary skills are limited at best. I can get dewormer in a sheep, and that's about it."

"You wouldn't have to do it all by yourself." The sing-songy tone in Auggie's voice caused her to give him a sharp look. "Just have Josh handle it. He's there a lot of the time, anyway."

This wasn't a secret, of course, but Melinda was clinging to her last nerve. And Auggie just stepped on it. "You seem to be quite the expert. How do you know so much?"

"Oh, I have my sources." Auggie hid his smirk behind his coffee cup. "You know I pal around with Ed."

Living in the middle of nowhere, a half-mile from the nearest farm, apparently gave Melinda no promise of privacy. She'd had more autonomy in Minneapolis. Everyone in her three-story building had been friendly, but their close quarters meant no one put anyone under the microscope for too long.

Josh's truck wouldn't fit in the garage with her car, given the structure's modest size and the piles of stuff inside. The back of the machine shed was Lizzie's spot. There was nowhere for Josh to park that wouldn't attract attention. She just had to accept it.

The other guys waited for Melinda to give Auggie a good talking to. But when it became clear she was too tired, or too annoyed, to make an effort, Doc stepped up to the plate.

"Who watched the Cubs' home opener last night? What a game, huh?"

* * *

"I have the housewares aisle restocked." Roger passed the counter with an armful of empty boxes. "Where do I take these again?"

"Back to the wood shop." Melinda gestured at the door. "Just flatten them and add them to the big bin." She reached for one of the empty boxes. "Oooh, that's the perfect size for something I need at home. Could you take it upstairs and set it on the break table? Thanks!"

A middle-aged man laughed as he set his purchases on the counter. "You know you're getting old when you start collecting cardboard boxes. We have a whole stash at home," he added in answer to Melinda's surprised expression. "Well, I'm glad I found a space right out front so I don't get too soaked. That rain doesn't seem to quit."

"That's for sure. We always have paper bags, of course, but I'm guessing you'll want plastic today."

Roger returned, looking worried.

"Oh, no." Melinda braced her palms on the counter. "What is it now?"

"I put the box on the table, and then I heard this *plop, plop, plop.* So I looked around and, there in the front, by the windows? Honey, I hate to tell you this, but the roof's leaking."

Esther had been in the display window, organizing the shiny-new garden shovels and rakes. But now, she hurried to the register. "Are you serious?"

"I'm afraid so." Roger shook his head. "I can go back up there, see what I can do."

Melinda came out from behind the counter, but left her apron on.

"Let me see if I can deal with it. I'll have to someday, anyway, as it'll all be on me. And Bill," she added hastily. Bill was off that afternoon.

"Just watch the register. If nothing else, I'll set out some buckets."

"I'll come." Esther followed her to the stairs. "Let's see what's going on."

Her dad was right; four dark spots had taken hold on the plaster ceiling. All of them were up front, but thankfully none were too close to Miriam's desk. Two were hanging on to each drop for dear life, but the other pair dripped in a steady rhythm that made Melinda's heart pound. There was no carpet on the floors, but the old oak planks certainly didn't need a bath.

"We have buckets in the storage room." Esther tipped her head toward the space behind the break area. "I'll bring six, just in case."

"I'll grab the mop and some old towels. I think there's a spare sheet of plastic around here, somewhere. Let's try to get the floor dry before we put everything out, at least."

Esther nodded with satisfaction when they were done. "That should fix it, for now."

"Seems like Frank and Miriam had some leaks repaired, maybe five years ago?" Melinda rubbed her temple. "I vaguely remember them talking about it once, but that's all. I wish I'd been paying more attention."

"Why would you?" Esther asked kindly. "They take care of things around here. Don't worry, the roof can be patched."

"I know. But it makes me wonder, how many years before it'll need to be replaced? This building's over a hundred years old. I love it, but it's as big of a responsibility as an old house. More so, in fact. I don't know if ..."

She looked around. "Do you hear that?"

They both glanced at the ceiling. Esther frowned. "I don't think it's coming from there."

Melinda pointed at the bank of windows that looked out on Main Street. They were narrow and tall, original to the building.

She ran over to the wall, touched one of the bottom sashes, and swore. "This shouldn't be wet! Oh, no. Look!"

Beads of water waited where the top of the frame met the brick wall. "Some of those drops sliding down the window are inside, not outside! I'll get more plastic, maybe we can tape it under the top of the frame and let the water run down it, so it doesn't ruin everything."

"Cut it nice and long," Esther suggested. "We'll feed the plastic into this other bucket, keep it from hitting the floor."

They stood back to study their work. "Well, that'll take care of it. For now." Melinda crossed her arms. "I'll call the roofing company, see when they can come by."

"I doubt they'll want to get up there until this rain stops. When did Auggie say it would?"

"Might get a break Friday, but then it's supposed to rain all weekend. At least, that was this morning's forecast. But he seemed pretty sure of himself."

"When doesn't he?" Esther rolled her eyes.

"Good point."

Esther studied the boxes filled with screwdriver kits, which were thankfully out of the drip. "So, the next problem is, what are we going to do with all of those?"

"When it rains, it pours." Melinda peeked in the top carton, as if there might be an answer inside. "I think we can sell a few, but not a ton."

"You know, I was looking at them while I was eating lunch today. Hubby has his own tools, and I don't use them much. But I swear, when I do need something, he has them strewn all over the basement and the garage. It takes me longer to find what I need than to fix whatever I'm fixing. Maybe I'd like one of these. And I wonder if my daughters-in-law might want some, too. I mean, Mother's Day is barely a month away."

Melinda's head jerked up. Suddenly, things didn't seem so gloomy.

"That is a wonderful idea! We could market them for Mother's Day, put up a display somewhere."

"How much do you think people would pay?"

"I don't know. But I'll snoop around online, see what the big box stores sell them for."

"If we only have to return part of them, that would be a big help," Esther reasoned. "Restocking fees on the whole kit and caboodle is the problem, right?"

"Yep." Melinda glanced down at her dark-green Prosper Hardware apron, and over at Esther's matching one. "Oh, hey, what about this? A screwdriver set, an apron, and a pair of nice work gloves. Nothing too expensive," she added quickly. "But maybe some that aren't so ..."

"Ugly?" Esther laughed. "Like those hideous yellow things? We carry some nice cream canvas ones, or those brown pairs."

"Either would look great paired with one of our aprons. They're not much more than the tees, at wholesale. Our branded clothing is great advertising for the store. Why not sell aprons, too?"

"They'll be in high demand." Esther chuckled. "An exclusive offer. Otherwise, you have to be an employee to get one. What about baskets? Should we package everything in baskets?"

The women discussed tying the bundles with dark-green ribbon, but decided that might be a step too far. Besides, they were trying to save money. The store already had several spools of cream twine, which could be used to bundle the items. The effect would be rustic, yet refined. And most of the shoppers picking up these special offers would be men. Baskets and ribbon wouldn't mean much to them.

Esther mulled this over for a moment. "But we could offer to wrap them for a fee. Do you have spare paper at home, anything springy or cute? I have more than I care to admit."

"Yeah. I think Mom does, too. And Miriam's trying to clear out the clutter at home before they move."

Melinda started for the stairs, and there was almost a spring in her step. "Esther, this is brilliant! And it's perfect that Dad is here today. He's our target demographic, let's see if he gives this a thumbs-up."

* 16 *

Just as Auggie predicted, the sun came out again. The co-op's gravel parking lot still shimmered with a series of puddles when Melinda turned in the following afternoon, but she didn't mind the ruts.

She'd brought Lizzie to town that day because she needed feed, and the old truck could navigate the mess far better than her hatchback.

Lizzie's mud-splashed sides fit right in with the other vehicles, and Melinda smiled with triumph when she found a free space. And then she laughed at the sign anchored to a can't-miss location close to the front door.

"SLOW DOWN! Duck Crossing. Violators will be dealt with."

"Another sign? I'm guessing that threat's for the lead-footed customers, not the feathered residents." Melinda hoped for a glimpse of Lucy and Desi, but came up empty. "This sign's less controversial than the last, at least. And much smaller."

Auggie had erected a massive plywood banner along the highway to protest the federal government's plan to close Prosper's post office. The threat was gone, and the sign's sections had been removed. But the posts remained, and Auggie promised to press them into action when the next challenge arrived.

The outside of Prosper Feed Co.'s retail building was squat and dull, a single-story structure clad in beige siding with only two small windows on the front.

Its face wasn't the most welcoming, but it didn't need to be. Customers were drawn inside by the wide selection of animal food and medicine, the sometimes-heated conversation, and the jolting coffee.

The aisles were packed with shoppers today, and the yeasty smell of animal feed mixed with the earthy aroma emanating from worn jackets and muddy boots. But the place had a comforting vibe that Melinda found appealing. Maybe it was because a visit to the co-op always made her feel like a real farmer. In the same way a trip to her favorite boutique in Minneapolis had always made her feel fashionable.

Auggie was behind the counter, ringing up orders while keeping up his ongoing commentary on just about everything. Dan, his assistant manager, was off stocking shelves, but Auggie did have backup from his feline employees. Mr. Checkers lounged on the counter near the vitamin display, his orange-and-white coat confidently displayed for anyone wishing to offer a belly rub of greeting.

His lady friend, Pebbles, sat in a Sphinx pose on the far end of the counter. That required her loyal subjects to make more of an effort, but she accepted the affections of anyone who couldn't resist her thick, smoky-gray fur.

Melinda was thrilled to find an empty cart, but decided to leave it be. The sheep's feed would be loaded outside, and the rest of her purchases could be carried in her arms. The place was packed, and a cart would just slow her down.

Her hunch was right, as the small-animal aisle was blocked halfway down by two men, a woman, and a pair of carts.

One man told the others how his dog needed vaccinations, and he hoped to get those done before his family went out of town next week. But Doc and Karen were swamped, and their few available in-clinic slots over the next two days were being held for emergencies.

"It can wait, I know." He leaned on his cart's handle. "But Sparky loves to run around in the yard, now that the weather has turned. It's fenced, of course, but what if he gets into a tussle with something while we're gone? My son's going to come twice a day to check on him, but he'll be on his own most of the time."

Melinda reached for a bag of cat food. "Why don't you call Doctor Vogel, over in Swanton? He partners with Doc and Karen on calls these days."

The woman nodded. "That's right, I heard that." She turned to the man. "See if Josh can work him in. I hear he's done wonders with that practice since he took it over. He's getting quite a good reputation around here."

She suddenly gave Melinda a wide, knowing smile, and Melinda's cheeks started to burn. The woman looked familiar, but Melinda wasn't quite sure of her name. However, she had a feeling the lady knew an awful lot about her.

Melinda beat a retreat between their carts, turned her back, and focused on the dog section. The trio's conversation moved on, thankfully, and they soon did as well. She flinched when Dan bumped her with an elbow.

"Way to put in a good word for Josh." Dan cradled a shipment of dog snacks in his beefy arms. "You know, it's like those romantic movies my wife likes to watch on that one channel. See, you were from the city, and you moved back to the country. And then this hunky veterinarian arrives and, well, it's happily ever after, right?" He gave her a sly wink. "I say, if he's staying over that much, maybe you should just ask him to move in."

She stared at Dan. "Oh, really? You seem to know an awful lot about it."

"I hear things." He shrugged, but his eyes cut to the counter, where Auggie was still engrossed in conversation. "Good to see you happy. Well, I better get these restocked. Want a few? Twenty percent off through Saturday."

Melinda swiped three pouches before she stalked away. The line was long, and she had to keep shifting her items so they would stay in her arms. She should have grabbed that cart, but that wasn't what made her simmer while she waited. Auggie meant well, most of the time, but this was too much.

"I need to talk to you." She bit off her words as she dropped her items on the counter. "Right now."

He raised his eyebrows. "Now?"

"Yeah."

Auggie looked away, but not before Melinda saw the guilt on his face. "Hey, Dan," he called out in a chipper voice. "Get the register for a moment, will ya?" He set Melinda's purchases aside and waved the next customer forward, then met her at the end of the counter.

"In the office," she hissed.

Pebbles and Checkers followed, their tails up with curiosity. Once all four of them were inside, Melinda shut the door and took the tattered chair across from Auggie's desk.

"I saw you talking to Dan." Auggie's tone was casual, but there was a wariness in his eyes. "Did he ... say something?"

"You bet he did! Dan seems to know an awful lot about my personal life these days."

Auggie sighed. "Nothing's a secret around here, so ..."

"And why can't it be?" Mr. Checkers bounded into her lap, but his purr wasn't enough to ease her frustration. "Why can't I, or anyone else, get even a little bit of privacy now and then?"

"What does it matter?"

Melinda gave a bitter laugh. "You're not even going to deny you're the one babbling things around. Who else have you told?"

He didn't say anything. Pebbles settled into his arms, her queenly presence unshaken by the tension in the room.

"Fine," Melinda finally said. "The horse is already out of the barn. But how about you put it back in, and keep it there? No more."

"All right. Sorry. But Ed said that ..."

"Yeah, and I'll be calling Mabel and telling her about all of this."

That made Auggie's eyes widen.

"Ed's going to get his hand slapped, too. And I won't even have to do it myself. I know people around here are nosy, and this place is one big fishbowl." She gestured around them. "But I'm just saying: Don't blab my business around anymore than you would your own, OK?"

Auggie nodded. "You got it." Melinda thought he'd get up from his chair, but he stayed seated. Maybe he wasn't in a hurry to dethrone Pebbles. But was there something else?

"What is it? Oh, no. What now?"

"Well, since you're already in here, and the door is shut." He paused a moment to rub Pebbles' plush fur. "And, since we have some spirit animals with us ..."

She frowned and looked at Mr. Checkers, who was almost asleep in her arms. "Spirit animals? I love cats, but I'm not sure if ..." Then she laughed. "Auggie, that's something else entirely. I think you mean 'emotional support animals.'"

"Yeah, OK. But you know what I'm saying." He hugged Pebbles close. "Now, I know I'm not supposed to be meddling in your personal life, but I wanted you to know: Evan and his family are going to be here this weekend, and part of next week."

Melinda was suddenly glad for Mr. Checkers' comforting weight in her lap. Auggie's son and young daughter had turned up in Prosper during the holiday season two years' ago, and Melinda and Evan soon became acquainted. Evan was separated from his wife at the time.

Nothing happened between Evan and Melinda; or at least, nothing that mattered in the end. But he'd moved back to Madison without so much as a goodbye, and it had stung. Evan wasn't on the best of terms with his parents, but she'd wondered from time to time if she would ever run into him again.

That seemed like forever ago. And now, with Josh, it didn't matter anymore. But she'd felt a sick kick in her stomach at the mention of Evan's name. And by the way Auggie studied her now, he knew it.

"So I see." She absentmindedly rubbed Mr. Checker's ears. "Yes. Thanks for telling me."

"They're getting in Friday, staying through Wednesday." Auggie seemed about to say more, then waited. Melinda decided not to ask. When she didn't, Auggie hurried on.

"Anyway, they'll be staying at the house, and they'll be around. I'm thinking if they need anything while they're here, we'll probably head into Swanton."

Melinda was relieved by that, but wasn't sure if she really should thank her friend. After all, he hadn't said the plan was specifically to keep Melinda and Evan from bumping into each other. And she was still upset with him, anyway.

While Auggie was nosy and blunt, he could be cryptic when it suited him. "I see what you picked up for Hobo and the barn cats," he blurted out now, and Melinda knew the uncomfortable topic had been set aside. "How are you doing on sheep feed?"

"I'm going to get a few bags while I'm here. It'll get me through a few weeks, at least."

"Good." He looked relieved. "You shouldn't have to come back next week. Well, that's settled then."

Pebbles gave a small growl of irritation when Auggie shifted in his seat. "Oh, stop it. I need to get back to the counter. You can have the chair, if you want."

"As long as she gets her way, she'll be happy." Melinda tried for a smile. "I guess it's the same for me." Mr. Checkers bounded down and now waited by the door, ready to mingle with his admirers. "Thanks for the heads-up. I appreciate it."

"See, sometimes there's an advantage to having someone all up in your business." Auggie reached for the doorknob. "How else would you get that kind of information?"

* * *

Sunny popped through the barn's pet entrance as soon as the plywood scraps were fastened in place.

"Much smaller, huh?" Melinda rubbed Sunny's fluffy orange coat. "Only you and Stormy can squeak through here now. Hobo has to stay out for a while. Unless I'm in there with him."

She set her tools aside and looked around the yard. The lawn was finally a soft shade of green. Tender shoots dotted the farmyard's perennial beds, and the sky was a gentle blue. But she sighed as she stared down at the road, and wished she felt as hopeful as the day appeared. Hobo wasn't going to like losing his easy access to the barn, but he'd get over it. If only a disappointed dog was her biggest concern.

"Josh was the one who said I shouldn't take on so much." She reorganized the metal toolbox and snapped it closed. "And now, he's bringing me one of the biggest challenges I've faced in a long time."

Stormy trotted around the corner of the barn, and his tail dropped when he spotted the updates to his barn entrance. "I know, I agreed to this plan. I said yes, and I'll see it through. Narrowing your doorway was the easy part. I just put back the pieces we use in the winter to keep the wildlife away. But getting the west feeding area cleaned out? That was a lot of work."

The sheep had been out to pasture, but ambled inside when they spotted Melinda doing the same. "Think something's going on? You're right." She handed out nose pets while Stormy catwalked the ridge of the main aisle's fence. "We have a visitor coming, and I'm not sure how long he's going to stay."

She put away the toolbox, then checked the fence across the aisle one more time for any broken boards. But it was strong and true, and high enough that it would do. The gate's old latch, however, was another thing entirely, and she'd added a second, larger bolt last night. She'd used this area to wean the lambs last spring, so at least there weren't decades of dust to clear away. The pitted concrete floor was now swept clean, or as clean as she could get it, and mounds of fresh straw were spread on the floor.

"The feed trough is set up, the water buckets are ready." She made sure the pails were securely fastened to the new hooks in the wall. This visitor, or rather, this patient, was known for being smarter than just about any other barn critter.

"And that includes you, Annie," she called out as she went back down the aisle. "You just wait and see."

Hobo soon burst through his door on the back-porch landing and began to bark. Josh's truck, with a small stock trailer hitched on behind, was just about to turn up the drive.

"Well, he's here," she told Stormy. Hobo's alarm had the cat tense with anticipation. "We might as well make him feel welcome."

Melinda reached for Hobo's collar and took him over to the picnic table. Josh drove slowly into the yard, mindful of his cargo, then carefully angled the trailer's back gate as close to the barn as he could.

Melinda decided to lock Hobo in the house, then started for the barn. Despite her misgivings, a smile spread across her face when Josh climbed out of the truck.

"Hello, beautiful." He gave her a quick kiss before he reached for his chore gloves. "I've said thanks already, and you have Doc and Karen's infinite gratitude, but I'll say it again: this means more than you can know."

She nodded. "I just hope it goes OK."

"Sure, it'll be fine. He's on a lead, so let's see how this goes."

Melinda peered through the trailer's back gate, searched the shadows to get a better look.

"His name's Pepper." Josh dropped the ramp. "They said he has specks in his coat, but I don't see them. Anyway, let's bring him in."

Josh stepped out of the trailer with the saddest-looking donkey Melinda had ever seen. Not that she's seen many; just Gus, the brash guy who loved to be the center of attention at Prosper's annual live nativity. Pepper's dark eyes went wild at the sight of a strange barn and the nervous woman hovering near its doorway. He let out a raucous neigh and gave an irritable stomp with one front hoof.

"Easy, boy," Josh whispered. "You'll be OK here."

Pepper's physical state gave Melinda pause. Along with a swollen back leg, which Josh said was a bad sprain due to a tussle with a board fence, his brown coat was worse than shaggy. Clumps of fur were missing here and there, and under all the dirty mess, his flanks were too thin.

"He's neutered, right?" She slipped around Josh to get into the barn aisle first, but tried not to make sudden movements. Pepper was in a strange place, with people he didn't know, and he was on edge.

"Of course. We wouldn't have taken him in like this if he wasn't. He'd tear this barn up. Doc thinks he's around seven years old, so his personality has settled some."

As Josh attempted to guide the donkey through the gate to the convalescent wing, "stubborn" seemed to be the right word. He stomped a hoof, more than once, and snorted his disapproval. Or maybe, just his fear.

The ewes across the aisle sniffed the air cautiously, but even Annie was too shocked to offer a greeting. When Pepper gave another holler of protest, all the sheep ran for the open pasture door.

"They'll get used to him, in time." Josh's shoulders relaxed once the gate was shut and Pepper's journey was at an end. Melinda had a feeling, though, that hers was just beginning.

"I hope there's enough straw on the floor to cushion his leg." She slipped through the gate, but didn't step any farther than the fence. "Will he have to stay tied?"

"No, and he wouldn't like that one bit. The sprain's bad, and he shouldn't be running around much until it heals, but he does need to keep moving."

Josh looked around and nodded. "This space is perfect! The stalls in the back are a little small for him. This way, he won't feel hemmed in."

Josh rubbed Melinda's shoulder as he passed by. "I'll get the oat straw and his hay, it's in the trailer. Why don't you go say hello?"

Now that Pepper was inside her barn, Melinda could really see how big he was. Not the size of a horse, of course; but far larger than any of her ewes. She took a few slow steps forward, and tried to make her chore boots land softly in the fresh straw.

"Hey, mister," she whispered. "How are you?"

The annoyed twitch of Pepper's tall ears said he'd been better. His sharp eyes evaluated her from top to toes, and his twitching nose picked up on her scent. He let out another bray, and she wondered if she should feel accepted or challenged.

He didn't flinch, but she wasn't sure if he trusted her, or his leg simply bothered him too much to make an effort. The sight of the straw and hay in Josh's arms, however, perked Pepper up considerably.

"Here you go, buddy." Josh filled the feed bunk. "The rest of it is out in the aisle," he told Melinda, "although maybe we should tuck it in the grain room. The regular hay you feed the sheep is too rich for Pepper, he needs to eat this other stuff."

Sunny and Stormy were now perched on the fence, their eyes and noses working overtime. "What do you think?" Melinda asked them. "You have a new roomie, at least for now. We're not sure how long he'll stay."

"I consulted with Doc." Josh leaned against the fence. "Maybe three, four weeks? Will depend on how things heal."

"I'm sure his family will be missing him." Melinda pulled a small plastic bag of carrot chunks from her jacket pocket and turned toward Pepper. When Josh didn't answer, she looked back.

"Well, I don't know about that." He looked down.

"They were concerned enough about the sprain to call Doc, and they'll pay the bill. But Doc got the impression Pepper was an impulse purchase from the Eagle River sale barn. His owners don't have other donkeys, just a few cows. Pepper's been bored and lonely, and he started chewing on things. As you can see, he's underfed. We didn't want to leave him there."

"You think they don't want him anymore?" Melinda's wariness melted as she looked into Pepper's dark eyes. "Oh, Pepper, I'm so sorry."

Doc and Karen would ask around to try to find Pepper a better home. Josh would, too, but most of his clients lived in town. But the donkey had one thing working in his favor: unlike some of his kin, he was good with dogs. His owners had two, and Doc had witnessed them interacting with Pepper. Even so, Melinda and Josh wanted to keep him away from Hobo until everyone adjusted to the change.

Melinda was thrilled when Pepper finally accepted a chunk of carrot from her outstretched hand. "Hey, isn't there something about donkeys, and sheep and goats? That they can act like watchdogs for the flock?"

"I think I've heard that, too. And llamas." He winked. "Sorry to say, we're fresh out of those."

"Well, let's get him on the mend. He might like to get outside once he's feeling better. But the only way that'll happen is if he shares the pasture with the sheep. I wish it was sectioned off, but it's not."

"Let's not get ahead of ourselves." Josh laughed. "That could work, or it could turn into a crazy rodeo." He held the gate for Melinda, then checked both latches were secure. When he turned around, his expression was more serious. And cautious. "Have you given any thought to what we talked about yesterday?"

She gave pets to Sunny and Stormy while she weighed her words. "I don't know if that's a good idea. Not just yet."

"It would only be for an hour or two. We can do whatever you want, go wherever, or just stay at my place. Aiden will be here Friday night, and he doesn't go back until Sunday afternoon."

"You haven't seen each other for a few weeks, won't I just be in the way?"

Josh shook his head. "It's not like that at all. I didn't tell him yet, I didn't want to get him excited about a new friend when ... I'd really like it if you'd come over while he's here."

There was a pleading note in his voice that made Melinda's chest tighten. Their conversation at the nature walk had been rehashed a few times in the past weeks, but Aiden's impending arrival meant Melinda couldn't brush her concerns aside any longer. She'd hoped her misgivings would vanish on their own, but they hadn't.

There didn't seem to be any way around it. "I know you'd like us to meet, but are you sure this is the right time?" She reached for Josh's hand and took a deep breath. "This will sound harsh, I know ... but are you just trying to keep up with Amber?"

"What?" Josh's brown eyes flashed with surprise. "You think this is some sort of competition? I would never do that! Are you sure this isn't really about you?"

Melinda wasn't about to bring up anyone from her past, no matter how tenuous the connection had been. But Evan's upcoming visit had reminded Melinda about another young child who had found herself, too many times over, caught in the drama of her parents' chaotic lives.

Evan's wife struggled with addiction, and he'd brought little Chloe with him when he temporarily moved back to Prosper. The girl was sweet and well-mannered, but it had made Melinda's heart ache to see how world-weary she seemed.

Aiden also needed the comfort and security of a regular routine. And to know, without a doubt, who in his life belonged where. Melinda wasn't about to make his life more complicated that it already was.

She didn't know how to explain this without coming off wrong. If she wasn't ready to become a part of Aiden's life, she certainly had no clearance to tell Josh how to handle the situation.

"I know you have only his best interests at heart," she finally said. "But adults' relationships can be so complicated, and it's not always easy for children to understand them. And, well, we've only been dating four months. Actually, not even quite that. It just seems soon, I guess. And what if ..."

"Is that what's going on here? Do you think we aren't going to work out? That it's not right to let Aiden get to know you because ..."

"No! Not at all." She started to cry. Suddenly, it was all too much. It felt like Frank and Miriam had been gone forever, but they still wouldn't be back for another week. Taking in an injured and lonely donkey would add to her chores, even with Josh's help. And then, worst of all, she was fighting with the man she loved.

"Look, you know how I feel about you." She took two steps forward, and was relieved when Josh didn't hesitate to open his arms to her. "I just think we're getting a bit ahead of ourselves," she said into his tee shirt, comforted by the steady beat of his heart. "I'm not going anywhere, I promise. And if you're not either, then, what's the hurry? I'm not saying no, not saying never. Only, maybe we wait a while longer, OK?"

Josh kissed the top of her head. "All right. I'll keep asking. And one day, I hope you say yes."

"Agreed." And then she kissed him.

"I suppose I should get going." Josh sighed, clearly eager to stay. "I need to drop off Doc's trailer, then get back to Swanton."

The fight was over, but the negative emotions still lingered between them. She would see him tomorrow night, but all Melinda wanted right now was to keep Josh with her, if only for a few minutes' more.

"Please come in, for just a bit. The coffee's on in the kitchen." She took his hand, he smiled, and they started for the door.

17

Doc's arrival the next morning brought the rest of the guys to the windows. "What's up with him?" George wanted to know.

Melinda was behind on her opening chores and didn't have time to gawk. "As long as his boots are reasonably clean, I'm not sure I care. I just swept the floor."

"I'm talking about what he's carrying." George pointed. "Is that a hula hoop?"

Jerry gave Doc another once-over, shrugged, then went to fill his mug. They'd find out the details soon enough. "Maybe he's training some patients for an agility contest. Me, I'm desperately in need of caffeine."

Auggie reached for his jacket. "More stuff! Looks like he could use a hand. Melinda, the store's not selling beach balls, is it? Wherever did he get that?"

"Not this time of year. Not ever, actually."

Auggie ran out in such a hurry that he didn't even hear her response. Melinda knew Doc's game plan, and it was funny to see the regulars caught off guard. She smiled at her dad as she reached for the dust cloth.

Roger knew all about Pepper, of course, and was also enjoying the suspense. These morning conversations at Prosper Hardware were so entertaining, he'd said, that he was already dreaming up ways to invite himself back after Frank returned. At least, once in a while.

The bell above the door announced Doc's arrival and Auggie's return.

"Now, what do you have there?" Jerry smirked. "Welcome home gifts for Frank and Miriam? Those'll remind them of their days of sun and sand, for sure."

Doc laughed as he set the hoop and ball by the counter. "Melinda's doing Karen and I a huge favor, with an assist from Josh." He turned to Melinda. "I can't thank you enough. He needed a place to go, and it was wonderful of you to take him in."

"What happened to Josh's house?" George frowned with confusion. "Why can't he stay there?"

Auggie looked ready to say something smart, but Melinda shut him down with a stare.

"George, check your hearing aids," Jerry suggested. "Josh isn't homeless, they're talking about someone else." He looked to Doc and then Melinda. "Who's this?"

"A donkey," Melinda explained. "There's a donkey in my barn. Not named Josh. His name is Pepper."

The men listened as Doc explained the situation. And the need for the hula hoop and beach ball. "Donkeys are smart. Pepper's not feeling himself yet, but it's better to find ways to entertain him before he starts getting into things he shouldn't."

"How long is Pepper going to stay?" Auggie asked. "Is this a permanent arrangement?"

"Oh, no," Melinda said quickly. "Just for a few weeks, until his leg heals."

"We could use your help there," Doc said. "We're asking around, trying to find Pepper a new home. Know anyone?"

Auggie thought for a moment, then shook his head. "Not right now, but I can make some inquiries, if you like." It was clear Auggie couldn't wait to do just that. He had a new story to tell, information that would be fresh news to his regulars down at the co-op.

George took a sip of his coffee. "You know, when Mary and I were still on the farm, we had a neighbor down the road

with sheep. There were always coyotes around, being so close
to the river timber and all. You know what our neighbor did?
He got a llama. Put the guy right in there with the sheep, sort
of a guard-dog situation."

Melinda knew where this idea was going, but she just let
George roll. He was enjoying himself too much.

"A llama?" Auggie asked. "Don't they get mean and spit a
lot? I suppose that'd keep the coyotes away."

"Wait a minute." Roger held up a hand. "Coyotes can't
climb fences, last I heard. Was that really necessary? I mean,
I could see it if there were mountain lions around."

"Oh, there are." Auggie seemed to know all about it.

"People do the same, sometimes, with donkeys," George
continued. "Melinda, why don't you just keep Pepper? He can
run around with your ewes."

This wasn't the first time Melinda had had this
conversation, of course. And, while she wasn't ready to admit
it to the guys, she'd given the idea some thought.

She had agreed to this plan with more than a little
hesitation. What did she know about donkeys? Nothing. But
the more time she spent with Pepper, it was clear he was
settling in at her farm.

He had been lonely at his last home, and even just talking
to him over the aisle fence seemed to raise his spirits. Melinda
could now sense the emotions behind his various brays, and
that eased her concerns about getting in with him when Josh
wasn't there.

"I don't know if it's the right thing to do," was all she said
for now. "Besides, you've all cautioned me to not let my little
farm put me in the poorhouse, and donkeys need food and
care like any other animal."

"So, who's taking care of him, then?" Jerry asked. "I
mean, medically."

"Karen and I are going to help out," Doc answered, "but
Josh's offered to do most of the work. I don't know what we'd
do without him. He's busy with his own practice, but this
sharing agreement's been a godsend, for all of us."

Melinda knew the men were staring at her, waiting for her to jump in with some praise for her boyfriend. Doc was right, of course; Josh was a very talented veterinarian.

But right now, she didn't want to talk about him, or think about their tense words yesterday regarding his son. They had smoothed things over, but it was a topic that wasn't going to resolve itself.

Doc broke the awkward silence with a kind offer. "I can take these toys upstairs for you, if you like."

"Oh, that would be great, thanks. Just put them by the break table."

Roger also sensed his daughter's reticence, and reached for the still-bagged newspaper under his chair. Melinda's parents subscribed to the Des Moines daily, and Roger's willingness to bring it along when he subbed at the store had instantly made him a member of the club.

"Well, now, let's see what's going on in the rest of the world." He shook out the main section with a rattle loud enough to get all the guys' attention. "I'm sure there's something in here for us to discuss."

* * *

As the conversation wound down for the morning, Auggie set his cup on the sideboard and came to the counter. "I'll wash up in a bit. Let's go take a look."

"Hey Dad, can you please unlock the door and watch the counter?" Melinda finished checking the register's tally from the night before. "I'll be right back."

The buckets and plastic sheets had been set aside once the weather changed for the better, but Melinda hadn't put them away, just in case. The days of rain had put the roofing company behind during one if its busiest times of the year, and they hadn't been out yet to give Melinda an estimate. Much less say when they could do the work.

"They'll be here tomorrow, probably late morning." She gestured at the now-dry beige spots on the plaster ceiling. "I have no idea what they're going to say."

She'd been glad when Auggie offered to give his not-quite-expert evaluation of the mess. However, it was good the roofers wouldn't arrive too early tomorrow. The thought of having Auggie underfoot while the guys tried to do their assessment made her cringe.

"Uh-huh, I see what you mean." Auggie crossed his arms and studied the ceiling. "Well, there's four, so ... no, a fifth spot over there. And you said the one window's leaking, too?"

"Do you know when the roof was replaced last? Mom wasn't sure, just that it's been a while."

This was one time when Auggie's nosy knowledge might come in handy. He'd worked at Prosper Hardware all through high school, for Melinda's grandparents. That was forty years ago, but he'd been friends with Frank and Miriam almost as long.

"Yeah, I remember your grandpa saying it needed to be done. Let's see. Probably at least thirty years?"

Auggie was working at the co-op then, even though he had yet to purchase it from the previous owner. Grandma and Grandpa Shrader were glad they took a gamble and replaced the roof when they did, he recalled, even though the farm crisis had meant money was tighter than ever.

"The economy was terrible around here, and it was several more years before it began to bounce back. But this was one less thing to worry about. At least they had a roof over their heads, so to speak."

It was a bright, clear day, and the open windows brought in a fresh breeze full of promise. But Auggie's face was temporarily shaded with gloom, and Melinda felt a chill on her shoulders as she looked out over Main Street.

"Thirty years sounds like a long time to let a roof go." It pained her to say anything critical about her aunt and uncle, but she knew Auggie could keep things to himself when it mattered.

"I know it's a commercial building, not a house; not quite the same, but still." She pointed over their heads. "And it's nearly flat, right?"

"As a lopsided pancake. Just enough grade to roll off the water. Much different project than what you want to do out at the farm, for example."

Melinda hadn't had time to even think about the farmhouse's roof lately. But she was looking ahead at home, thinking of the future as much as repairing the wear and tear from the past. Prosper Hardware would be around for a long time, hopefully, and so would she. Perhaps a bigger change was needed.

"Maybe I should get an estimate for a full tear-down while the guys are here. Would be good to know what we're up against, at least. What about those steel panels you have on the co-op's office? I'm thinking about those for my house. Frank and Miriam will be back in about a week. If they can see the value in it, maybe ..."

Auggie's brows were tilted at an angle that said he had something to say, but didn't know if it would be well-received.

"You're awfully quiet, all of the sudden." She tried to prompt him. "And that's unusual, to say the least. What is it?"

"Miriam and Frank aren't ones to do things half-way," he finally said. "They know the long-term value of staying ahead of maintenance around here. With a building this old, there's always something."

"Oh, I know," she said quickly. "I wasn't trying to imply they're careless, or bad with money. They're not trying to run this place into the ground. Far from it."

Auggie thought for a moment, then tried another tactic. "Look, let's say this: If they had the money to replace the roof before now, don't you think they would have?"

She stared at him. "Well, yeah. But it's a huge project, it has to be incredibly expensive. They're probably saving a little here and there for it, setting aside a chunk of the profits every quarter, or whatever. I'm sure it's on their radar." She nodded, her decision made. "I'll get some options, and we can talk them over when they get back."

"Running a small business is very difficult, especially these days. It's never been a great way to make money, for that matter." Auggie rubbed a hand through his short gray hair, and looked away. "If I were you, I'd only get the estimate for the patch job. Don't worry about the rest."

She stared at him. "You know something! Why won't you tell me what it is?"

Auggie went to the top of the stairwell, and listened. Roger was chatting with someone at the counter while the scanner beeped each purchase. Several other customers were already wandering the aisles, as there was a general hustle and bustle in the background.

When he was certain the coast was clear, Auggie came back to where Melinda stood, now nearly frozen with anxiety, next to Miriam's desk.

He tipped his head at the darkened monitor. "Have you looked at the accounts since they've been gone?"

"No, I haven't needed to. Miriam did payroll before she left, and the shipments are automated." She gave a small sigh of irritation.

"Look, I know they aren't millionaires, but it's not like the place is on the verge of bankruptcy." But she waited, barely breathing, to see his reaction.

"It's not," he said quickly. Melinda was relieved, but still reached for the edge of the desk for support. She needed something solid to cling to right now, as it was clear Auggie had more to say.

"I mean, that's not the point. Prosper Hardware isn't going anywhere, and I know you're planning to take things over one day. You and Bill."

Auggie glanced around nervously, as if he'd already said too much. "It's just that, retail's a tough world, and I wouldn't want either of you to … have unrealistic expectations, I guess." He gave her a level stare. "I don't know all the details, I swear. But you should. Maybe not Bill, at this point, but you. You have the passwords, right?"

Auggie's meaning was clear. And suddenly, she wondered if the leaky roof was the real reason he'd been so eager to come up here this morning.

"Yeah, I have them." She looked away. "Miriam gave them to me before she left." She raised her chin and straightened her shoulders. "I don't think they're trying to hide anything. It's not like ..."

"I would agree." He pointed at his temple. "But forewarned is forearmed, right? They won't be back for several more days, so there's time. You don't have to do it right now. But I'd give it some serious thought, if I were you."

Melinda couldn't believe what she was hearing. Was Auggie serious? He really thought she should go behind Frank and Miriam's backs and snoop around in the store's finances while they were out of town?

However ... Miriam had given her the passwords, and seemed to have no qualms about doing so.

Do whatever you need to do while we're away, she'd said. *Everything's an open book around here. At least, within the family.*

But still.

Of course, her aunt and uncle spoke freely to Melinda about the business in general. Good years, tight months, spectacular sales that should be repeated, and so on. Prosper Hardware turned a profit. At least, enough of one to keep Frank and Miriam comfortable, and pay the bills. There was no doubt about that.

What exactly was that profit margin, though? Melinda hadn't thought too hard about this before, as it hadn't been her direct concern. But given Auggie's wariness about the roof repairs, she suddenly realized things might not be as rosy as she thought. And it now occurred to her that perhaps Miriam wanted her to have a look, or at least wouldn't mind if she did. Melinda's mind spun with all the possibilities, with all the things she didn't know.

Auggie was waiting for her to say something. So she did. But she didn't give away what she was thinking, or feeling. This dilemma would take some time to sort through.

"Thanks for the ... for the tip. I know that wasn't easy for you."

"Well, us business owners have to stick together. Past, present and future." With their awkward conversation over, Auggie was back to his usual sort-of-good humor. "Don't worry, I'm sure it's not too terrible. And besides, sounds like Josh's practice does really well. If you two ..."

Melinda closed her eyes for a second. While Auggie meant well, this whole situation had her on edge. And she'd heard that line before. "You know, you're not the first person who's said that to me, and I'm sick of it."

Vicki's observation from a few weeks ago still burned bright in Melinda's mind. Why did it keep coming up? Why couldn't people just let her make her own way? Or, at the very least, assume she could manage on her own, no matter how much, or how little, money she had. Because she could.

Auggie wisely looked for a chance to change the subject. "Have you heard anything about what's going on with that vacant property?"

He went back to the windows, and Melinda was relieved to follow him. There was nothing wrong with a little gossip, especially when it didn't concern yourself.

"No one seems to know, but lots of people are asking about it." It was a hot topic among Prosper Hardware's customers, and Melinda was almost glad Frank was still gone. There was no chance she had any inside information about the council's plans, so people weren't pressing her for details.

"Well, if you can keep a secret, I'll let you know what I know." It was clear this would benefit Auggie as much as herself, since whatever it was, he was about to burst. Telling someone would lower his internal pressure.

"Yep. You might as well share it."

"You know Emmett and Patricia Beck, of course. I saw Emmett the other day." Auggie leaned in. "He cuts my hair, you know."

Melinda nodded, and wondered if men had the same secret-sharing rapport with their stylists as women did. "Did he have some good gossip to share while you were in the chair?"

"Oh, no, not then. Just said he wanted to call me later, to discuss something. Well, turns out, he and Patricia are planning to buy that building." Auggie's brown eyes lit up with excitement. "He's not ready to retire yet, but decided it would be great to have his shop right here in Prosper. Save the commute, you know."

Melinda reined in her laughter. Emmett's "commute" was a ten-minute drive down a state highway that saw very little traffic. But she could see how that would get tiresome as he aged, especially in winter. In Prosper, on nice days, he could walk to work.

"That would be wonderful! Does he think his clients that live in Swanton would want to come here, though?"

"Yeah, he thinks most of them will. They're loyal. And, he thinks he can pick up more people right around Prosper that are driving to Eagle River, or even Charles City. He leases now, and they raised the rent again. It's always been too high, anyway. Really puts the squeeze on his budget. And this place? He can steal it for a song."

"Wow. That would be great to have another business in town."

"And, that's not all. He might look for a lady stylist, at least part-time to start, to get more customers. Besides, someone has to take the business over when he retires, right?"

Melinda nodded. "I see a theme here."

"But don't say anything," Auggie cautioned her. "It's still a secret. Jerry knows, and maybe the council does." He sighed. "With Frank gone, I really don't know all the details."

"Mum's the word. Well, I better get back downstairs, and you need to get over to the co-op."

Auggie eyed the bundles laid out on the office's round table. "Are these the hardware sets you were talking about, for Mother's Day?" He inspected one, and gave an approving whistle. "These should go fast. A little tool kit, some gloves, an apron. Everything a woman needs, and a little store branding to boot."

Melinda couldn't help but smile as she started a stack. Sometimes, necessity was indeed the mother of invention. As were steep restocking fees.

"Esther and I cooked this up. We're going to make the best of an imperfect situation, and maybe even clear a little profit. At least, that's the plan. I'm putting them out today, so we'll see how this goes."

Auggie made another, taller pile. "Here, I'll help you carry them down. Are they going on that end cap, near the register? I saw it was cleared off, wondered what the deal was. That's the perfect place for them."

When they reached the stairs, he stopped short. "Look, I didn't mean to upset you. I just think you should know the real deal. But if you keep coming up with good ideas like this one, you're going to do just fine."

✳ 18 ✳

Melinda didn't have a free moment alone until her midday break. But she couldn't bring herself to sign on to the accounting system. She sat at the round table with her sandwich, and the appetizing lunch she'd packed that morning settled like sawdust in her stomach.

Finally, she approached the computer and made herself sit in Miriam's chair. She needed to check email, anyway; the proofs for the store's weekly ad in the Swanton newspaper would be waiting, and they had to be approved by two.

She wasted as much time as she dared but, just as she was about to log all the way in, Bill bounded up the stairs. They chatted while he rummaged in the refrigerator for his lunch, and she was glad when he sat down to eat rather than rush back to the wood shop. She checked the ad spreads, sent them back to the newspaper, and was relieved to look up and see that her break was over.

When she clocked out for the day, Melinda was at last left alone with her conscience and the passwords. But by then, she was too rattled to look. She packed up her things, went back down to the store's welcome hustle and bustle, and said goodbye to Esther and her dad as if nothing was wrong.

And maybe it wasn't.

At least, that's what she tried to tell herself that night as she wrestled with her dilemma. Josh came over for dinner and to check on Pepper, but was soon called away on a farm emergency. Normally Melinda would have been a bit disappointed, but this gave her the chance to pace and worry and think. She took Hobo for a walk down to the creek, just before sunset. The fresh air and exercise helped a little, but even the sight of the eagle parents on their nest couldn't ease her mind.

She was exhausted, but sound sleep still eluded her. Hobo sensed her angst, and watched from his spot at the end of the bed with worry in his dark eyes. Hazel and Grace also noticed something was up, and curled their soft backs near her shoulders in a comforting embrace.

At some time during the wee hours, Melinda decided: She had to take action. She would look, even for just a few minutes, and see what she could see.

And she'd do it first thing in the morning. She'd make sure to be at the store twenty minutes before even Auggie arrived, and get it over with. What she'd find, or how she'd feel about it, was something she'd have to deal with later. With her mind finally made up, she quickly fell asleep.

She was exhausted in the morning, but resolute. Whether Miriam had implied her permission to do this, or hadn't, Melinda wasn't sure. But today, before she did anything else at Prosper Hardware, she would get some answers.

The computer chirped to life, and Melinda realized she was holding her breath. She let it out, logged into the accounting system, and waited. Her weary eyes scanned the spreadsheets as her heart thrummed in her chest. No one would walk in on her, not at this time of the day, but she was desperate to get this over with as quickly as possible.

The situation wasn't dire, at least. Just as Auggie had suspected, Prosper Hardware wasn't in any serious jeopardy. But the figures were less than what Melinda expected. And, if she was honest with herself, far lower than what she'd hoped to find.

She closed her eyes and leaned her head in her hands. Her aunt and uncle had never lied about the business' finances. They never hinted Prosper Hardware was well off, or anything close to that. But this ...

They managed, barely, and that was it.

Melinda's fingers shook as she logged off, as much from anger with herself as shock about what she'd seen on the screen. She hadn't been doing her homework, hadn't been asking enough questions. Her only concerns about taking over the business had revolved around working with Bill, how to make sure they both were happy going forward.

Uncle Frank couldn't work full time anymore, and Melinda knew Prosper Hardware needed her almost as much today as it would in the future. But it was now clear just how deep their employees' salaries cut into Frank and Miriam's bottom line. No wonder they were downsizing from their sprawling Victorian to a modest ranch home.

Miriam and Frank had never been careless with money; but then, they'd also never had children. Melinda thought about Bill, and how he and Emily were expecting their third child. And even if Melinda never had kids, she and Bill both had decades of work ahead of them. Could they keep this business going? Would it ever be enough?

The front door's bell sounded below, and snapped her out of her reverie. Auggie was here, thank goodness, so she was no longer alone with her circling thoughts. Surely there'd been some odd incident at the co-op yesterday, or something he'd spotted around town on his way in this morning, that would force her to set her worries aside.

One thing, though, had already been decided. She would tell no one what she'd found.

Her parents were not active partners in the business, despite their ties to the family's store. What did her mom know? Melinda wanted to find out, but was afraid to bring it up. Maybe Miriam had confided in Diane over the years; maybe Diane simply knew the situation.

But how long had things been like this? What if Miriam had kept it quiet? That was a can of worms Melinda wasn't about to open.

Bill was a big no, of course. Unless something changed, he'd still be an employee someday when she became owner. Maybe Bill didn't care, even. As long as his salary was secure, and he had some creative freedom and general input, he'd continue to be as satisfied as he seemed to be now.

It would do Melinda good to confide in a friend, someone who didn't have a hand in the store's future, but she didn't feel right about that. Josh, of course, would listen. She loved him, trusted him, but money was something they didn't discuss. At least, not yet.

And, to top it off, he was another local business owner. The last thing Frank and Miriam would want is for anyone in the business community to know the real inner workings of Prosper Hardware.

Melinda still wasn't sure they even wanted her to know. She'd been counting the days until they came back, eager to hand over the reins and get her life back to normal. But now, she saw the price she would pay for her new knowledge.

Things would never be quite the same. Auggie had been right, however: It was better to know, than not. Melinda was no longer in the dark, and maybe it would push her to find ways to brighten Prosper Hardware's future.

It seemed she was alone in this, at least for now. However, there were a few special, furry friends that knew her better than anyone, but would never reveal her secrets.

"I don't know what to do," she said to Hobo as he watched the driveway from the kitchen window. It was Sunday afternoon, and they were expecting company. "I know, we've been over this a hundred times. There's nothing I can do, or should do. Other than tuck this information away, and count myself lucky for knowing it at all."

Hobo wagged his tail, but he wasn't responding to Melinda. Karen's truck had turned up the lane, and he'd spotted Pumpkin riding proudly in the front seat.

"Don't forget to greet your guests," Melinda sarcastically called after Hobo as he lunged through the first doggie door into the back porch. "Make them feel welcome."

It was a beautiful day, almost too warm for the middle of April. Cotton-ball clouds chased each other across a bright blue sky, and there was a hint of humidity in the breeze. The air was filled with birdsong. Tender buds had recently appeared on the lilac bushes, and the tulips had joined the daffodils in the flower beds on the sunny sides of the house. It was almost time to put the wire cages on the peonies, as the bushes had shot up significantly in the past week.

Best of all, Melinda decided, was the sight between the house and the garage: She'd done laundry that morning, and it was finally warm enough to hang her sheets and towels on the clothesline.

Karen and Pumpkin's arrival woke Sunny and Stormy from their naps on the picnic table, where they had their stomachs stretched out to the sun. The friendly collie merited only a few sniffs of curiosity from the cats, who were content to stick to their post and collect pets and coos from Karen. Pumpkin and Hobo, however, had already left for the windbreak.

"Well, I have my grubbies on." Karen looked down at her ratty tee shirt and faded jeans. "Nothing like hauling manure to make you dress down."

"I'm so glad you were willing to come out." Melinda waited by the truck's tailgate while Karen grabbed her medical tote. "It's so hard for us to find time to get together these days. This won't be the most glamorous afternoon, but it'll be good to get the barn cleaned out again. And catch up."

Karen laughed. "Someday, we are going to put on nice clothes, maybe even skirts or dresses, do our hair and makeup, and then go somewhere for a nice lunch and some wine. You know, like civilized people."

"Makeup?" Melinda made a shocked face. "I hardly remember how to put it on, seems like. Well, it's a beautiful day. Isn't the fresh air invigorating?"

"Oh, it is out here." Karen looked around the farmyard and smiled at all the signs of spring. "But somehow I think it's a different story in the barn."

The ewes hurried inside as soon as they saw Melinda and Karen head that direction, although the tote in Karen's hand brought a few wary stares from over the aisle fence.

"No, girls, it's not for you today." She stopped to scratch a few noses. "But we will kick you out to pasture in a bit so we can do a little spring cleaning. First, though, I need to check on your new buddy over there."

Pepper let out a noisy neigh of greeting when Melinda opened the gate. "He seems much better, I've noticed him putting more weight on that back leg." She couldn't stop the smile of pride from spreading across her face. "And his coat's improving, I think. He let me brush him the other day. Just for a minute."

"Really?" Karen was impressed. "Well, I'd say he's taken a liking to you, then." Stormy came down from the haymow to watch the show from the ridge of the aisle fence, and Sunny soon hustled in through the now-smaller cat door in the outside wall. He sniffed the back of Karen's boots, then rubbed against one of Pepper's front legs.

"Look at that! Seems like everyone is getting along." Karen knelt next to Pepper and gently felt along his sore leg.

"Sunny and Stormy got used to him sooner than I thought they would." Melinda stayed by the gate so as not to distract Pepper.

"I guess when your personal door is in Pepper's pen, you have to make friends quickly. And besides, that beach ball Doc sent home? The cats were drawn to it right away. If Pepper isn't nosing it around, I've caught the boys batting it about on their own."

Karen stood up and rubbed Pepper's back. "Do you share with the kitties? I think they like you." She reached into the tote and pulled out a tiny bag of apple slices, which Pepper was eager to accept.

"The swelling's gone down. Quite a bit, actually. I know Doc and Josh are hesitant to let him roam too much yet, though, and I agree. We want to move forward, not backward."

Melinda knew exactly what Karen meant, in more ways than one. Spring was a season of change, but not all of it was easy.

And some of it, like what waited on the other side of the aisle, was just dirty and messy. "Well, I have the pitchforks and the wheelbarrow out and ready to go."

"Let's get started." Karen latched her medical tote and set it in the grain room. "It might actually get hot this afternoon, so that manure's not going to smell any better than it does right now."

The wheelbarrow was filled again and again, and pushed around the outside of the barn to the fermenting pile just beyond the back pasture gate. Decayed sheep manure was mellow and rich with nutrients, and in high demand with gardeners prepping their plots for the growing season. Melinda's phone was already ringing with calls from Horace's repeat customers, all of them eager to swing by and purchase several bags' or buckets' worth from the already-decayed side of the pile.

As the sun rose higher in the sky, the women started to sweat from their efforts. The barn's front stoop faced north, and provided a bit of shade and a chance to rest. A duet of barks echoed from the windbreak, and Karen laughed.

"Oh, Pumpkin, I bet she's found a country squirrel to torment. They probably aren't as tame as the ones in town, but they can scurry up a tree just as fast."

"They all know Hobo." Melinda wiped her face with the inside of her tee shirt's hem. The outside wasn't up to the task. "And they know they have him outsmarted, as well as outnumbered. Josh texted this morning, wondering if you and Eric are still up for dinner next weekend. Friday night, right?"

"As far as I know. There's a new Mexican place in Mason City we'd like to try if you're up for it. It's a drive, but I hear it's worth it."

"Sounds good. Might run some errands while we're up there, then." Mason City was forty minutes' away, but it was the closest town with a wide selection of big-box stores, as well as a variety of restaurants.

"Eric and I were thinking the same. Civilization, at last! Who needs to go to a movie when there's that kind of entertainment available?"

"So, how are things? I mean, with Eric." Melinda took a swig from her water bottle. "Are you still talking about moving in together?"

Karen sighed. "Not anytime soon, I guess. I have my house, and I love it. He has one, too. Neither of us is willing to budge and be the one to sell. He's across town, of course, but in Prosper, that's maybe five blocks at the most. We've decided, what's the rush? Why mess with a good thing?"

But from the wistfulness in Karen's voice, Melinda wondered if she was really fine with delaying that next step. When her friend didn't say more, Melinda thought it best to turn the conversation toward herself.

"Funny you mention that, because Josh and I are at a crossroads, too." Melinda had already told Karen about Josh's eagerness for her to meet Aiden. But when she shared the latest update, Karen raised her eyebrows.

"He thinks you may not be as invested in this as he is? He said that?"

"Well, sort of. That's not true, though! I love him, so much. But this is a big leap, especially when it's only been four months. It's ..."

"Scary." Karen finished the thought. "You can't imagine your life without him, but you can't quite see into the future." She gave a rueful laugh. "Wow, that sounds familiar. I guess here's the big question about Josh: Do you trust him? Trust him to do what's right? Can you rely on him, no matter what? Because if it's not one thing, it's always another. Do you think the two of you can work things out, whatever they are?"

"Yes." Melinda didn't hesitate to answer. A warmth spread through her chest, and lifted her spirits until they were as high as the spring sky. "Absolutely."

"Well, then, I predict good things to come. I see what you

mean about Aiden, though. No need to rush things. That's a lot of change for one little boy to grasp."

Melinda looked around her wonderful farm and shook her head. "I can't believe it's been almost two years since I came back, since I moved here. It was the best thing I ever did, even though, at the time, it was the last thing I expected to do." Her shoulders dropped. "You know, sometimes I can hardly remember what my life used to be like, in Minneapolis. It's like it all happened to someone else."

"I get it." Karen pushed the stray hairs out of her face and scuffed the edge of the concrete slab with the heel of her chore boot. "I feel like I was just drifting around, one job to the next, wandering my way through life. And then, Doc was hiring, and I decided to come out and see what the deal was." Then she smiled. "And, well, here I am."

"Yeah, here we are." Melinda laughed. "And somehow, I think here is where we are both going to stay."

"It's a deal." Karen stuck out her hand, and they shook on it. "You know, speaking of errands, I was in Swanton the other day, and ... oh, I don't know if I should say anything!"

"What?"

"Well, there I was in the superstore, loading my cart with a bunch of stuff I didn't really need, when I came around the corner and saw Nancy and Richard."

"I know there's a few more light fixtures to replace in the community center. We put most of that money into the vintage-style ones for the main room. They must have been scouting for bargains."

Karen smirked. "Maybe I should clarify. I saw Nancy and Richard holding hands."

"Oh." Melinda sat back and took in this news. "Oh!"

"Right there in the snack aisle. And not buying light fixtures. More like stuff for grilling out. I steered myself away before they saw me."

Stormy had arrived, and Melinda paused to scratch his ears. For one puzzle, at least, the pieces were starting to fit together.

"Well, she's been absentminded lately. More than one person has commented on it. But she's also seemed happy, content. I didn't think anything was wrong, so I didn't ask."

"That's what I was wondering, if she'd said anything to you. Do people know? Is this some big secret?"

"It might be." Melinda grinned. "Remember at book club? She was in a big hurry to leave. Now, it makes a lot of sense. Richard's widowed, she's divorced. He seems like a nice guy. They've been spending a lot of time together since the community center project started."

"Well, I hope it works out." Karen leaned back against the rough wall of the barn and closed her eyes. "She deserves to be happy. I guess we'll just keep our mouths shut, then. She'll tell us when she's ready. Just goes to show, I guess, you never know what people are keeping to themselves."

Melinda turned her head away and tried to keep a straight face. She could confide in Karen, about the store ... but no. The decision had already been made.

"That's true, you never know." She gently put Stormy out of her lap and stood up. They'd better get back to work before they lost all ambition and succumbed to the lazy afternoon. "Let's push through and finish the barn. And speaking of snacks, I have chips and salsa waiting in the kitchen."

* 19 *

Melinda smiled at the man as she rang up three of the tool sets. "They're a great deal. Would you like Esther to wrap them?"

"That would be great." He reached for his wallet. "Small price to pay to not have to do it myself. My wife and daughters are going to love these."

Esther already had the wrapping paper out from behind the counter. "Well, if you find any more female relatives or friends between now and Mother's Day, just stop back."

The guy chuckled. "I think I have my family tree's branches untangled, but I'll let you know if anyone else shakes their way out."

He looked over at the refrigerated case. "Melinda, have your hens been producing much lately?"

"They sure have. Brought three dozen in this morning." She pointed out the egg cartons that were hers.

"Great. Put me down for one. Oh, and a gallon of skim milk." Then his eyes caught the display of Prosper Hardware merchandise. "Hmm. My caps are getting pretty worn. Time for a change." He lifted one off its hook.

"I thought we'd just make a little extra wrapping these up," Esther whispered to Melinda under the rustle of the paper. "But he's not the first guy to make impulse purchases while he waits."

"Two birds with one stone. Or maybe three." Melinda's spirits lifted with every beep of the handheld scanner. It had been a solid week for sales and, even though the store had been open for less than an hour, it was already crowded.

"Hey, there's Vicki." Esther leaned around Melinda to get a closer look. Vicki nearly collided with another woman on the sidewalk in her rush to reach Prosper Hardware's front door. "Doesn't Meadow Lane open in a few minutes? I'd think she'd be ..."

"Melinda!" Vicki's perfectly highlighted hair was coming loose from its manicured bun, and her face was flushed. "I need to talk to you. Right now!"

Several customers looked up in surprise, but most of them smiled and went back to their browsing. Vicki was well-regarded in the community, but her mercurial moods were well-known, too.

"What's going on?" Melinda noticed something, or rather, someone, was missing. "Oh, no! Where's Francesca?"

"She's fine." Vicki tried to take a calming breath. "Sorry to scare you. I left her at the shop with Bethany. I had to come over, right away, but I wanted to wait until all the coffee guys were gone. They're a terrible bunch of gossips."

"That's the truth," one woman said as she passed by, shopping basket in hand. "And they always say it's the women that can't keep a secret. Hah!"

"No kidding," Vicki told her, then turned back to Melinda and Esther. "And that's just it. I found something out last night, something shocking! It's been a secret so far, from what I can tell."

Melinda gripped the counter's edge for support as her mind began to spin. What did Vicki know? Surely she couldn't have found out about Prosper Hardware's finances; no one knew, even if Auggie suspected. And he would never stoop that low. Was this about Emmett's plans to relocate his barbershop? Maybe. Or, what about Nancy and Richard?

For once, Melinda wished there were fewer people in the store. She tried to focus her thoughts and stay calm, as Vicki seemed incapable of doing the same. And wondered how, exactly, she'd become the vault that held everyone else's secrets.

"How bad is it?" Esther leaned on the counter, the scissors still in her hand. The man was in no hurry to leave, as he was now catching up with a friend by the display window, so Esther had time to get the scoop.

"It's terrible!" Vicki was nearly in tears.

"I'm so shocked, I just can't believe it. And what a scandal! If people only knew."

Customers were staring again. And this time, they weren't looking away. Melinda edged around the counter and gently took Vicki by the arm. "Let's go in the back."

She hurried her friend down the main aisle, and hoped she could get the wood shop's steel door between them and everyone else before Vicki blurted out her news.

What if it was about Arthur? Melinda's heart nearly skipped a beat. Was he ...

Bill looked up in surprise, his safety goggles settled over his face and the skill saw still snarling in his hand. Melinda waved him on, then steered Vicki into the corner of cut lumber.

"OK, take a deep breath." She had to raise her voice over the whine of the saw. "Just slow down, and tell me what's going on."

"I was doing research for the founders play last night." Having to shout to be heard only intensified Vicki's worries. "Oh, God, I don't know what to do! That scoundrel! How he ever thought he'd get away with it is beyond me!"

"Who?" Melinda felt a little better, since it was now clear the person at the center of this mess was no longer among the living.

"Charles Fisher, one of the town's founders!" Vicki spat out his name as if it left a bad taste in her mouth. "I can't believe it, but he ..."

The saw kicked into a higher gear, and Melinda didn't catch the rest of it. "He what? Sorry, I can't hear ..."

Suddenly, the saw cut off. "He was a bigamist!" Vicki shouted. "That rat!"

Bill set the safety on his saw and joined the conversation. No matter how long ago this alleged transgression occurred, it was certainly an interesting one.

"Are you serious?" He started laughing. "That dirty dog! Wait. How do you know for sure?"

"I followed him all the way back to Germany." Vicki crossed her arms. "I'd already figured out he'd been married twice, some of his children were significantly older than the others. Old enough they couldn't be Sarah's kids."

Hours of exhaustive research had put Vicki on a first-name basis with these long-ago residents, and she spoke of them with the familiarity usually reserved for old friends. "Well, I assumed his first wife died in the Old Country, that he came over with his little brood after that. A single father, making his way alone in a new world." Vicki punctuated this comment with a sweeping gesture.

"But then, I found the passenger list. He came by himself! I thought, what did he do, leave the kids with relatives until he found success in America?"

"People did that, you know," Melinda reminded her. "They sent for their families once they settled."

Vicki rolled her eyes. "Not this guy. Last night, I was digging around online, and I found his first wife's death record. She died in Germany, all right, but only after she lived to be eighty-seven! Nobody got divorced back then, so you know what that means. There's no record that she ever remarried, either."

Bill raised an eyebrow. "Wow, that's terrible. What a loser."

Vicki's research showed that Charles Fischer, as he was first known, dropped the "c" from his last name before he got on the boat. It was common back then for families to "Americanize" their surname when they started out for the New World, but to Vicki, that was just one more strike against him. He settled in Wisconsin and accrued an impressive amount of farmland (by what means, Vicki couldn't say for sure, but you know he was up to something shady) before he sold out to further his ambitions in Iowa. Six short months after his arrival in Hartland County, he married Sarah, who was barely eighteen, and they had nine kids.

"Can you believe it?" Vicki narrowed her eyes in disgust. "Left Ingrid back in Germany like she was a pile of rags. None of the older children turned up here until they were in their twenties. And it was only the boys that came. The daughters stayed in Germany."

"Maybe they were married themselves by then," Melinda suggested. "Maybe they didn't want to come over."

"Or maybe they wanted nothing to do with their deadbeat dad! The trouble is, now what am I supposed to do? Charles Fisher's hard-luck journey was to be the centerpiece of the Founders Day play. His story, or what I thought was his story, pulled at my heartstrings. Turns out, it was all a lie."

Bill shrugged. "Well, maybe it wasn't a lie, at the time. Maybe people knew."

Vicki's expression said she highly doubted Bill's version of events.

"He wouldn't be the first scoundrel, I guess." Melinda tried to give Vicki some perspective. "Maybe he had a 'ruthless charm' that made people believe this little town, which only existed on paper at first, was the place to be. Sometimes it's the crazy ones that get the most done. Can't you just leave his family drama out of it?"

"Rewrite history, you mean." Vicki shook her head. "Oh, no, I don't feel right about that. I have to tell the truth. It's on me to set the record straight, I can't whitewash these things."

"I understand. But these parts will be played by children, so I don't see how you can include any of this. Shelby and Amy would not give it the green light; I can't imagine the principal would, either."

Vicki was as deflated as she was outraged. She'd worked so hard on this project, only to hit a wall. Melinda knew what that felt like.

"At least you found something interesting. Kevin and Jack have tried for weeks to decipher that old ledger I found under the floorboards, but no dice. Kevin gave it back to me Sunday when I met up with him at Horace and Wilbur's. I don't think we'll ever get any answers."

"See, Vicki, your search went somewhere, at least." Bill repositioned his goggles, ready to get back to work. "But you'll have to write a G-rated version. No blood, no guns, no scandal. Besides, there must be people in town today that are related to this family. They won't want to see their dirty laundry on display."

"What does Nancy say?" Melinda tried another tactic. "Does she know what you found?"

"That's the worst of it! I called her this morning. She said not to worry about it, it's no a big deal. Everyone has a right to their privacy, she said. She didn't seem shocked or concerned. Not one bit. What has gotten into her?"

Melinda only raised an eyebrow, then glanced at the clock over Bill's cutting table. "Who knows? But I think you'd better get next door. It's almost nine."

* * *

Hobo yawned and stretched his paws when Melinda appeared on the back porch's steps, but stayed in the shaded spot under the picnic table.

Even the sight of Melinda loading a rake, trash bags and several pairs of old gloves into Lizzie's flatbed wasn't enough for him to abandon his nap plans.

"I'm glad you're not interested in coming along," she told him. "Because unfortunately, dogs aren't invited. The members of the sort-of Fulton Friendship Circle are, however, and I hope several of them come out to help today."

Volunteers were gathering at Hawk Hollow that afternoon to clean up the tiny cemetery in the long-ago abandoned community. While Hawk Hollow had once boasted a creamery and small general store, a historic iron-framed bridge was all that had been visible at the site for decades.

But the pasture along the creek had kept a secret for much longer than that. The discovery of three pioneer-era graves last fall caused quite a commotion in the rural neighborhood, as well as the surrounding towns.

When it was determined the bodies were not the result of any modern-day foul play, the yellow "caution" tape had been removed and a quick fence of metal posts and cattle panels erected to protect the plot. With the support of the Hartland County Historical Society, the township's trustees began a capital campaign to preserve the cemetery and recognize the site's historical significance.

Mason Beaufort was on the township board, and Adelaide had asked Melinda to contribute some snacks, as well as sweat equity, to this afternoon's activity. When she went back into the house for a container of cookies, Melinda paused to admire the Hawk Hollow Creamery milk bottle that held a place of honor on her kitchen counter. She'd found the glass bottle on a dusty basement shelf, and it served as a reminder of her home's past as well as that of the township.

"A hundred years ago, the Schermanns took their milk to that creamery." She smiled as she picked up her purse. "And now, we're going to bring that history back to life. For today, at least, Hawk Hollow is going to be hopping."

It was a pleasant, sunny day, and seeing the farmers planting their fields along the way made Melinda itch to work in her garden. But it would be a few more weeks before the dirt was warm enough for delicate vegetables and flowers. Which was why today's work at Hawk Hollow was so crucial to restoring the pioneer cemetery.

The farmer who owned the pasture donated the small plot to the township late last fall, then mowed the tall grasses down to the ground before the snows came. Once volunteers cleared away winter's orphan sticks and decaying leaves, and uprooted any early signs of invasive plant species, the ground would be tilled and reseeded.

The township trustees had chosen a specialty mix that reflected the native prairie from this part of the state and, if all went well, coneflowers, milkweed, goldenrod and other hardy plants would fill in the plot.

While it was common practice to burn off large sections slated for prairie restoration, the trustees had decided against that in this case. The area was so small that any fire could easily spread into the farmer's pasture, or ignite the trees and bushes that lined the waterway.

The highlight of this afternoon was sure to be the installation of the cemetery's new wrought-iron fence. Donations from several of the region's residents, along with proceeds from the historical society's holiday open house, had made it possible to purchase the fence from a Waterloo landscaping company.

Several cars and trucks were parked on the west side of the road, near the farm gate that provided access to the cemetery. A few more were in the pasture, but Melinda wasn't about to test Lizzie's temperament and instead chose the safety of the gravel shoulder.

"Watch your boots," Adelaide suggested as she accepted the cookies. "The grass isn't tall enough yet to give the cows much to graze, but they've been out here quite a bit already. And busy, if you know what I mean." She pointed out a pile of dung just inside the pasture gate.

Melinda grabbed her gloves and shouldered her rake. "Where are they today?"

"Closer to home." Adelaide gestured to the farmstead up the road. "And out of our hair."

Melinda spotted Donna and several other now-familiar faces, and gave them a wave. "Look at this turnout! And I'm glad to see the women's club well-represented. We should have this cleaned up in no time."

"Come see what's in the back of our truck." Adelaide could hardly contain her excitement. "Mason had the honor of picking it up the other day."

"Oh, this is beautiful!" Melinda touched the delicate scrollwork that danced along the top of the black iron fence. The posts were already turning warm in the afternoon's bright sun. "It's perfect for the period; you could almost imagine it was here from the beginning."

"That's the idea. We're going to try our best to set things right. Hawk Hollow has a fascinating history, and I'm sure we don't know the half of it yet. But it's been neglected for far too long, and those poor people never had the respect they deserved."

"I'm just glad the historical society put their weight behind the project. The trustees never could have afforded this fence on their own."

Adelaide sighed. "I'm optimistic, but there's so much more work to do. We still need to find the money for three headstones. And we'll have to keep an eye on the prairie once the plants begin to emerge. They're supposed to be tough, but we're starting from seed. I think there's going to be some serious watering and weeding in our future."

She shaded her eyes and looked back toward the road. "And I'd love to see a historical marker up on the gravel, perhaps by the bridge, in addition to getting a sign for the cemetery itself."

"Baby steps." Melinda followed Adelaide over to the snack station, which was laid out on another truck's tailgate in the shade. "We'll get there."

While the resident cows were absent, the volunteers still had plenty of supervision. Several indignant squirrels discussed the situation from the trees along the waterway. A few blue jays, as brash and bold as their brightly colored wings, swooped over the site to offer their comments. The rest of the area's feathered residents, however, merely sang the praises of the lovely spring afternoon.

Adelaide pointed into the top of a tall oak tree. "Guess who I saw when we pulled up? Mister Hawk, or maybe the missus. It flew off as soon as we bumped and thumped into the field."

Melinda scanned the trees, which were just starting to fill in with delicate new leaves. "Oh, I'm sure we're being watched. This is their home, after all."

Mabel waved from one edge of the plot, where she and Ed were filling a wheelbarrow with fallen twigs. Her white curls were perfectly in place under a straw hat, but the humidity was trying to take its toll.

"Goodness." Mabel wiped her brow. "I'm glad we're in a bit of shade, over here. Guess it's a good reminder that summer's not far behind. Did you see Donna, and Harriet? Angie's running late, but she hopes to bring Maria with her."

"Looks like the Fulton Friendship Circle is alive and well. At least, in the way that counts the most." Melinda reached for the broken tree limbs near her feet. It was good to chat, but they were here to work.

"I'd say Anna and your mom, and the rest of the former members, are smiling down on us today. I came by Bart's on the way over here. How's he doing, have you heard?"

"The same." Ed chucked some sticks into the wheelbarrow. "He's himself, always has been. Marge likes her place, I heard, but Bart? Still says he's not about to budge."

"The kids are trying." Mabel shook her head. "I'm not holding out much hope, though."

Adelaide directed Melinda to bring her rake along to the back side of the property, where several volunteers were trying to corral last year's leaf debris and bag it up for removal. Melinda spotted Lauren working with the fence crew, holding a post steady while one of the trustees poured concrete mix into the hole.

"How's Lauren doing? Did she get that interview?"

"It's next week. I'm sure she'd do great as a home health care aide. She has the certification for it, and the patience, too. But even if she gets the job, and I really hope she does, we've told her she's welcome to stay on as long as she likes."

"She'll want her own place, eventually." Donna joined their group. "But this has been a great way for her to get back on her feet. Besides, you certainly have the room. How are the renovations coming along?"

As Adelaide filled Donna in on the grand house's ongoing updates, Melinda studied the pasture. A solitary tree here and there broke up the view, but the cluster of sturdy oaks closer to the road caught her eye.

Was that where Mr. Peabody's house had stood? It was a grand home, from what Horace had said, and its front parlor had even served as a post office for a few years around 1900. But it was destroyed in a mysterious fire in the 1960s, and what little had been left of Hawk Hollow at the time was razed soon after.

Word was the builder of the Beaufort's stunning farmhouse had also constructed the Peabody home, and Melinda tried to imagine what it might have looked like. Surely there were gracious porches on every side, maybe gingerbread trim on the cornices and roof peaks.

There would have been a hitching post near the front entrance, and an impressive carriage house just beyond. Mr. Peabody had been a very successful farmer, so the barn and outbuildings had surely been substantial.

Then she studied the side of the property that followed the creek's bank. Somewhere, tucked back from the prying eyes of the gravel road, had sat the speakeasy George and Horace remembered.

Melinda tried to imagine this now-peaceful pasture on a summer night in the twenties, with a few rows of roadsters parked by what surely wasn't more than a souped-up shed. Did the place only offer contraband booze, or did raucous bands bust out jazz tunes inside its weathered walls?

Melinda sighed and turned back to her raking. She'd probably never get answers to any of her questions.

There were no photos of the Peabody house, as far as anyone knew, or of the store and creamery across the road. And after Kevin's efforts to decipher the ledger came up empty-handed, any connection between Peabody's speakeasy and the Schermann family also looked to be lost to time.

Kevin reached out to members of his extended family, as promised, but hadn't turned up anything more than rumors the Schermanns distilled liquor on the side. Exactly how they peddled the stuff and who bought it, which would have been a secret even back then, would be nearly impossible to trace today.

But there was Harriet across the way, chatting with a man digging holes for the fence posts. It was worth a try. Melinda was ready with her questions when Harriet passed by on her way to get a bottle of water and a cookie.

"Oh, honey, I'm sorry." Harriet shook her head. "I do remember the Peabody house, but that's all. It was run down, even when I was a child. I don't recall any talk about a speakeasy. I'm sure anything is possible, but it surprises me that old Mr. Peabody would have been involved with something like that, even in his younger days. They were a fine family, from what my parents always said. I don't know if he seems like the type."

"Well, from what I hear, the Schermanns were among the finest people you'd ever want to meet." Adelaide paused to brush the stray hairs out of her eyes. "Kevin and Melinda haven't been able to prove it yet, but it seems they were breaking the law six ways from Sunday."

Melinda laughed. "I think it's a great story, and I'm thrilled that it might be true. We have a similar tale in my family, that at one time the Shraders sold illegal booze from the back room of Prosper Hardware. These old rumors keep things interesting, at least."

She thought of Vicki's discovery about one of Prosper's founders. In that case, there seemed to be enough facts to back the rumor. But did it matter now?

Charles Fisher had seen the potential in the wide spot in the road that would become Prosper. If he hadn't had that vision, the town may have never incorporated and evolved into what it was today. Maybe nothing would have taken root there but a railroad crossing and, like Hawk Hollow, Prosper might have faded off the map.

She wanted to tell her friends about Vicki's discovery. It was a good story, and it was even better that the story was apparently true. But Melinda had no idea who might be related to the Fishers, and she didn't want to upset anyone with this juicy tale. The trustees were doing the right thing, marking this pioneer cemetery and honoring the few people buried there. But the rest of it? Maybe it was best to leave it all in the past.

Adelaide leaned on her rake. "You know, I really hope those rumors about Peabody are true. And the Schermanns. And your family, Melinda. All of it." Then she grinned. "I've always said, it's not much fun to go through life toeing the line too closely. Sometimes, you have to step over it."

"Agreed." Donna nodded in Lauren's direction. "And it just goes to show, people are more complicated than you think. You never know what might be in somebody's past. And whatever it is, it doesn't have to control their future."

✳ 20 ✳

Diane leaned on the oak showcase and smiled at her daughter. "Honey, you've polished this counter three times already. It's fine."

"I just want everything to be perfect when they get here." Melinda did put the dust cloth away, but then reached for the broom again. Was that more dirt inside the front door? The last of the coffee guys had just arrived. Would they ever learn to wipe their feet on the mat?

"And it will be. Don't worry." Diane nodded encouragingly, then began to fuss with the garden-seed display across from the register.

"So, what are you doing?" Melinda paused on her way to the door, broom still in hand.

"Oh, just straightening up a bit. Some of the peas were tucked in with the annuals, and ..." Diane sighed. "OK, fine. I'm nervous about their return, too." Her arms dropped to her sides. "Everything went somewhat smoothly while they were away. No one got injured, I don't think we chased off any customers. No true disasters, natural or otherwise."

Melinda had been reciting a similar mantra to herself the past two days. It was also the gist of what she'd told Miriam every time her aunt texted to see if everything was OK.

"It's been good to be back at the store." Diane looked around, and gave it a brief nod that said Prosper Hardware passed inspection. After a burst of extra cleaning yesterday by Esther, the place really did look sharp. "Your dad and I come in a lot, of course, and help with special events. But it's been years since I've put in this many hours here. And this store is so full of memories."

"Well, I'm sure if you'd like to volunteer in the future, Aunt Miriam would love it. No matter how hard we work, there's always something left undone."

"She said the same thing when we talked last night, but I don't know." Diane rubbed her back. "Don't tell her, but I'm exhausted. So's your dad. There's a reason we retired from our own careers when we did."

Diane pointed to where Roger was planted in the coffee circle, laughing about something with Auggie and Jerry. "But I have a feeling he's going to show up here in the mornings on occasion. You'll have to keep his chair handy."

Auggie managed to keep one eye on the street while he had both ears invested in conversation. "That's their car, they just drove past. They're here!"

"Thank God!" Diane pressed her palms together and looked at the ceiling. "The captains of the ship have returned." She squeezed Melinda's shoulder. "Give them a day or so to get their land legs under them, and you'll be free to get back to your usual routine. Take a few days off. You've earned it."

Melinda didn't answer. Her mom was right, relief was just around the corner. Or, more accurately, coming in the back door right this minute. But her stomach was filled with butterflies and her mouth was dry. She wasn't going to say a word about what she'd discovered about the store's finances. But it was one thing to push the facts aside, and another to look her aunt and uncle in the eye and act as if she didn't know anything.

The initial shock had worn off over the past few days, at least, and there'd been plenty of other things to think about. It didn't really matter, at least not now. And thankfully, it wouldn't any time soon.

Melinda took a deep breath and smiled at Frank and Miriam. It was only a smile of relief at this point, but it would do. And how good it was to see them saunter up the main aisle, looking refreshed and relaxed.

"Melinda!" Miriam gave her niece a huge hug. "I'm so glad to see you! And you're still upright."

"Well, barely." Her worries melted away at the sight of her aunt's kind face. "Welcome back! You must be exhausted."

"Well, yes and no. We napped all the way home on the plane, and got back at a decent hour yesterday. The trip was wonderful, but there's nothing like sleeping in your own bed." She looked around Prosper Hardware with shining eyes. "I've missed this place so much. Didn't think I would, but I did. Oh, here." She reached into the canvas tote on her arm and pulled out a lei of silk flowers.

"One for everybody!" She plopped it over Melinda's head. "Bill, you too."

Bill's eyes widened at the wreath of fake flowers in Miriam's hand, but Melinda shot him a look. *Put it on.*

"Uh, thanks, Miriam. Glad to see you're both back, safe and sound."

Miriam threw her arms around him. Bill was momentarily shocked, but then leaned into her hug. She patted his cheek as if he were a little boy. "How I've missed you! How's the family? How's that baby coming along?"

"Everyone's well. Really well." Melinda saw her own relief echoed on Bill's face. "We've been busy here. Wood shop's been booming ever since you left."

"And I'm sure you're doing a great job." Miriam smiled at him again, then turned to Melinda. "Both of you. You've earned every dollar of those bonuses, and then some."

Bill and Melinda exchanged bemused looks. The last few weeks were rough, but they made it through. And then Melinda felt another stab of guilt, as she now knew how much those extra checks had cut into the store's slim profits. But Miriam had been so proud to offer them, and Melinda wasn't about to hurt her aunt's feelings by trying to give hers back.

Frank was soon on his way over to greet them both. "Look at you!" Melinda gasped. "You're so tan!"

"Oh, a few weeks of sun and surf will do that to you. Well, the sun, anyway. I didn't get too far into the water." He spotted the display of women's tool kits near the register. "Hey, what a great idea! How'd that come about?"

"It's a long story, I'll tell you later." Melinda waved Frank back toward the rest of the group. "Looks like Miriam has treats."

It wasn't long before everyone, including Auggie, was sporting a lei. Miriam passed around pieces of what she called Tropical Cake, which was topped with vanilla pudding and crushed pineapple. Diane and Miriam soon retreated to a corner for a sisterly chat, and Frank began to entertain his friends with tales of their adventures.

"But Frank," George broke in, "you haven't asked us what's been going on around here."

"Don't say you forgot about your old friends while you were off at the islands." Doc gave a mock pout. "We've been here the whole time, trudging along, keeping the fires burning."

"OK, then." Frank looked around the circle. "What did I miss?"

Auggie thought for a moment. "Um, not much, really. Lucy and Desi are back."

"Melinda got a donkey!" Bill snickered.

"Now, you were supposed to tell us if something major happened while we were gone," Frank said to his niece. "I assumed it was as boring here as ever."

"Hey!" Auggie frowned. "We might get stuck in a rut, sometimes, but we're never dull."

"You know what I mean." Frank waved him off, then turned to Melinda. "What's the deal?" She explained about Pepper, then waited to see if anyone else shared any news.

Auggie rested his chin in one hand. "It seems like there's been so much going on. But, now that I look back, I can't remember what else there was."

"It's all been sort of a blur." Melinda meant it. And she was glad it was over.

"Oh, actually." Jerry sat up straighter in his chair. "Frank, you're just in time. The council needs to start talking about painting the water tower this summer. I have some paint chips across the street."

Frank groaned. "Maybe I'm not as glad to be home as I thought. You remind me of Miriam, going on about what colors she wants to paint which room at the new house. Can't a guy get a day to unwind before he's back in the thick of things?" Frank glanced over his shoulder to look out the windows. "I'm not even sure what time it is. Good thing the sun's out. That helps."

"OK, fair enough. But there's something else, city-related, that I bet you'll find interesting." Jerry explained Emmett and Patricia's plan to purchase the empty storefront and relocate the barber shop. That made Frank's eyes light up, but then he frowned.

"The council meeting's not until next week, so the agenda won't be out for a few more days. Does everyone really know?"

"Of course, we do." Auggie raised his chin. "We always know everything. Besides, Emmett's the only one that placed a bid. It's not like he had any competition."

"I know you've been away for a few weeks," George told Frank, "but don't tell me you've forgotten how things work in our little town. There's no such thing as a secret, at least not for long."

Melinda enjoyed another bite of her cake, and tried not to laugh as she looked across Main Street toward city hall. Nancy's car was already out front, as usual.

How long had things been percolating between Nancy and Richard? No one seemed to know. In fact, no one seemed to know anything. As far as Melinda could tell, only she and Karen knew the truth. Or at least, what passed for it until Nancy confessed.

Oh, George was wrong. Very wrong.

* 21 *

Josh was about to start the movie when he paused, remote in hand. "You OK?" He gently ran a finger along Melinda's cheek, then lifted her chin to look into her eyes. "Want to tell me what's going on?"

"Oh, I'm fine. Just tired, is all." She was glad when Josh didn't turn away and turn on the film. He was listening, like he always did; and maybe she needed to talk.

"The store was crazy today. And Grace and Hazel were up half the night, sprinting back and forth in the hallway like their tails were on fire."

She pointed to the rug in front of the silent fireplace, where the cats were curled in a sisterly ball of fluff, sound asleep even though it was barely past seven. Hobo was still outside, enjoying the last rays of daylight on this pleasant late-April evening.

"I don't know what the girls were up to last night. I swear I have the mice population under control, they're moving out of the house now that the weather is warmer. So, it shouldn't have been that. The full moon, maybe?"

"Well, animals are sensitive to those kinds of things. But they seem pretty content right now. And I don't think that's all that's bothering you."

Frank and Miriam had been back for five days, and the fragments of Melinda's routine had slowly settled back into place. A few extra days off had done wonders for her mood and energy levels but, despite her best efforts to set it aside, what she'd discovered about Prosper Hardware's bottom line continued to weigh down her conscience as well as her usually optimistic outlook.

She and Miriam had gone for lunch at the Watering Hole yesterday as a treat, but also to run through everything that happened while the Langes were on vacation. Miriam had praised Melinda and Esther's pivot on the tool sets, which were flying out the door. She'd sympathized with her niece about cranky customers and leaky roofs, and admired how all three employees worked together, with Diane and Roger's help, to keep the store going in her absence.

But further discussion about the roof, which couldn't be avoided, made Miriam squirm. She was obviously relieved when Melinda didn't mention the possibility of a full tear-down, which only confirmed what Melinda discovered. But then, there was something else: a small hint of hope in Miriam's eyes that Melinda would keep talking about money, and some disappointment when she let the roof discussion drop. It was as if Miriam wanted Melinda to ask her something, and she wanted to give her niece honest answers. But between Melinda's reticence to admit what she'd found, and too many listening ears in the restaurant, she'd quickly changed the subject.

She still had so many questions. Has the business always been this lean? Did one thing happen to put the store in this situation, or had it just evolved over time?

All Melinda had heard, all her life, was Prosper Hardware was a cornerstone of the community and her family enjoyed a comfortable existence as its sole operators. That wasn't a lie, not really. But how frugal did past generations have to be to keep the store going? Could she do the same? Or, more honestly, was she willing to do the same?

Josh was still waiting for her to say more. And as she looked into his eyes, Melinda suddenly knew just what it should be.

He was always there for her, just as she was for him. Or at least, she tried. And she should try harder. In the past, she would have turned to her parents or friends with her troubles. And now, when that didn't seem to be the right way to go, she was reminded of the special place Josh held in her life.

She could trust him. Not just to share her worries, but to keep them to himself.

"I need to tell you something." She took a deep breath and leaned against him. "I haven't talked to anyone about it yet, and ..."

"Oh, God." Under her palm, she could feel his heartbeat speed up, just a little. "What is it?"

She almost laughed at the shocked look on his face, and quickly kissed him for reassurance. "Don't worry, it's not ... monumental, I guess. But something has been really bothering me."

With her head still on his shoulder, Melinda told him what she'd discovered. Josh wrapped his arms around her and simply listened, which was all she needed him to do. She didn't get into hard numbers; there was no point to that, and Josh probably wouldn't have felt comfortable knowing them, anyway. It was the dilemma that mattered.

"I can't stop thinking about it." The tears came, but most of them were from relief, not worry. "Did I do the right thing? I just don't know. And the irony of it is, this is such valuable information for me, going forward. I guess I'm not sorry I uncovered it; I just don't know how I'm going to keep it to myself."

"Well, the good news is, I think it's already too late." There was a lilt in Josh's voice that made her look up. "And speaking of cats, I'd say this one is officially out of the bag."

Then he turned serious. "I won't say anything, you know that. I'm glad you told me. That's a hard thing to carry around, on your own."

She kissed him again, and for a few minutes, all her worries were forgotten. "What would I do without you?" she finally asked.

"Oh, I'm sure you'd be miserable." Josh reached for his can of soda as he considered the situation.

"You know, I would have been tempted to do exactly what you did. As you said, such an opportunity had never presented itself before, and isn't likely to again. The curiosity would be too much. And Miriam gave you the passwords, it's not like you went behind her back in that way. Besides, it sounds like Auggie made a pretty persuasive argument. He's very skilled at that."

"Yeah." Melinda sat up and wiped her eyes. "Thanks, honey, I feel so much better. I guess I'm just a little worried about tomorrow, though."

Miriam had asked Diane and Melinda to come over and help her box up things in the attic. She and Frank would close on their new house in two weeks, and wanted to move things as they found the time. Their Victorian wasn't on the market yet, so they didn't need to hurry.

"We talk about everything, which is usually great," Melinda explained. "I just hope I don't let my guard down and say something I shouldn't."

"You have a lot of questions, and no easy way to get answers. It's going to be tough, I can see that. I guess keep yourself busy, and when you feel the urge to blurt out something, stick your head in a cardboard box and count to five."

That made her laugh. Josh could always find a way to make her laugh.

"And there's something else." She put a hand on his arm. "I want to meet Aiden. I think I should."

"Really?" Josh's brown eyes lit up. "Are you sure?"

"I am." She nodded emphatically and squeezed his hand. "He's a big part of your life, and I need to let him into mine, somehow. I mean, without getting in the way ..."

"You're just a friend, as far as he'll know." Josh's shrug was casual, but she knew he was thrilled. "That's all it has to be, at least for now. We'll go to the park, get lunch." He tipped his head and rested it on top of hers. "And, I was thinking;

you said Miriam wants you to take a long weekend sometime soon. How about the two of us get away for a few days?"

"Get away?" Melinda widened her eyes in mock alarm. "Do you think we could manage it? That's a logistical nightmare."

"Doc and Karen would cover any emergencies at my clinic. You can take off from the store. Ed usually does chores when you're gone; do you think he'd be willing to work with Pepper?" The donkey's stubborn streak was more pronounced now that his leg was healing, and he was increasingly prone to sudden movements and mischief.

"Ed's not as spry as he used to be, but he might. John Olson and his son brought over straw and hay yesterday, and Dylan was taken with Pepper. He got right in Pepper's pen and tossed the beach ball around. John practically had to drag him back to the truck."

"We just might make this work. Why don't we start the movie, and think about it later?" Josh picked up the remote again. "I've had a long day, too. I don't know if I'll be able to keep my eyes open after ten."

* * *

Miriam waded through the sea of crates and boxes to reach the small window in the attic's closest peak. "We need some fresh air in here." The sash stuck even though the lock turned easily, but the sweet smells of spring finally drifted in the window. "I haven't been up here much lately. I wish we were further along with our packing."

"Well, you were on vacation," Diane reminded her sister. "I think that gives you a good excuse. At least you don't have to hurry to clear out. When are you thinking of putting this place on the market?"

"Maybe June." Miriam looked around with searching eyes, and shook her head at what she saw. "It's going to take a lot of work to get it empty and ready to show." She took a deep breath and reached for the nearest box. "And I'll need at least that long to be ready to say goodbye."

Melinda busied herself moving a stack of Christmas totes to the "keep" section near the stairwell. She was emotionally attached to this grand house as well, between its ornate loveliness and the years of family gatherings held inside its walls. It was hard enough for her to let go; she couldn't imagine how tough this was for Frank and Miriam.

"You can always visit this house." Diane tried to find something positive to say as she reached for a broom. "Prosper's not exactly a big city, you'll only be two blocks' away. And it'll be exciting to see who buys it. What if it's someone from out of town?"

"New faces in Prosper are always a big deal." Melinda reached for her water bottle. Despite the now-open window, the attic's spot at the crown of the house made it stuffy and close. "Who knows who might turn up? I know Frank's already hoping for that."

Miriam laughed. "He's really hoping someone comes along who wants to get involved in civic matters, not just add a few more ticks to our population count. Serving on the council is interesting, but he's found that while it's easy to get elected, it can be hard to step away."

The Langes' new home had a small room in the basement for Frank's hobbies, but he would have to pare down his stash. He was out in his garage wood shop, supposedly organizing his tools, but Jerry's car parked in the alley probably told a different story.

The ladies worked in silence for half an hour, then Miriam looked up from behind her fort of boxes. "Let's take a break. I wanted to show you something I found in those file cabinets over there." She gestured at a nook on the other side of the attic, then started to make her way in that direction.

"It's not the Fulton women's club records, is it?" Melinda asked with mock surprise. "They are still missing, likely lost to the sands of time. At this point, I wouldn't be surprised if they turned up in the last possible place anyone would look."

"Sorry to disappoint you." Miriam made a sad face, then laughed. "I don't have them. But there's plenty of other neat stuff. Frank and I moved most of the store's old records up here several years ago, once he got the papers scanned and organized. I decided I'd sleep better at night with the digital and real files in separate locations." She reached into the top drawer of a file cabinet and pulled out three large, leather-bound ledgers whose pages were yellow with age.

"Take a look at this!" She handed one to Diane. "The store's accounts from way back when. You have the stuff from the early thirties, I believe. And Melinda, here."

The book was heavier than Melinda expected, and she could feel the weight of her family's history in her arms as she found a seat on a discarded footstool. Her fingertips tingled with excitement as she traced the lines of old-fashioned ink, the numbers and notations in an unfamiliar, slanted hand.

"These are from the early twenties!" she gasped. "Who did the books back then? Do you know?"

"Maybe our grandpa?" Miriam looked to Diane for support, but Diane only shrugged. "Grandma was very involved in the business, of course, and I think they had a clerk or two. But when I knew them, much later, Grandpa always took pride in doing the accounts himself."

"Look at all these transactions." Melinda slowly turned the page, careful to not crease the fragile paper. "After getting such a close-up look at our deliveries over the past month, it makes me wonder exactly how that was done back in the day. I'm guessing they got shipments by train, to start, then eventually by truck. But did they source more products locally?"

"I believe so." Miriam opened the other ledger. "The railroad's arrival drove the creation of this town, so of course it was instrumental to the start of Prosper Hardware and other businesses, too. But I'm sure several suppliers were from the region, like you said. Not to mention that many farmers traded eggs, as well as butter and produce, for credit over the years."

"I remember that still going on when we were girls," Diane added. "For many customers, it was the most-consistent way to get the supplies they needed. Many farm families didn't have anyone working off the land back then, and money was always tight."

"Those running accounts for customers are in separate books." Miriam tipped her head toward the file cabinets.

"I'm sure our parents, and especially our grandparents and great-grandparents, were willing to put things on credit when times were really hard. It was part of being a good neighbor, of looking out for each other. We don't carry customers anymore," Miriam added quickly. "But the good-neighbor thing? It's still part of what we do."

Melinda paged through the store ledger in her lap and wondered about Prosper Hardware's financial history. The amounts listed were so small by today's standards, and offhand she didn't know the calculations to adjust them for inflation.

There was no easy way to compare this picture to the store's current state, but maybe it didn't matter. As much as she was fascinated by history and her family's legacy, she had to keep her eyes on the future.

Miriam broke into Melinda's thoughts. "Speaking of ledgers, did you bring that other one with you?"

"I sure did." Melinda set the store's volume carefully aside and went to the deep window ledge in the stairwell landing. She'd left the Schermanns' little book there for safety. "I know you're excited to see it, since you weren't at the store when I brought it in. I wish I had more details to share. Kevin and Jack followed some leads, but unfortunately, too much time has passed."

"And there was so much secrecy to begin with," Diane gently reminded her daughter. "I'm sure the Schermanns made just enough notes to keep their numbers straight, and nothing more. I guess we'll have to be content with the stories you've heard about the family's side hustle, as the kids call it these days. But the details? It's likely too late."

Miriam came back to the center of the attic, a stack of much-smaller books in her arms.

"Oh, I don't know," she said breezily. "You never know what you might find when you're poking around."

She thumbed the fronts of a few volumes and handed one to Melinda. "Why don't you look in there, see what you can find?"

Melinda stared at her aunt. "What?"

"Just look." Miriam raised an eyebrow as Diane leaned in, her face full of questions.

Melinda did as she was told. "These are alphabetical, looks to be by surname." Miriam was beaming now; she obviously knew something.

When Melinda reached the "S" section, her heart started to race. "Oh, look, here they are! And this volume is from ..."

"The twenties." Miriam pointed. "That's twenty-one."

Melinda ran her finger down the page. The Schermanns were frequent shoppers at what was then Prosper Mercantile, and paid for many of their purchases in trade.

There were frequent barters with eggs and butter, and notations for tomatoes and other produce that would have been valuable to town residents who didn't bother with, or have room for, a garden.

But one of the bartered items seemed odd. Even more so because it was frequently noted.

"Applesauce?" Melinda frowned. "There are some nice apple trees on one end of the windbreak, and they still produce like crazy. I know the Schermanns were big on canning, but, are you serious? They traded it at the store?"

Diane shrugged. "I guess you bartered with whatever you had. Making applesauce is messy and time-consuming, I bet some people didn't want to bother with it. But whatever the Schermanns canned was surely better than anything from a factory."

Miriam burst out laughing, unable to stay silent any longer.

"I thought the same thing! But the more I studied it, it didn't really make sense. There are numbers there, sure, but I couldn't tell what measurement they were using. Quart or pint jars? Single or by the dozen? So many transactions. And even when apples weren't in season."

"Canned goods last a year, you know," Melinda reminded her.

"Yeah, but still. Frank and I were talking about it last night, and I decided to do some searching online. Many slang words were invented in the twenties, several of which we still use today. But not all of them."

Miriam looked at her sister and her niece with a glint in her eye. "Any guesses as to what 'applesauce' really means?"

"I have no idea." Melinda was on the edge of her seat.

"Absolutely nothing!" Miriam crowed. "It literally meant 'nonsense.' Well, I thought that was odd, so did Frank. Almost like, it was a secret code for something." She pointed at the Schermanns' ledger. "Frank said he saw initials and dates in that little book, and not much else. But do you think ..."

Melinda handed the Prosper Hardware book to her mom, suddenly in such a hurry she nearly dropped it. "Oh, if this is the missing link ..."

She paged through the little ledger and eagerly scanned the dates. "Your Grandpa Shrader's name was Anton, right?"

"Yes." Diane leaned in. "Find anything?"

And sure enough, there it was. Or, more accurately, there they were. Several transactions, noted by date, a cash amount and the buyer's initials.

The women huddled over the books, exclaiming with excitement, as they matched up one deal, then another, and another.

"They were sneaky, too." Miriam pointed at the Schermanns' little book. "The dates in there are always two days' behind the ones in the store's records. At first glance, it doesn't make sense. But the pattern is there."

"Wait a minute." Melinda was excited, but something still didn't add up. "If the Schermanns were selling liquor to Great-Grandpa Anton, and he was taking it in trade under the table, where are the sales he made to his customers? Money in, money out, right?"

Miriam thought she knew the answer. Booze trades into the store had to be tracked somehow, since they were the basis for the running account the Schermanns held at Prosper Mercantile. But the liquor sales, which Shrader family lore said took place in the back room?

Miriam's eyes danced. "I would bet that was strictly a cash job."

"I just can't believe it!" Melinda looked from one ledger to the next and back again, and tried to take it all in. "Who would have thought our families were linked like this? Oh, I know we can't prove it one-hundred percent, but it has to be true."

"Well, I say we believe it, and enjoy it." Diane rubbed her hands together. "And honey, I've said this before, but I'll say it again: It was no accident when you saw that 'for rent' sign pointing down Horace's gravel road. You felt compelled to turn off the highway, see where that little detour would take you. And look where you landed."

Melinda closed the tiny ledger with careful hands. She'd found it fascinating before, but now it held so much more meaning. It was a tangible link between her family and the Schermanns, between the past and the present.

"I'm going to take this out to the car, away from all this packing and these boxes. And as soon as I get home, I'm going to call every single Schermann I know and give them the astounding news." She reached for her phone. "In fact, I'm going to call Kevin right this minute."

* 22 *

Nancy adjusted the purple tablecloth one more time, then nodded with approval as she studied the community center.

"We're as ready as we're ever going to be." She looked to Melinda for support. "I didn't think I'd be this nervous! It's just a group of ladies, and easygoing ones at that. Not much different than our book club, really."

Melinda laughed. "Sam might feel a bit slighted by that, but I know what you mean. This is the center's first paid event, though, so it's a milestone. I just keep reminding myself we pulled off a New Year's party for over a hundred people, so this isn't really a big deal."

She went over to one of the tall windows, and adjusted the blinds so they were perfectly level. "The Red Hat Society's bringing their own food and drinks, and promised they'd clean up after themselves when they're done. Easy as pie."

Every last detail had been taken care of in the past few weeks, including the kitchen sink. While the main room was the star of the show, with its historically accurate light fixtures and freshly scrubbed windows, the two back rooms were also prepped and ready for future guests.

Some others, thankfully, had moved out. The bat wranglers returned just a few days' ago, this time to much less fanfare, and pronounced the upstairs empty. And, thanks to a last round of cleanup, the bat dung was gone, too.

"I have to say, it does look good." Nancy's smile widened as she glanced around the front room. "It's amazing what six months and several volunteers can do."

"And a big chunk of change from Delores. Let's not forget about her."

Nancy groaned. "I don't think that's possible. She called me yesterday and insisted I come over here, right then, and give her a private tour of the entire building. I guess since we didn't do a formal ribbon-cutting and open house, she wanted to make sure everything was just right."

"And?"

"It passed inspection. I was so relieved. She pulled a little notepad from that gigantic purse of hers before we started, and I thought, 'I hope I don't have to call Richard and have him run over here and fix something last-minute.' He's already worked so hard on this project."

Melinda hid a smile. "He certainly has. And he's done incredible work, all at cost. Thank him again for me, next time you see him. We never could have come this far without his help."

"Hmmm." Nancy hurried to the bank of windows at the front of the building, and looked up and down Main Street. "I don't see them yet." She glanced at the grand clock on the far wall. "But then, they don't have the booking until ten. And we were early."

"We might as well relax." Melinda pulled out two of the chairs gathered around the rectangular table. "Have a seat."

"Don't mind if I do." Nancy stretched out her legs and flexed her ankles. "Now that the center's ready, the next big project on my list is Ryan's graduation party. It's coming up in only a month." She put her hands over her face. "I've barely gotten started. There's the cake, and the sandwiches to order. I have to get the garage cleaned out, see where I can borrow some tables."

"Why don't you have the party here?"

Since the committee hadn't been sure when the place would be fully functional, Nancy had held off on signing up renters beyond the Eagle River women's club. But now, with the doors about to open, she planned to make an announcement on the city's website tomorrow and run something in the Swanton newspaper at the end of the week.

"Oh, that's an idea." Nancy put her elbows on the table. "I'm not sure that's the right thing to do, though. I suspect we'll be flooded with requests once the word gets out. I don't know if I should budge ahead of the line like that."

"That's true, I guess. Why don't you check with Jerry? If he's cool with it, I'd say, go for it. Put yourself first; you've more than earned it."

Nancy laughed. "You sound like ... well, someone else has been telling me that very thing lately."

"If it makes you feel better, I've been trying to do that, myself. Not take on too much, if I can help it. But there's always so much going on, so many things I want to be a part of, and it's hard to say no." Melinda shook her head.

"It's been wonderful to have Frank and Miriam back, in more ways than one. But I still have a donkey in my barn, and I need to start lining up crews to paint and shingle the house, and the plant swap's next weekend. I haven't even started to weed through my transplants, if you will, and figure out what I can bring."

The clock ticked comfortably on as the friends sat at the table and enjoyed a few moments of peace. All of the sudden, Nancy spoke up.

"I have something to tell you. But, now, you have to promise you won't say anything. Not yet."

Melinda had hoped this was coming, had expected it would. But she'd already decided to pretend to be pleasantly surprised, so she simply listened as Nancy discussed her relationship with Richard.

"It was just so unexpected." Nancy glowed with happiness. "I don't know where it's really going, or what I want." She shrugged. "It just feels right. You know, with Ryan graduating this year and Kim doing the same in two years, my nest is going to be empty soon. I'd been thinking about that a lot. Dreading it, really. It's going to be a huge change, and I was wondering how I would ever fill all that free time. I just didn't think much about trying to date again."

"But then, Richard came along." Melinda gestured around them. "Or really, the community center came first. And that came about because of Delores."

Nancy gave a sharp laugh. "The last thing any of us needs is Delores thinking she's Prosper's fairy godmother. Although, in some ways, she is. Anyway, Richard and I are keeping things quiet, at least for a while longer. His kids know, of course, as do mine. So, when are you going to meet Aiden, is it this weekend?"

"Next weekend. Just for an hour or two, see how it goes."

"I'm sure it'll be fine." Nancy patted Melinda's hand. "Things will sort themselves out. Aiden's so young, he probably won't ask a lot of questions. Now that I think about it, our kids didn't ask too many, either. But that's teenagers and young adults for you. They don't seem to care what their parents are up to, in general. We're boring."

"Well, meeting Aiden is something new for me." Melinda looked around. "Kind of like the community center opening, for the town. A new chapter."

Nancy thought for a moment. "You haven't asked for my advice, but I'll give it anyway: Take this next step with Josh and Aiden, and don't look back. Who knows where it might lead? Life is hard enough sometimes, as it is. We have to embrace happiness where we can find it, when we find it."

"Thanks. That's what I'm going to do, no matter how nervous I am."

The community center's vintage windows were in good condition, but a faint echo of outside noise still seeped into the space, especially when the interior was this quiet. They soon heard car doors opening and closing, and a rush of lighthearted voices.

"They're here!" Nancy jumped out of her chair.

Melinda was so excited, she almost beat Nancy to the vestibule.

"Are you ready to greet our first official guests? It seems like we've been waiting for this day forever."

"Here we go." Nancy opened one of the front doors, and Melinda took the other. Four elderly women, decked out in red and purple with jaunty hats tacked to their freshly styled hair, laughed and chatted as they trotted up the sidewalk.

"I think it's fitting the first group to rent our community center is one based on friendship," Nancy told Melinda as they waved the women forward. "Ladies, hello! Come on in!"

"There's five more on the way," one of the women called out as she sheltered her hat against a sudden breeze. "They're younger than us, but we drive faster."

Melinda laughed and filed that one away for safekeeping. Someday, when her hair turned gray and there was a shuffle in her step, she wanted to have special friendships like these ladies did. Or, actually, like she did now.

The post office was about to open. Glenn was out front, pretending to adjust the flags, but Melinda knew it was all a ruse to evaluate the society's ladies and their colorful gear. Just past the corner, she could see Esther sorting the sale items in Prosper Hardware's display window. The grass was green at last, and young leaves were filling in the trees along Main Street. Melinda took a deep breath of the fresh air, and had no trouble returning the women's enthusiastic smiles as they scaled the community center's freshly scrubbed steps.

The front room was silent no more. Instead, it was filled with laughter and exclamations of awe as the women took in the refurbished space.

"Oh, I've been anxious to get in here and see this." One of the women paused to wipe her red shoes on the new floor mat. "But I almost didn't want to come inside. Isn't it a beautiful day?"

"Yes, it is." Nancy smiled and squeezed the woman's arm. "It certainly is."

WHAT'S NEXT

More to come! Come along for another visit to
Prosper! Book 10, "Firefly Season," will wrap up this series
when it arrives in fall 2021. Read on for a sneak peek! After
that? Well, I have ideas for a few more series set in the same
area, so look for more titles in 2022 and beyond.

Recipes: Discover three more delicious dishes at
fremontcreekpress.com. Just click on the "Extras" tab to
enjoy all the recipes inspired by the series. This time around,
enjoy a citrusy muffin, a spring-flavored cake, and a hearty
chicken pasta.

Stay in touch: Be sure to sign up for the email list when
you visit the website (you'll find it under the "Connect" tab).
That's the best way to find out when "Firefly Season" will be
available for pre-order.

Thanks for reading!
Melanie

SNEAK PEEK: FIREFLY SEASON

Early May: Melinda's farm

"Uncle Horace," Kevin called into the living room, "come see this stuff, you won't believe it!"

"Hmmm." Horace barely looked up from his newspaper.

The Schermanns had gathered at Melinda's farm to celebrate the discovery of the Fulton Friendship Circle's historical records. Much to everyone's surprise, including her own, Horace's sister Edith had them at her place.

With Edith moving to a senior-living complex and Jen, her granddaughter, planning to buy the house, everything was in turmoil. But the records had been found.

"What's new at Scenic Vista?" Edith called to her brother. "Haven't talked to you since last week. How's that new therapy for Wilbur? Is it helping?"

Horace let out a barely audible sigh, and Hobo thumped his tail on the rug in sympathy. "Oh, I don't know. He doesn't know what day it is, hasn't for some time. But the nurse lady is really nice, and she's patient with him."

The lift in Horace's voice made it clear patience was a quality he greatly admired.

Edith shook her head at Ada, but there was a hint of a smile at the corner of her mouth. Beyond farming or the weather, Horace wasn't much of a conversationalist. Edith tried again. "What else is going on?"

"Oh, not much. Maggie called last night, she thinks we should get married."

Ada's shriek of surprise made Hazel bolt upright from the couch's cushions, her once-sleepy eyes wide with alarm. Hobo studied Horace's face for a reaction, but there wasn't one. Nobody else moved.

"Get ... married." Edith's tone, low and cold, was the opposite of Ada's. "Have you lost your mind? And here I thought Wilbur was the one ..."

"Well, I didn't tell her yes. Not yet."

Not yet? Kevin and Melinda stared at each other. Jen crossed and uncrossed her arms, unsure what to do. The club's papers were quickly forgotten, and the group drifted into the living room.

"Start at the beginning," Ada demanded, as Horace was unnervingly silent. "Tell me ... tell us ... exactly what happened."

Maggie and Horace had been in love as teenagers, but time and circumstance pulled them apart. Last summer, Melinda helped Kevin and Ada track down Maggie, who was now widowed, in Cedar Falls. The two saw each other regularly and talked on the phone several times a week.

This idea, however, would change everything. Maggie pointed out that if they got married, they could share her assisted-living apartment and split the cost. Wilbur's spot in the adjacent dementia unit would be expensive, of course, but the care was excellent.

"Maggie's always been awfully headstrong, she likes to have things her way." Horace shrugged, but the set of his jaw reminded Melinda that, despite his quiet ways, he was the same. "Guess I'll have to think on it."

"Well, who knows?" Kevin rubbed his hands together. Despite his smile, Melinda knew this conversation was far from over. "Jen, maybe you're not the only one in the family getting married this year."

Out of nowhere, Jen began to cry.

"What is it?" Melinda reached Jen before Kevin could. "Planning a wedding is stressful, but you're so organized."

"There's not going to be any wedding." Tears ran down Jen's cheeks. "Everything's a mess! I don't even know ..."

"What did he do?" Edith's tone was sharp and protective. "No one's signed any papers for the house yet. Andrew has no claim on it. It's all yours if you want it."

"No, it's not that. We're good; wonderful, in fact. But everything else is ruined! My venue coordinator called last night to say they're going bankrupt." There were more tears.

"Can you find another location?" Melinda suggested. "Surely they have to give you your money back. I know it's only two months' away, but ..."

"Everything's booked up, but that's not the worst of it. We went with this place because it was all-inclusive, to save money and stress. They were handling it all: the flowers, the dinner and cake, the open bar, the decorations. I have my dress, we have the rings and that's about it."

Jen was a practical woman. But in this case, it had worked against her. She'd put all her eggs in one basket, and now there weren't many left.

And then ... Melinda had an idea. She took a mental step back and considered it carefully, as Kevin, Ada and Edith continued to offer Jen support and suggestions.

Melinda looked out the picture window at the expanse of lawn and the lush trees, and remembered how lovely her acreage was in the full bloom of summer. There was plenty of room for a tent, the guest list wasn't outrageous; if they had to, people could park in town and carpool to the farm.

Even so, it was a big commitment. Melinda couldn't do it alone, would never have considered it. But she knew people who would love to help. Maybe Jen's big day wasn't going to be a bust, after all.

"Jen," she finally said, "there might be something I can do. In fact, if this works out, I'd love to do it." Melinda took a deep breath. "What would you say to having the wedding here? A tent, food, dancing, the whole works."

Jen blinked, and her mouth dropped open. The next round of tears was one of happiness. She looked out the window, and a smile spread across her face. Melinda wasn't the only one who could see the potential.

"Here, at the farm?" Edith clasped her hands together. "Oh, that would be perfect. Only trouble is, will people want to drive out here? It is forty minutes from Hampton."

Jen considered that. "Most of them won't mind. And if some of them don't want to, well, that'll cut the list down a bit. We were talking last night, we might have a casual celebration at a bar later on, for our extended circle of friends. People could attend that, instead."

Jen gave Melinda a hug. "And here I thought we would end up at the courthouse! Let me talk to Andrew tonight, but I think we might be interested."

Melinda went to fetch a pitcher of iced tea, and Kevin followed her into the kitchen. They leaned on the counter and tried to process what they'd just heard.

"I can't imagine Horace marrying Maggie!" Melinda whispered. "She's sweet, but I don't know what to think."

"Well, there's still time for him to come to his senses." Kevin clearly had his doubts. Then he laughed. "Be careful, or you might take on more than you bargained for. A double ceremony, right here at the farm. But somehow, I don't think that's Jen's idea of a dream wedding."

"And I'm glad." Melinda motioned for Kevin to grab the cookie jar. There was so much to discuss; treats were a must. "Because it sounds like a nightmare to me. I just want Horace to be happy, but ... one wedding at a time."

"Firefly Season" arrives in fall 2021.
Visit the "Connect" tab at fremontcreekpress.com
and sign up for the email newsletter to find out
when Book 10 will be available!

ABOUT THE BOOKS

*Don't miss any of the titles
in this heartwarming rural fiction series*

Melinda is at a crossroads when the "for rent" sign beckons her down a dusty gravel lane. Facing forty, single and downsized from her stellar career at a big-city ad agency, she's struggling to start over when a phone call brings her home to rural Iowa.

She moves to the country, takes on a rundown farm and its headstrong animals, and lands behind the counter of her family's hardware store in the community of Prosper, whose motto is "The Great Little Town That Didn't." And just like the sprawling garden she tends under the summer sun, Melinda begins to thrive. But when storm clouds arrive on her horizon, can she hold on to the new life she's worked so hard to create?

LOOK FOR BOOK 10 IN FALL 2021! FOR DETAILS ON ALL THE TITLES, VISIT FREMONTCREEKPRESS.COM

BOOK 2

BOOK 3

BOOK 4

Songbird Season

BOOK 5

The Bright Season

BOOK 6

Turning Season

BOOK 7

The Blessed Season

BOOK 8

Daffodil Season

BOOK 9

Firefly Season

BOOK 10

✳✳✳

A TIN TRAIN CHRISTMAS

The toy train was everything two boys could want: colorful, shiny, and the perfect vehicle for their imaginations. But was it meant to be theirs? Revisit Horace's childhood for this special holiday short story inspired by the "Growing Season" series!

CPSIA information can be obtained
at www.ICGtesting.com
Printed in the USA
LVHW090747160421
684695LV00022B/254/J